The Desperate Viscount

The Desperate Viscount

Gayle Buck

Five Star • Waterville, Maine

Buc

Published in 2003 in conjunction with Gayle Buck.

The text of this edition is unabridged.
Other aspects of the book may vary from the original edition.

Set in 11 pt. Plantin by Myrna S. Raven.

Printed in the United States on permanent paper.

Library of Congress Cataloging-in-Publication Data

Buck, Gayle.
    The desperate viscount / by Gayle Buck.
      p. cm.
    ISBN 0-7862-5619-2 (hc : alk. paper)
    I. Title.
    PS3552.U3326D47 2003
     813'.54—dc21   2003052927

The Desperate Viscount

Chapter 1

The dawn was chill. A light drizzle had begun to fall, making the grass slippery under the feet of the intent swordsmen. Under the watery gray sun, the steel whipped like so much dull silver.

The dance woven by the flashing blades was too swift for the three intent spectators to follow. One of the silent gentlemen held in his hand an open pocket watch, at which he periodically glanced. At the feet of another of the gentlemen was a small black valise. He coughed, then mumbled an apology when the third gentleman, an extraordinarily tall and fashionably dressed personage, threw an irritated glance at him.

The coatless swordsmen engaged in a long deadly ballet. It was parry, turn, leap, thrust, circle, over and over. The blades flitted, flirted, retreated, only to return to hungrily probe again. The swords rasped together, the sound falling unpleasantly on the ear.

One of the swordsmen lost his footing on the slick grass. He went down on one knee, throwing up his sword defensively. Immediately the other swordsman stepped back and dropped his point. His breath fogged the cold air on his harsh command. "Get up."

The flicker of a mocking smile crossed the downed swordsman's face. "Much obliged." He leaped up, setting himself firmly.

The sword points flashed up in mutual salute, then down to meet with a resonance of clashing steel.

The duel was resumed more furiously than before.

Heavy breathing cut the peaceful morning air, punctuated by an occasional terse, pungent curse.

There was a flurry of incredible action, the white shirts and swords blurring together. "Good God, they'll spit each other at this rate," said the tall gentleman, with more irritation than concern. He did not heed the disapproving glance cast him by the owner of the black valise.

Suddenly one of the swordsmen leaped back, clapping his hand over the blood swiftly darkening his pristine shirt. "Damn you, Weemswood!"

The other swordsman dropped his bloodied point to the ground and leaned lightly on the hilt. He dashed the perspiration out of his cool gray eyes. A smile flashed over his thin face. "I am satisfied. And you, my friend?"

"Oh, aye," said the wounded man in disgust, tossing aside his sword.

The seconds had conferred softly over the open watch before converging on the combatants to hand them their coats. The doctor opened his valise and bound up the wounded gentleman's shoulder, quietly recommending a rare steak for breakfast to replace the small loss of blood.

"Here you are, Hargrove. I'll play the valet this once," said the tall gentleman.

"My thanks, Connie. I don't believe I could manage otherwise. It's a deuced awkward cut," said the wounded gentleman, allowing his second to ease his coat over the pad of bandages. He flexed his shoulder cautiously, grimacing.

"You'll survive, Hargrove?"

Captain Hargrove, on leave from his company on the Peninsula, looked round to meet his former antagonist's amused gray eyes. "Indeed I will, my lord. It is a mere trifle. I congratulate you. Nicely pinked; but I believe outside the time allotted. What say you, Lord Heatherton?"

The second thus addressed, who had already put away his watch, shook his head regretfully. "All too true, my lord. Captain Hargrove has won by a scarce half minute."

Lord St. John, Viscount Weemswood, threw back his head in a rare display of laughter. When he looked across at his former opponent, he said, "Well done, Hargrove. You have succeeded in surprising me. I shall have my man of business forward the draw on my account."

"A pleasure doing business with you, my lord," said the captain, grinning. He started to offer his hand, but wincing, he thought better of it. "Though I must admit it was a deucedly harder bet to win than I anticipated."

"A compliment, indeed," said Lord St. John. "Will you join us for breakfast? We've bespoken a table at the small inn up the road."

"Thank you, my lord. We will be happy to do so," said Captain Hargrove, speaking for himself and his second, Mr. Conrad Dennard.

The gentlemen separated to their various carriages. Lord St. John shook out the reins of his phaeton, while Lord Heatherton got up into it, and then set out with a flourish of his whip. Captain Hargrove and Mr. Dennard followed in a barouche. The good doctor left in his gig, shaking his head over the so-called intelligence of well-bred gentlemen who thought nothing of an illegal sword duel at dawn to settle a bet.

Lord St. John breakfasted with his three companions. Then taking leave of Captain Hargrove and Mr. Dennard, he returned to town with Lord Heatherton. After dropping Lord Heatherton at their club, he whiled away the day by making a few social calls, boxing a few rounds at Gentleman Jackson's saloon, and buying a new horse at

Tattersalls. In the evening he attended the theater in the company of a slightly scandalous lady, whose widow's weeds did not prevent her from indulging in a heavy flirtation. The viscount was not adverse to pursuing a more intimate acquaintance with the lady and accepted her invitation to come up for a late coffee when he had escorted her to her door.

It was after midnight when Lord St. John left the lady's town house. Restless and not inclined to return home, he went to his club, where he eventually found himself involved in a card game with a gentleman whom he detested. Perhaps at any other time Lord St. John would have quietly folded and relinquished his place at the table. However, Sir Nigel Smythe was known as a regular card shark and that evening he had already made several remarks touting himself every bit as good as his reputation had painted him.

Lord St. John found the gentleman's boasts distasteful. He was not precisely a gamester himself, but he did possess an extraordinary affinity for the cards. He could not resist the temptation to pit his skill against the man, with the object of serving the gentleman just such a defeat as he was all too willing to dispense to others. One by one the other gentlemen at the table gradually realized that the game had become a contest and withdrew, leaving the viscount and the self-proclaimed card shark to it. The news swiftly traveled the club and soon spectators stood two deep round the table.

Lord St. John surveyed his cards with boredom. He sprawled in his chair in a careless fashion, his thin lips curled in a lazy half-smile. A small pile of coins and scribbled vowels sat next to his elbow. Beside his other hand was a half-full wineglass.

"Well, my lord?" His opponent's voice was impatient, almost eager. "What is it to be?"

Lord St. John lifted his gaze to stare at his opponent's smirking expression. He smiled, slowly and mockingly. Without a word he pushed the entire pile of coins and vowels to the center of the table.

Sir Nigel Smythe's eyes momentarily bulged. Then his face turned expressionless. He studied his cards again.

There was a guffaw from one of the gentlemen ringing the table. "Weemswood has called your bluff, Sir Nigel."

The baronet flushed. "We shall see which of us is bluffing," he snapped. He pushed his own measure of coins to add to the pile already in the middle of the green baize. He spread out his cards. "Your cards, my lord!"

Lord St. John laid his cards down. Sir Nigel and the spectators craned to look at the viscount's hand. Then laughter rose again.

A gentleman clapped Lord St. John on the shoulder. "Well done, Sinjin! Oh, well done!"

The baronet's mouth stretched in a tight smile. "Indeed, my lord. It was extremely well done." The acknowledgment was grudging but with scarce-veiled anger.

Lord St. John smiled again, mockingly. "The game is done, Sir Nigel," he said softly.

Sir Nigel swept what little he had left of his winnings into his pockets and left the table. The spectators drifted away, while the viscount's friend dropped into the chair vacated by the baronet. Mr. Carey Underwood gestured at the viscount's winnings. "You've a small fortune there, Sinjin."

Lord St. John shrugged. He tossed off what was left of his wine. When he looked across the table to meet his friend's eyes, he said, "A fortune tonight or penniless tomorrow. It's all one to me, Carey."

Mr. Underwood frowned slightly. "You've a damned uncaring outlook, Sinjin."

Lord St. John laughed quietly. "Uncaring, Carey? Hardly that. It is boredom, my friend, nothing more. I cannot recall when I last felt anything but this deplorable ennui. The turn of the cards, a horse race, a woman—these are temporary respites at best. Pleasurable but all too fleeting."

He abruptly stood up, regretting his revealing confidence. "I've enough of gaming this night. My head needs clearing of brandy fumes."

"I'll walk with you," said Mr. Underwood, also rising. He caught the viscount's forearm as that gentleman turned away from the table. "Sinjin, your winnings."

Lord St. John smiled crookedly. "I had forgotten. I must be more disguised than I thought." He swept up the heavy coins and vowels into his coat pockets. With a grimace, he observed, "I am weighted down like a millwright."

"All the more reason for me to walk with you. Footpads are not as likely to take on two gentlemen," said Mr. Underwood.

The gentlemen left the club and, followed by the porter's "good night," sauntered down the sidewalk. The driver of a hackney called to them, offering to take them up, but Lord St. John waved the carriage off.

"That fellow Hargrove has been talking up the wager he won from you all day. It seems the fellow stands in considerable admiration of your courage and skill," said Mr. Underwood.

Lord St. John laughed somewhat sardonically. "The captain has reason to be generous. An inordinate sum passed from my hands to his this morning."

"Then I am glad that I did not hear of the duel until I returned to town. It would have annoyed me to have lost on the outcome," said Mr. Underwood.

"Your loyalty warms my heart," said Lord St. John with heavy irony.

The gentlemen continued down the walk in companionable silence, finally broken by Lord St. John. "I am something of a fool, Carey," he observed dispassionately. He paused on the curb, lifting his heated brow to the cool night air. His eyes closing, he murmured, " 'Vanity, vanity, all is vanity.' "

"What was that, Sinjin?"

Lord St. John opened his eyes and shook his head. "I was but recalling the text of a sermon I once heard. Strange how the most unexpected memories come back to tease one's mind."

"Sermon?" Mr. Underwood stared at his friend. "You in church, Sinjin?"

"I do occasionally attend for the sake of my immortal soul."

At Mr. Underwood's expression, Lord St. John laughed and clapped his palm against Mr. Underwood's shoulder. "Absolve me of false piety, my friend. The last time I stepped foot inside hallowed walls was at the insistence of the duke. I suspect the text on that particular occasion was chosen specifically for my benefit. His grace disapproves of my extravagances and heedless hedonism. In any event, the sermon was from Ecclesiastes, which teaches that, absent God, everything in life is fleeting and without meaning."

"Good God!" said Mr. Underwood blankly.

Lord St. John gave a crack of laughter. "Exactly! You should make certain that I get home this evening, or rather, this morning, Carey. I have the most lowering suspicion that I am four sheets to the wind."

"At least, if you are mulling over a sermon," agreed Mr.

Underwood. Following his own train of thought to its logical conclusion, he asked, "Do you go to see his grace, then?"

Lord St. John grimaced. "Aye, today. I have not yet made my quarterly pilgrimage, having put it off until the duke's communications have become quite pointed."

"A pity that the old tartar does not kick up his toes and leave you in peace. Bad *ton,* that's what it is," said Mr. Underwood darkly.

"You're drunk, too, Carey," said Lord St. John.

"Well, it ain't natural that his grace should last this long. No, nor that he should possess that fine ladybird. What the devil does that gorgeous female see in that old reprobate?" said Mr. Underwood.

Lord St. John's smile twisted. "I suspect that in the lady's eyes the title overrides the duke's obvious octogenarian infirmities."

Mr. Underwood digested the viscount's statement for a moment. He shook his head in true regret. "Women are fickle creatures at best. There is no depending upon their loyalty. Why, I have myself enticed several ladybirds away from their previous protectors. The pretty creatures, for all their softer attributes, all have a sharp nose for gain."

"You would know better than I," said Lord St. John indifferently.

"Aye, I've a vast experience with the females," Mr. Underwood agreed with modesty. "It's a pity that you have not a portion of my charm, Sinjin. You could have lured that luscious little piece out from under the duke's long nose long before this."

"You forget, Carey"—Lord St. John yawned, with scarce interest in the conversation.—"the title."

Mr. Underwood wagged his finger. "You mistake my

14

meaning, Sinjin. One tryst, followed by the duke's discovery of same, and in the blink of an eye the lady would be cast out the door. She'd be willing to take up with you then."

"I am betrothed. I don't wish to take on a mistress as well."

"Oh. I had forgotten." Mr. Underwood was silent for a long moment. "How is Lady Althea?"

Lord St. John shrugged. "Beauteous as ever."

Mr. Underwood nodded slowly, then observed, "Lady Althea's mother has preserved well, though a colder woman I have yet to meet."

"Lady Althea is not given to emotional displays, if that is what you are hinting at, Carey. It makes for an uncomplicated relationship." Lord St. John slanted a mocking glance at his friend. "It is not at all your business."

"Of course, it is not," said Mr. Underwood, displaying affront. "I would not presume to question your judgment, Sinjin."

Lord St. John smiled and his eyes gleamed coldly in the light cast by a street lamp. "Forgive me, Carey. I thought I detected a quite inordinate curiosity in my affairs. As for Lady Althea, I am satisfied that we shall deal well enough. She will have her interests and I, mine."

"That reminds me, Sinjin. Do you race on Saturday next?"

Lord St. John laughed quietly. "Are you angling after the odds, Carey?"

Mr. Underwood smiled. "Of course, I am. How else am I to protect my interests?"

"Yes, I race."

The gentlemen had reached the steps of Lord St. John's establishment. Mr. Underwood declined an invitation to come in for a drink and went on his way.

Lord St. John let himself into his town house and went upstairs to his bedroom. His valet was waiting up to prepare him for bed, but St. John waved the man away after giving up his coat and boots. Then calling the man back, Lord St. John said, "We are leaving town at noon."

"Very good, my lord." The valet exited the room.

Lord St. John tumbled into bed as the first fingers of the dawn began to streak the sky. It had been twenty-four hours since he had last seen his bed.

Chapter 2

Lord St. John left London in the company of his groom and his valet. His head felt likely to split open, so he was not inclined to conversation.

Upon leaving the town house the viscount's groom had cast his lordship a comprehensive glance and known it was not a morning to comment on the fair weather or the superb movement of the horses. So he sat silently on the seat, appreciatively watching the viscount's capable working of the reins. The groom had been with the viscount for five years and before that been head groom with a large stable. He had yet to see any other gentlemen who could handle horses the way his present master did. The viscount had also a healthy understanding of what it took to keep a decent stable and his lordship begrudged no expense when it was a matter to do with his horses. It was very pleasant employment, for all of his lordship's sudden moods, the groom thought contentedly.

Lord St. John maneuvered his phaeton deftly, almost by second nature, through the congested streets, putting the carriage through such fine judgments of space that, to the casual onlooker, it seemed that he must come to grief. However, the phaeton invariably whisked past other carriages and the draft wagons unscathed.

The valet, however, was not witness to these miraculous escapes as he preferred to either keep his eyes squeezed tightly closed or else would fix his desperate gaze to the viscount's wide back so that he could not see the disasters coming.

It was a relief to Lord St. John to come out of the London traffic, leaving behind the raucous shouts of street vendors, disputing tradespeople, and the striking of hooves against the cobbles. Entering into the less-traveled roads, Lord St. John put the horses to a swifter pace. The resultant rush of air cooled his face and abated his headache to a degree.

Lord St. John made very good time and turned in the gates to the Duke of Alton's country estate in time for tea.

The valet was exceedingly glad to have arrived. He was never a good traveler and the viscount's way of putting his horses invariably upset his digestion. He heaved a profound sigh of relief and loosened his rigid hold on the seat railing.

Lord St. John had always liked the ducal estate. The lands surrounding the old manor house and grounds were pleasing to the eye. For all his careless manners and seeming indifference, the viscount was appreciative of the beauty inherent in the stately setting.

But as the phaeton bounded over the potholed gravel carriageway, Lord St. John felt a sense of disgust. He ran an assessing eye over the grounds surrounding the manor, before turning his critical gaze on the manor itself. As long as he could remember, the twining vines of ivy had covered the windows and two walls of the house, giving an impression that it was slowly being swallowed whole. Roof tiles were missing in places and coping stones had fallen. From past visits, Lord St. John knew that the garden was so overgrown and choked with weeds and undergrowth that it had become practically nonexistent.

As for the remainder of the estate, he knew if he rode over it he would find other such blatant signs of neglect, particularly with the tenant buildings. The duke's tenants had a miserable lot and little hope of improvement.

18

Pulling up at the front steps, Lord St. John stepped down from the phaeton, leaving his groom to take care of it and the horses. The groom was already grumbling under his breath about the conditions he was likely to find in the tumbledown stables, but Lord St. John paid no heed. A footman had come down the manor steps to get the luggage and the whey-faced valet revived instantly at the opportunity to issue orders to a lowly manservant.

Lord St. John did not wait for guidance or invitation, but strode swiftly up the steps and entered through the open door. At once he was struck by the gloom that no number of candles could have penetrated, even if the duke had been willing to put out for the expense, and the strong smell of must, mildew, and mothballs that pervaded the house. His jaw worked.

He detested these visits, which he was obligated to make out of family duty. He was heir presumptive to all that he surveyed on these infrequent visits, but it was of little pleasure to him to see the worsening condition of the estate. He knew that the majority of the rooms of the manor were shut up, with the furniture under dust cloths and that it was unlikely that anything had been done about the damage done by a leaking roof.

The last time he had come, he had also discovered that several window casings were no longer properly sealed and damp rot had invaded the long gallery and some of the other rooms. He had had a blazing row with the duke over the state of the manor, which had only ended when he had slammed out of the house and returned to London.

He had put off returning to the ducal estate as long as possible. There was, after all, no love lost between himself and the duke. The gentlemen were opposites in many respects, having differing opinions on politics, religion, and what constituted physical comforts. But their strongest disagreement had always been about the condition of the estate holdings and the duke's total indifference to the fact that all was falling into complete disarray and disrepair.

The aged butler took Lord St. John's driving coat, beaver, and gloves, informing his lordship where the duke could be found. As Lord St. John strode toward the front parlor, he recalled quite distinctly what the duke had said on the occasion of their last blazing row.

"The running of the estate is my business. If I choose to bleed it dry before I die, it is my right to do so," the duke had said coldly. "Aye, you may look as murderous as you please, Weemswood, but I shan't oblige you just yet. No doubt you have wished my death these last ten years so that you could get your hands on the income that I have saved and made into a fortune, and gamble it away just like your father frittered away his own inheritance! *That* is the real reason you counsel prudence and economy."

"If I counsel you, your grace, it is for the sake of the tenants. They live in hovels. They do not have the means to work the land properly, either for themselves or for the estate. This income you speak of is in danger of disappearing altogether. What then of your fortune? Even you must agree that there is only so far that one may economize," Lord St. John had returned bitingly, casting a glance at the poorly lit dining room and the ill-prepared fare on the table.

He had gestured at the woman sitting beside the duke. Her slender throat and arms had been adorned with glittering emeralds and diamonds. "Those pretty baubles would be the first to go."

The woman had not paid attention to the argument, but at the viscount's observation she had narrowed her eyes, then turned her face to the duke. She had placed her fingers on the duke's arm. "Your grace, perhaps his lordship has a point after all. It certainly is not right that he should question your decisions, of course, but perhaps a word with your steward might be in order. Those lazy tenants must be made to work."

The duke patted her clinging hand. "Never you mind, my lovely. I shall see that you have all that you could ever wish. As for you, Weemswood, your gall is the height of insult. Look at your own estate—mortgaged to the hilt and has been for years. At least my poor management has not gotten me into the claws of those bloodsucking merchant bankers!"

It was an unanswerable argument, though an unfair one. The duke knew perfectly well that when Lord St. John had come into the viscountancy, his inheritance had consisted of a pile of debts and an already mortgaged estate. The viscount's late father had been an improvident man in all respects, as well as being very unlucky at cards and at betting the races. It was generally agreed in society that it had been something of a relief when the gentleman had broken his neck trying to jump a horse over a too-high wall, or otherwise there would have been nothing at all for his only offspring to inherit.

Of course, Lord St. John's own style had never been parsimonious. He had lived just as wildly as his father, perhaps because he had never had anything remotely bordering on a steadying influence in his life. His mother had died when he was a small boy and his upbringing had been left to a succession of pretty nurses whose main occupation had been more to see to the late viscount's comforts rather than to the needs of his lonely young son.

As a consequence, Lord St. John had grown up undisciplined and wild to a fault. He learned early that his father would only bestow attention on him if he showed an aptitude for the gentleman's own interests. Thus he had applied himself to riding and playing cards. He had become an expert at both, quickly surpassing his father's skills, much to that gentleman's mingled pride and displeasure. Later had come driving, and in it Lord St. John had discovered a ruling passion. Whenever he sat up behind a powerful, fast team, he felt in control and fleetingly free of the unhappiness that always haunted him.

By the time Lord St. John was sent off to boarding school, he had already absorbed a worldly education that should by rights have been possessed only by someone at least twenty years older than himself. He was not popular with the masters and earned harsh discipline for his wild ways and disrespect.

Yet boarding school was the making of Lord St. John. His was a keen mind and suddenly he discovered the whole world was opened to him by learning. Despite the problems that he presented to the masters, because his marks were solid, few could quite bring themselves to condemn him outright and recommend his dismissal. It was hoped, even during the worst of times, that Lord St. John would eventually come round and make a decent showing of his life.

He had gone on to university and distinguished himself both in his studies as well as in any sort of sporting event. From that standpoint he was popular, but his cold, seemingly unfeeling manner and his biting tongue kept all but a privileged few from becoming fast friends.

When his father died, Lord St. John returned to the place of his birth. He felt nothing for it because it had never been home to him. Over the years he had rarely gone back to Rosethorn because he had spent school holidays with the families of friends. But the estate was his responsibility, and perversely enough, he had felt that duty.

He had done what he could to improve the lot of his tenants, recognizing that they could produce better with the proper housing and tools. His rent income deriving from the estate had thus improved, but the majority of it went right back into the land and into repairs and maintenance on the old manor house. He had no hope of ever retiring the mortgage but at least some day the place might be liveable again.

Always at the back of the viscount's mind had been the faint glimmering of a dream—more an impression, actually—of a woman with a welcoming smile and a child or two clinging to her skirts standing at the door of the manor at dusk, a welcoming light spilling out from behind them.

Whenever it had risen to his conscious thoughts, he had irritably brushed it aside as a childish yearning not firmly enough buried. He was a man grown. He had no need of anything but the pursuit of his own pleasures. He had seen enough of his father's liaisons to have developed a distrust of women and disillusionment in the sincerity of their expressions of affection to either young boys or to the man who bedded them.

Now, as Lord St. John entered the front parlor, a sardonic smile touched his face at sight of the Duke of Alton and his mistress taking tea. His grace's mistress was bejeweled and attired in a fashion more befitting an evening function than an early afternoon tea, presenting a picture of vulgar ostentation. Nor was there anything refined in the woman's heavily rouged face or the bold manner in which her gaze met the viscount's own. Despite the drawbacks of her dress and unfortunate love of the gaudy, she was an undoubtedly beautiful female and she simpered under Lord St. John's smile, mistaking it for admiration.

Lord St. John had recognized the woman for what she was the first moment he had laid eyes on her. He did not condemn her, for it was a matter of indifference to him what she managed to wheedle out of the duke. The estate had already been in such poor condition that a little more could not be said to be any great drain on its resources. Then, as now, he felt little more than a stirring of distaste toward the woman.

He greeted the duke and his grace's companion. "Your grace; ma'am."

The Duke of Alton stared at the viscount from under bushy white brows. There was no softening friendliness or welcome in his hard expression. "It's you, is it, Weemswood? Well, we've enough tea to spare another cup. I know why you've come and I warn you that I'll not countenance any of your tempers."

"Your graciousness never fails to surprise me, sir," said Lord St. John. He seated himself and accepted the cup of tepid tea that the woman poured for him.

The duke chuckled reluctantly. "Aye, I surprise myself. But these days I am mellowed, and all due to my sweet duchess." He squeezed the woman's arm possessively.

Lord St. John froze for an infinitesimal second in the act of touching the cup to his lips, then proceeded to sip the tea as though with the greatest calm, even through his thoughts had slipped with shock. "Your duchess, sir? I had no notion."

"Then why the devil have you come down, if it was not in response to the announcement I sent to the *Gazette*?" asked the duke irritably.

"My lamentable filial duty, I suppose," said Lord St. John.

He was not looking at the duke, but at the woman. Lord

24

St. John could not believe that the duke had been so lost to good sense that he had actually married the grasping doxy.

The woman smiled with a hint of smugness, as though reading Lord St. John's mind. "The ceremony was done quite sudden-like, my lord. But there was no stopping his grace once he had gotten out of me the truth."

Lord St. John's gray eyes narrowed. "The truth, madam?" he asked softly.

"Aye!" The duke laughed and flung his arm around the woman's softly rounded shoulders. "She carries my whelp, Weemswood. What think you of that, eh?"

Lord St. John felt the room tilt from under him. He held himself perfectly still, his face totally expressionless. "Indeed! I must felicitate you, then."

The duke laughed again, but maliciously. "Oh aye. I will accept your felicitations, Weemswood. You are a gentleman to the bone. Not a hint of the bitter disappointment of losing sight of all this." He waved a gnarled hand to indicate this once sumptuously decorated room that was now faded and dusty and hopelessly out of fashion.

Lord St. John set down the cup and rose from the chair. He sauntered to the mantel, saying, "Quite right, your grace. It is a bitter disappointment indeed to be freed of the responsibility for this decaying pile." His voice was mocking, as was his expression.

The duke's face mottled purple. "Out! Get out! You will not spend this night or any other under my roof! Get out!"

"Well spoken, your grace. I am held at once in admiration of your hospitality as well as your foolishness. I suppose it has not occurred to you that the woman may be lying about the child?" asked Lord St. John.

The woman jumped up and pulled her dress close against her stomach. The undeniable evidence was starkly displayed. "There, my lord! *That* for your wicked disbelief," she said triumphantly.

"I never doubted that you are increasing, dear lady, merely the paternity," said Lord St. John dryly.

The new duchess flushed. A flicker of fear flashed in her eyes. How dare you, my lord!"

"Aye, that will be insult enough! You'll leave now, sirrah, or I shall have you horsewhipped from the grounds!" the duke swore.

"Never more gladly, your grace," said Lord St. John, his lips twisted in a contemptuous smile. He strode out of the parlor, shouting for his bags and his phaeton.

Chapter 3

The announcement of the Duke of Alton's marriage to his ill-bred mistress came out in the *Gazette* on that same day. When Lord St. John returned to London, he read it for himself when he sat down at dinner.

The viscount's swift, unexpected return from the country had thrown the kitchen into an uproar because his lordship's exacting tastes were a byword in his household. Lord St. John had been known to return dishes not to his liking accompanied by a biting remark, and the cook waited with trepidation the reception of the ragout made from slivers of roast and various cooked vegetables, the barley soup, and fish cakes. There was, in addition, a tolerable tart and it was hoped that this particular item might go long toward reconciling the viscount to such a poor outlay.

After setting aside the newspaper, Lord St. John's eyes were so cold and his expression so forbidding that the footman serving the hastily prepared dishes did not dare to inquire what his lordship's preferences might be. In any event, the viscount seemed to have little appetite, eventually waving away everything but the wine bottle. As the various dishes were returned to the kitchen, the cook took consolation that his lordship had not sent down a blighting message but instead had taken a few bites of everything.

One of the manservants casually removed the discarded newspaper along with the rejected tart and carried it away to the kitchen so that the cause of his lordship's unholy humor could be determined by those of the household who could read. It was not long before the offending item was discovered and exclaimed over.

Lord St. John drank steadily as the black hours progressed, calling for a servant only when he wanted another bottle. His unseeing gaze did not see the darkening shadows, nor that a servant came in to light a few tapers. He sat sprawled in his chair, a brooding scowl heavy on his face.

Elsewhere in the house the servants whispered and speculated, somewhat anxiously, over what the viscount's change in fortune meant for themselves. The servant who had tiptoed into the dining room to light the candles reported that the master appeared to be caught fast in the throes of one of his freak tempers, except that he was unnaturally quiet. This, it was agreed, was a very bad sign. The viscount's tantrums were short and violent in character, as quickly over as they had arisen, and otherwise he was an easy and generous employer.

Though Lord St. John was considered a better master than most, it was felt that it would not prove possible for his lordship to maintain the same style of living that he had kept up in the past. Perhaps better than the viscount himself, the servants knew what it cost to run an establishment and they had also a fairly shrewd notion of what straits the viscount had gotten himself into over the years. The casual gossip that was always exchanged among household servants and tradespeople had made that information readily accessible. As one pert housemaid put it, they had all better look to their own skins; and though the butler and housekeeper both reprimanded the girl, the now-spoken thought remained uppermost in all their minds. It was not an easy night's rest for any of the household, and some resolved to begin looking for new employment the very next day.

When Lord St. John rose at last from the dining table,

the tapers had long since burned down and guttered. The dining room was cloaked in darkness except for a stripe of waning moonlight shining through a crack in the drawn drapes, but it was enough to allow him to make out the dim bulk of the furniture. He carefully maneuvered himself out of his chair, swaying slightly as he left the room and crossed the entry hall to the stairs.

"My lord? Is there anything I can do?"

Lord St. John looked round. He blinked before bringing into focus the form of his butler, who held aloft a flickering candle. The resulting play of shadows lent the butler a peculiarly pitying expression.

Lord St. John gave a bitter bark of laughter. "I'll do, Craighton. Go to bed." Clutching the balustrade and without waiting for acknowledgment of his order, he stumbled up the stairs and on to his bedroom. When he had safely reached his room, he sprawled across his bed fully clothed, already unconscious to the world.

The news of the duke's marriage had repercussions that reached far beyond Lord St. John's own household. The news spread with such rapidity that Lord St. John's tailor and his bootmaker, his clothier and his hatmaker, his glovier and his jeweler knew of the ill tidings before nightfall. The coachman, the butcher, the grocer, the chandler; the stables that housed his lordship's horses and carriages; the gentleman who struggled with the viscount's business accounts; and the ladies who had occasionally enjoyed the viscount's patronage—in short, anyone who had ever had any sort of dealings with Lord St. John greeted the news of his tumbled fortunes with dismay.

All the tradesmen who had ever extended credit to Viscount Weemswood were suddenly stricken by their own stupidity. They all knew that the viscount lived beyond his means—didn't their own books reflect the high-running tab that he had developed over the years and never paid? They knew that noblemen believed that tradespeople were the last that should be paid—had they not all learned that to their sorrow in their dealings with the aristocracy? But they had gambled on Lord St. John longer than they might have on another gentleman because he was heir presumptive to a dukedom of some means. It was well-known that the Duke of Alton had hoarded virtually every groat he could squeeze out of his estate and had thus undoubtedly amassed a tidy fortune. The tradesmen had thought of it as an investment, if not in monies, at least in prestige and goodwill.

Now, however, things had changed. Lord St. John was no longer heir to anything. All he had were his own mortgaged estates, his town house, his phaeton and horses, and his debts. Those tradespeople who had so eagerly extended his lordship credit just the day before were now anxious that the outstanding balances be paid in full, at once. Everyone knew that the viscount hadn't a feather to fly with on his own and so it behooved those who considered themselves savvy in business to get their own out of him before his funds were completely dried up.

The next morning an avalanche of bills descended upon the town house. Lord St. John's man of business and sometime secretary, Mr. Witherspoon, was unsurprised by the reaction to the announcement of the duke's marriage, but he was stunned by the steadily mounting totals owed by his employer. There were also some rather unpleasant confrontations between himself and others of the staff with a few of the more aggressive tradespeople who deemed a personal visit to be in order to collect what was due them.

Lord St. John was spared the majority of these embarrassments by the zealousness of the most loyal of his staff. When he came downstairs shortly before noon, however, he was instantly hailed by an individual in the entryway who was resisting being manhandled out the door by two sturdy footmen and the butler.

"I demands a hearing, I say! Your lor'ship—"

The manservants succeeded in thrusting the burly individual out the door, shutting it on his continued demands to be heard.

The butler, breathing rather harder than usual, bade the viscount a good morning.

Lord St. John, who had paused on the last stair to watch the outcome of the struggle, raised his brows and snapped, "If that is your notion of a good morning, Craighton, I shudder to imagine a bad morning."

"Yes, my lord. Will you want breakfast, my lord?"

Lord St. John was certain that his head was splitting open behind his eyes. His mouth tasted foul and his guts seemed to be tied in knots. He felt the very devil, but he willed himself to consider the suggestion of putting food in his mouth and of actually swallowing it. The prospect was not pleasing.

He said harshly, "Coffee, black; a small steak and some toast. I will be in my study. Send for Witherspoon."

A short while later Mr. Witherspoon and breakfast were ushered together into the study.

Lord St. John did not acknowledge with a single glance the tray that was put before him on the desk by the butler. Instead, his nostrils gave a barely perceptible quiver. His expression was sardonic as he addressed the gentleman who approached him. "Ah, Witherspoon. I am glad that you were able to join me."

At the viscount's gesture, Mr. Witherspoon sat down in

a chair placed in front of the desk. He said gravely, "I was anticipating your summons, my lord."

Lord St. John allowed his mouth to twist into a singularly bitter smile. "Of course you did. Everyone in the world must know about that damnable marriage by now. I saw a ruffian thrown out of my house this morning, Witherspoon. I assume that incident was but the tip of the iceberg."

"Aye, my lord," said Mr. Witherspoon unhappily.

Lord St. John turned deliberately to the coffeepot on the tray. The fragrant aroma of hot coffee rose on the air as he poured for himself. His head pounded abominably, but that was not the reason he sought refreshment. He found that his courage was failing him and though he despised himself for the weakness, he much preferred turning his gaze on the unpalatable food and drink than meet his secretary's mournful eyes a second longer. "Will you join me in coffee, Witherspoon?"

"Thank you, no, my lord. I breakfasted some hours ago," said Mr. Witherspoon. "But pray do not allow me to interrupt your own."

Lord St. John lifted his cup to his lips. The coffee was scalding hot, but he steeled himself against the burst of pain. His rage at himself was such that he almost took pleasure in it.

He lowered the cup, and without looking at his secretary, he abruptly asked, "How bad is it, Witherspoon?"

Silence greeted his question. He looked up swiftly. The expression in his secretary's eyes told him all that he had feared.

Lord St. John felt his own face stiffen. He set down the cup very carefully, trying to control the slight tremor in his hand. "I see."

"I am sorry, my lord. I wish that I had better tidings.

Naturally I shall do all in my power to preserve your interests and retire some of the more urgent debts, but—"

Lord St. John threw up his hand. Savagely he said, "Spare me the details, Witherspoon! Answer me just this one question. Is it to be Fleet Prison?"

Mr. Witherspoon hesitated. He had always prided himself upon the strict honesty of his dealings with his sometimes difficult employer, but never had he found himself put into the position of dealing what must surely come as a deathblow. "I . . . trust not, my lord. I have learned that India is not altogether barbaric in its amenities."

Lord St. John gave a crack of unamused laughter. His cold eyes regarded his man of business with a degree of respect that he did not often accord those in his employ. "Thank you, Mr. Witherspoon. Your discretion and tact are of the highest order. You have my permission to act on my behalf as you think best, up to the point that Rosethorn and my horses might be affected. You will naturally keep me informed on all matters."

"Of course, my lord. I understand perfectly."

Mr. Witherspoon did indeed understand. Lord St. John, Viscount Weemswood, would not allow himself to be taken off to debtor's prison. His lordship would prefer exile to all he had ever known to such an ignoble ending. Even so, the unburdening of his lordship's birthplace and his beloved horses would be the last of his possessions that he would countenance letting go to his creditors.

Mr. Witherspoon knew also when he was dismissed and he bowed himself out of the room. His last glance at the viscount, as he closed the door, convinced him that his lordship was not at all inclined to partake of the breakfast growing cold on the tray.

Lord St. John did not know how long he stared at the

opposite wall before he became aware once more of his surroundings. He was tired, discouraged, and made angry by
the circumstances in which he found himself. He could
think of no easy solution or escape.

None existed, of course. He had known that before he
had sent for Witherspoon. He had known it when the duke
had introduced his former doxy as the new duchess. With
the announcement of the duke's anticipated heir, certain
ruin had stared St. John in the face.

Lord St. John laughed hollowly to himself. Perhaps he
had sensed the change of fortune even before. That would
account, in part, for his increased sense of restlessness.

He had been challenging fate for a very long time. He
had lived hard and well, but in what he had at first dimly
begun to realize, and then become convinced, was an empty
fashion.

He had entertained brief thoughts more than once of
joining the army. The war on the Iberian Peninsula was said
to be hot and heavy; perhaps in the heat of battle a man
could feel again that he was really alive.

The army life was still an alternative. That, and
Witherspoon's notion of sailing for India. A man of wit and
physical stamina was said to have untold opportunities of
making of himself a rich nabob in those latitudes.

Certainly he was well-suited for either choice. Blessed
with extraordinary athletic ability and stamina, he was what
was known in society as a Corinthian. All the manly sports
came as naturally as breathing to him. Although driving was
his true passion and forte, he was a past master of boxing,
fencing, shooting, and riding. His allegiance to the sports
had graced his body with strength and endurance, certainly
an advantage if one was to go into battle or to spend years
building a nabob's fortune.

He had also been gifted with a high intellect. Though if he was to be judged by his lazy drift through the years, Lord St. John reflected dispassionately, he would quite possibly have been given low marks in that area. Nonetheless, he did not doubt that he could make a good cavalry officer or carve out a place for himself in India.

His hand, lying on the desk, slowly clenched into a taut fist.

Lord St. John let out an explosive oath, surging out of his chair. He took a swift turn about the study, his thoughts unwinding in turbulent fashion.

At length a sort of calm came over him. His future need not be decided quite at that moment. There was time to weigh his decision a bit longer. Witherspoon would see to that.

In the meantime, there was the business of keeping up appearances. As a member of the *ton*, he knew well that any hint of weakness on his part would be construed in the worst possible light and the jackals would rend his reputation into permanent disrepair.

Bleakness settled over his deeply carved grim expression.

It would happen in any event; but hopefully not before he and Witherspoon had had a chance to see exactly how badly things stood. He had at least the means to settle most of his debts of honor. After those debts were retrieved and, depending upon his reception at the hands of society, it would be time enough to decide the direction of the remainder of his life.

A peculiar smile lit his face, underscoring the bleakness of his eyes. He had any number of acquaintances. It would he interesting to see how many true friends he could boast among them.

Upon that thought succeeded another, and he returned

to the desk to pull pen and paper to him. He had pledged himself to call on his betrothed upon his return to London. The lady must be informed that he had not forgotten their assignation.

After dashing off a quick note, he got up from the desk to tug the bellpull. When a footman answered the summons, the viscount instructed him where to deliver the note. It would not be necessary for the man to wait for a reply. The footman left on his errand, carefully closing the door.

Lord St. John crossed to pick up the cold toast from the tray. He eyed it with distaste. If he was to keep up appearances and participate in all of his former activities, he had to consume a man's portion. More to the point, he should eat something in order to counter the roiling of his abused system. But he would be damned if he would muddle his insides with slop.

He tossed the toast back onto the tray and strode swiftly across the carpet. His eyes glittered as he wrenched open the door. He would have a proper breakfast in the breakfast room or know the reason why.

Chapter 4

Lord St. John had not been sitting at breakfast for many minutes before he had a visitor.

"That's all right, Craighton. I shall show myself in." On those words, Mr. Underwood entered the breakfast room. He greeted the viscount casually. "I thought I might find you in, Sinjin. Having breakfast, are you? I believe I might join you."

Lord St. John smiled slightly, the wintery look in his eyes dissipating ever so little. "Pray do so, Carey. I am not doing full justice to my cook's efforts this morning. It will gratify her no end if you were to empty a serving dish or two." He sat back at his ease, a faint smile playing across his lips and an amused light in his eyes, while Mr. Underwood made his selection from the sideboard.

Mr. Underwood declined the viscount's recommendation of the ale, but took coffee from the footman. He set to work on his plate in an appreciative fashion.

Lord St. John dismissed the footman with a curt word and, when the manservant was gone, he said, "Well, Carey?"

Mr. Underwood shrugged, not pretending to misunderstand the question. He cut another bite of thin steak. "I read the announcement. I never thought Alton would be such a dolt."

Lord St. John's tone became sarcastic. "So you've come to offer your condolences?"

Mr. Underwood looked at the meat speared on his fork. "You've a veritable curst tongue on you, Sinjin," he observed. He put down the laden fork and looked with a steady gaze across the table at the viscount. "If you must know, I came to offer you my support. I thought you might be feeling a bit blue, but I see that you are in as fine trim as ever."

"Devil a bit," said Lord St. John mildly, a faint flush coming up under his tan. He would scarcely admit it, but he was ashamed of his cutting words.

Mr. Underwood accepted the unspoken apology. He again started on the steak and eggs and kippers on his plate. "What do you mean to do?"

Lord St. John gave a short laugh. "Do? My dear Carey, what can I do? I am properly dished. I saw the evidence with my own eyes, though I harbor strong doubts that my esteemed relative planted the seed."

Mr. Underwood looked up quickly at that. "You mean the jade has done Alton false? The baggage! Shall you contest the marriage?"

"You know well that such a course would not suit my pride. I have little desire to set my name up as a byword, as assuredly it would be if I was to drag it through the courts," said Lord St. John, his brows drawing together. He rolled his tankard between his hands in a contemplative way.

"No," agreed Mr. Underwood, shuddering. "But still, it's a cursed shame. She's jockeyed you out of your inheritance and there's nothing to be done. I suppose it would do no good to appeal to Alton's reason?"

"I did do so. It was not a fortuitous confrontation. His grace very nearly went into apoplexy at the suggestion. Suffice it to say that the lady won game, point, and match," said Lord St. John sardonically.

Mr. Underwood uttered an emphatic curse. He ruminated for a moment, then said, "Well, there's nothing for it, then. You'll not want to be the object of all eyes, of course, so I expect that you will wish to beg off your social obligations for the next few weeks. Never fear that I shall not stand with you. I will put it about that you have left on a repairing lease—that you had business at Rosethorn. That will be believed readily enough, I think. It's known that you take an inordinate interest in the place."

Lord St. John stiffened in his chair. There was an odd, black expression in his eyes, which had gone very cold. "Your advice is doubtless well-intended, Carey; but I think not . . . solicited?"

Mr. Underwood lifted a startled gaze to the viscount's face. He also stiffened, very wary of the look in his lordship's eyes. "It was not my intent to insult you, Sinjin."

"Nevertheless you did, damnably." Lord St. John's voice became very low, almost dangerous in tenor. "I do not cry craven. I mean to remain in London and be damned to anyone with the impertinence to question my affairs."

"That I shall never do and well you know it! But I know too well your pride, my lord, and I do not think that you will care for the inevitable curiosity that will surely dog you with this reverse in fortune," said Mr. Underwood.

There was a moment's tense silence.

Lord St. John passed a hand over his face. With a wearied sigh, he said, "Forgive me, Carey. I should know better than to cut up at you. But you know what I am."

"Perhaps none better, saving Miles Trilby. Very well, Sinjin. I shall stand with you whatever course you choose. Even if it is to brave the very gates of hell itself, I shall do so," said Mr. Underwood.

Lord St. John threw back his head and laughed, his black mood lifted. "I am touched, Carey. I had no suspicion that your friendship was ingrained with such loyalty."

Mr. Underwood shrugged. He smiled suddenly. "Can I do less when you offered me such a handsome apology? I did not know until that instant how shaken off your pins you were."

Lord St. John made a noise that was half snarling, half amused. "Do not presume too much, my conceited friend. I shall still meet face-to-face with whatever fate has in store for me. Do you go to Tattersall's this morning?"

Mr. Underwood indicated that he was, and mentioned the new hunter that he had in mind to acquire. By tacit agreement the conversation was turned firmly into a long discussion of the finer points of horseflesh, and the question of the viscount's future abandoned.

When the gentlemen rose at last from the breakfast table, the morning was fairly flown and Mr. Underwood adjured his lordship to be swift. "I promised a little ladybird that I would take her shopping directly after one o'clock. It will be bellows to mend for me if I am late."

"You are bear-led by the petticoats," commented Lord St. John.

"Ah, but the petticoats have such a charming way of showing their appreciation for the mere price of a bonnet or a bauble," said Mr. Underwood slyly, as they emerged from the viscount's town house and sauntered down the walkway.

"You'll not think it so charming if ever one of those mantraps closes her sharp teeth on your ankle and you find yourself leg-shackled for life," said Lord St. John.

"Devil a bit," said Mr. Underwood cheerfully.

Lord St. John spent an agreeable two hours in Mr. Underwood's staunch company. If he noticed the reserve of some of their mutual acquaintances, or that certain conversations broke off as he came into sight, he did not allow it to show either in his expression or his manner. Instead he went out of his way to meet unflinchingly those sly grins and the scattered allusions to his reduced circumstances offered by some who had either never cared for him or who simply enjoyed inflicting insult when and where they were able, whatever the circumstances or party involved.

Mr. Underwood was all too aware of the rampant curiosity that hovered about them and he inwardly seethed at it. He was most angered by the scarcely veiled malice that underlay some of the comments made to the viscount. He found himself depressing the worst offenders, and wondered at Lord St. John's uncharacteristic forbearance. The viscount's black temper was famed, as was his quickness to parlay affront into a challenge for the boxing ring or a more deadly sort of duel. Surely Lord St. John's reputation could be counted upon to hedge off the less intrepid ill-wishers, and for a while that appeared to be the case.

Sir Nigel Smythe was also at Tattersall's, in the company of one of his cronies. Upon seeing Lord St. John, he tossed a word to his companion and with his friend in tow, sauntered over to make his greeting. His lips parted in a cold smile. "Viscount Weemswood. We are well met, my lord. You are acquainted with Rivers, I daresay. Underwood, your servant. My lord, it came as a shock to learn of your loss in the world. I offer you my sympathies."

"Your sentiments are fully appreciated, Sir Nigel," said Lord St. John, quite aware of the gleam of malicious satisfaction in the baronet's eyes.

Since the evening that Lord St. John had bested Sir Nigel at the gaming table, he had been the object of the baronet's intense dislike. Now Lord St. John's obvious indifference to Sir Nigel's false sympathy served to fuel the gentleman's ill-feeling to white heat.

The gentleman's antipathy was palpable, and his sneer unmistakable, but Lord St. John resisted the impulse to issue the cutting rejoinder that such insolence deserved.

"I was impressed with your skill with the pasteboards. Perhaps we shall meet again over the table in contest. Ah no, I forget; it would not be at all the prudent thing for you to indulge yourself in a costly game of chance, would it," said Sir Nigel, smiling still. He observed the flash of anger that heated the viscount's cold eyes, and his smile widened.

Mr. Underwood put up his quizzing glass and stared through it at the gentleman. His attitude was one of bored indifference. "I, for one, would hardly be interested in such a one-sided contest. The last quite pointedly showed up the greater skill."

Sir Nigel reddened. Too angered to utter a single word, he made a short bow and stalked off on his companion's arm.

"My dear Carey," Lord St. John said softly, "resist these efforts on my behalf. I am well able to bring myself out of a skirmish."

"Then do something about that poltroon. I shall stand your second whenever you say," said Mr. Underwood heatedly, dropping his glass. He stared after Sir Nigel, whom he considered had dealt to the viscount a high insult, no matter that it had been couched in friendly words.

"I do not make a spectacle of myself by engaging to duel with every fool in town," Lord St. John said shortly. There was a faint smile on his lips as he swept a contemptuous glance about the floor of Tattersall's. "I shall so honor only the *créme de la créme.*"

A laugh was startled out of Mr. Underwood, drawing the astonished attention of several gentlemen. However, Sir

Nigel appeared extremely annoyed. He snapped a word to his companion and left the vicinity altogether.

As for those who were not privy to the cause of amusement, it was to be seen that Viscount Weemswood was in fine form in order to be cracking jokes with his boon companion, Mr. Underwood. A grudging respect was accorded his lordship by many of the lookers-on and some, who had hung back in judgment of how Lord St. John meant to go on, were agreeably surprised. It was, naturally, to Lord St. John's credit that he was presenting such a well-preserved front. It showed the breeding of a true gentleman.

Shortly thereafter several gentlemen approached Lord St. John and Mr. Underwood, obstensibly to talk horseflesh but it was tacitly understood by all parties that, though never a word was said on the topic, there was approval of the viscount's manner and some sympathy at least for his predicament.

Lord St. John did not purchase a horse, not an unusual occurrence in itself, for he was known for his selectiveness, but noted nonetheless by his sharp-eyed peers.

Mr. Underwood bid for and acquired a showy gelding. After making arrangements for his new possession, he reminded Lord Sr. John that he had a previous engagement that he was rather anxious to keep. "It is not that I do not find your company agreeable, Sinjin, but you will shortly be *de trop*," he said with a grin.

Lord St. John laughed. "I shall not keep you any longer, then."

"Yes, I suppose you have a few calls of your own to make," said Mr. Underwood, his tone making of it a question.

Lord St. John's smile twisted. He assured his friend that he would indeed honor the remainder of his obligations that afternoon. His lips curled in self-derision. "I, too, occasionally accept my share of bear-leading from the fairer sex. I am engaged to drive Lady Althea later."

"Are you?" asked Mr. Underwood slowly. There was an inflection of surprise in his voice, which caused the viscount to glance sharply at him; but if Mr. Underwood had thoughts on the matter, he preferred to keep them to himself. "Well, I shall not see you again. Unless you mean to drop into the club later? Nana and I are meeting for dinner and I expect there will be a few other companionable spirits about."

"I have not made up my mind. I may attend Lady Pothergill's rout instead," said Lord St. John coolly.

Mr. Underwood gave a low whistle, signaling astonishment and admiration. "In for a penny, in for a pound, Sinjin?"

Lord St. John allowed his most cynical smile to light his eyes. "What else? Let them all stare and titter. It will run that much the quicker through the gossip mill."

"Will the beauteous Lady Althea care for being the center of all eyes at the rout? I assume, of course, that you are to act as her ladyship's escort," said Mr. Underwood.

Lord St. John gave a short bark of laughter. "Come, Carey! When has Althea ever balked at the prospect of garnering the attention of every eye? She'll want to attend the rout, never fear."

Mr. Underwood frowned, disturbed. "You have so few illusions, Sinjin."

Lord St. John again laughed, but this time with a bitter edge. "It is indeed a sad lack in my character, Carey. I am thought to be not quite human." He grimaced suddenly. "However, I will grant you this much of a glimpse of human

44

feeling. I hope to God that some other scandal will ascend onto the horizon."

At Mr. Underwood's changing expression, he instantly regretted the confidence. At once he reverted back to his usual sardonic manner. "In Tattersall's I had the devil of a time holding on to my temper, which is never of the best, as you know. The last straw was your infernal impudence to have objected to my opinion of that slab-sided tit you bought."

Mr. Underwood accorded his lordship a sympathetic laugh. "No doubt I shall rue the day that I laid out my blunt on it, but I had a fancy for the bay. I mean to give it to a friend, in any event."

"No one with sense will take it," said Lord St. John. He regarded Mr. Underwood's swift grin and raised brow, and with sudden comprehension, laughed. "Oh, she will like it, I don't doubt. The tit is showy enough. You must tell me sometime if appreciation for a horse far outstrips that for a bonnet or a bauble."

"That is what I mean to find out this afternoon," admitted Mr. Underwood. He laughed at the viscount's grimace and, with a wave of his hand, he left his lordship to his own devices.

Chapter 5

At five o'clock Lord St. John presented himself at a fashionable address in St. James Street. The note he had sent around to his betrothed, Lady Althea, some hours before had been to inform her that he had returned early to London and that he would be happy to wait on her at the usual hour. He was therefore unsurprised when he was immediately ushered into the house to await the lady's appearance.

He cut a commanding figure in a multicaped driving coat that fell to his heels. Underneath it he wore a coat of superfine cloth, cut close to his broad shoulders, and buckskins smoothed into mirror-polished top boots. Extra whip points were thrust through his lapel and he carried a pair of driving gloves.

He allowed the porter to take his beaver, but declined to give up his driving coat and the gloves, since he expected to be leaving the house again in short order. Lady Althea never left him to kick his heels for more than a quarter hour, for she understood that he would not allow his horses to stand any longer. On two occasions, the viscount had been known to leave a polite but terse message that he would appoint another afternoon more convenient for her for driving. Lady Althea had learned to her chagrin, carefully hidden but never forgotten, that she could not command the viscount's anticipation of her grand entrance while his cattle grew restless.

Lord St. John waited in the front parlor. He noticed without particular interest that the furnishings had been changed. He did wonder, however fleetingly, why he had been shown into the formal room when before he had always been received in the lady's private sitting room. He shrugged, thinking it but another conceit of his betrothed.

The seeming puzzle was solved when the door opened and Lady Althea entered the room. He had not realized until that instant that the blue silk hangings and blue-and-gold striped coverings on the gilded furniture would prove to be the perfect foil for her dazzling beauty. Lord St. John smiled, for he was no stranger to his lady's vanity.

Lady Althea offered her hand to him, the touch of her slim fingers cool on his. "My lord." She returned his smile, hers a bewitching sight to the male of the species.

Lady Althea had been blessed with unquestioned birth and beauty. The daughter of the Earl of Cowltern, she could look as high as she wished for a husband; but it was her beauty that made her remarkable. She was fortunate to possess a sylphlike figure that was the envy and despair of every other lady in society. Her guinea-gold hair framed a face of classical purity. If there was a lack of spontaneity in her smile or on occasion a hardness in her deep blue eyes, these faults were overlooked in the general concession that Lady Althea was a diamond of the first water.

Lord St. John was mildly surprised that his betrothed was not dressed to go out driving with him. Lady Althea wore a lovely dimity dress that enhanced her slender femininity and, while he was appreciative of the vision that she presented, he knew that it was not a dress suitable for the seat of a high-perch phaeton.

It had become an established habit that he should drive his betrothed at least once a week in the park during the fashionable hour and such was his intention for this afternoon. Lady Althea had never concealed that she thoroughly enjoyed the attention that she was thus afforded in being seen with such a notable whip as Viscount Weemswood and it had not mattered to him that she should take advantage of their betrothal to serve her own conceit.

As Lord St. John straightened from brushing a kiss across her fingers, he said quizzingly, "That is a marvelously fetching gown, but should you not exchange it for one more suitable since you are driving with me today?"

Lady Althea freed her hand and turned away, presenting her faultless profile to him. She stepped over to the occasional table to reorder the bloodred roses in an already perfect bouquet. "I have changed my mind, my lord."

Lord St. John detected a considerable coolness in her tone and her expression. Such was her reserve that he did not believe that she was referring to their driving assignation. He stiffened.

It had not occurred to him before that his own betrothed might not stand by him. If he had given any thought to Lady Althea at all, he had vaguely assumed that she would join him in his social exile. It was a matter of public record that they were betrothed and the date of their nuptials had already been announced. It was inconceivable that either party could gracefully exit the contract at this late date.

In view of the lightning bolt which had befallen him, Lord St. John had actually been thankful that that part of his life had already been decided. The dowry settled on Lady Althea would not cover all of his expenses, of course, but it would do much toward preserving his pride over the debts of honor that he owed to certain of his peers. That much of his reputation he could be certain of salvaging out of the mess, at least.

At Lady Althea's deliberate words, however, the conjecture that his betrothed had gotten cold feet definitely reared up its ugly head. Testing her, he said, "I had thought of escorting you to Lady Pothergill's this evening."

Lady Althea briefly considered him from out of bright, but rather hard, blue eyes before returning her attention to the roses. "It is good of you to offer. However, Papa has requested that I make one of his party this evening."

Instantly the expression in his gray eyes became completely shuttered. He leaned a broad shoulder against the mantel, stretching his arm along its length, his leather driving gloves crushed between his strong fingers.

He would not pretend to misunderstand her. It was not in his character to do so. "Indeed, ma'am. And to what do I owe this abrupt turnaround?"

Lady Althea lifted one slender shoulder. Her pure profile did not reveal anything to the gentleman who regarded her so closely. "I have heard disturbing news, my lord. It has quite overset me."

Lord St. John's mouth tightened. A hard light entered his eyes. "Perhaps you will be good enough to enlighten me as to the cause of your upset, my lady."

Lady Althea turned, holding a delicate stem between her fingers. Her slim blond brows rose. "Oh, Sinjin, must we fence like this? It is all over town. The Duke of Alton has married that creature—because she is increasing! I was never more shocked in my life."

She paused a moment, cocking her lovely head as she regarded the rose cupped in her hand. "And never more regretful."

Lord St. John slowly straightened away from the mantel. His expression had gone very still. "What exactly are you trying to say, Althea?"

Lady Althea put the fragile bloom to her exquisite nostrils. "My dear Sinjin, surely we are too well acquainted for you to mistake my meaning."

Lord St. John's lips twisted. He would be damned if he would ease the way for her. "Nevertheless, Althea, pray indulge me."

She sighed and turned to gently replace the rose into the middle of the bouquet. "How very vulgar of you, Sinjin. Very well; your suit is no longer acceptable to me. That is bald enough, is it not? I have already spoken of it to my father and he understands my feelings perfectly. I could not possibly contemplate marriage to you now."

Lord St. John spoke exceedingly softly. "Am I so different than I was two days ago, Althea?"

Lady Althea looked over her shoulder at him in incomprehension. "Of course you are, Sinjin. Two days ago you were heir presumptive to a dukedom. I would eventually have become a duchess. Now you are a mere viscount."

"Whilst you are the daughter of an earl," said Lord St. John with heavy irony.

Lady Althea regarded him with a gathering unfriendliness in her blue eyes. She turned slowly toward him. "Such mockery is beneath you, my lord."

"On the contrary, *I* am beneath you. Isn't that what you actually mean, my lady?" asked Lord St. John from between his tight-clenched teeth.

Startled by the blaze of naked fury in his cold gray eyes, Lady Althea took an instinctive step backward. The sharp edge of the occasional table stopped her retreat, reminding her of what she owed her consequence. She stretched to her full height and said coldly, "I think you should leave now, my lord."

"And so I shall, with alacrity, my lady!"

Lord St. John turned on his heel. Before he had quite reached the door, however, he whirled back to the earl's lovely daughter. "But first—"

In two swift strides, he had reached her and hauled her, astonished, into his arms. With one hand he forced up her chin. He kissed her ruthlessly, for several seconds, before thrusting her from him quite abruptly.

Lady Althea staggered as her hand brushed a chair back, and she clung to it for balance. Her eyes were huge dark pools as she lifted her other hand to touch her swollen lips. Her lovely face was flushed and a pulse beat openly at the base of her slender throat.

She had never appeared more beautiful, but her beauty left Lord St. John untouched.

"Think on that when you wed your dried, old stick of a duke, my lady!" said the viscount savagely. He strode to the door and flung it open. Without a backward glance, he exited. The door crashed shut behind him.

On the carpet, forgotten where they had dropped, were his driving gloves.

Lady Althea stared at the gloves, seeing in them the latent power of the viscount's fingers. She shuddered, slowly rubbing her bare arms, where the sensation of the bruising cruelty of his hands lingered.

Lord St. John left the Earl of Cowltern's town house without a thought given to where he was headed. Vaulting onto the seat of his phaeton, he whipped up his team, scarcely granting the boy holding his horses time to leap out of the way.

He was consumed with rage at this latest, and cruelest, blow. It seemed that everything that he had depended upon, everything that had undergirded his life, was but a hollow mockery. Society was riddled with hypocrisy—on the one hand touting birth and honorable qualities as the highest attributes, and on the other cutting at one stroke one of their number who had been credited with such, but who seemed to have lost all redeeming value together with his expected inheritance.

Lady Althea was the very essence of one of the favored ones. But he had fallen outside the shining circle, and she could not now be bothered with such as him. The betrayal was stunning for its very unexpectedness.

He had never been in love with Lady Althea, nor she with him. Theirs had been a cold-blooded agreement that would have served to ally two old and respected families. He had expected to acquire a suitable bride and hostess, one who would have brought a substantial dowry and would in time have produced the necessary heir. She had expected to become mistress of her own household and to enjoy the social position that her fortunate birth had decreed was hers by right.

Though there had never been a spark of feeling between them, neither had found the other physically displeasing. As for strength of personality, Lord St. John and Lady Althea had discovered that they were fairly evenly matched. Each had the determination and the selfishness not to be overtrodden by the other, and this had engendered a mutual, though tepid, respect.

On the whole, it had been a satisfactory arrangement.

One which had been blown to flinders.

Lord St. John drove for an hour or more. He gave no thought to his destination, only to the desire for constant movement, while his dark reflections occupied his mind. He stopped only to rest his horses at an out-of-the-way inn and there discovered a very tolerable Madeira.

It was full night when he returned to London. He

stopped only long enough at his town house to change and to give over his exhausted team into the care of his groom before he set his steps toward the club.

Mr. Underwood and Lord Heatherton were pleasantly surprised when Lord St. John appeared to join them for dinner. "I thought you would be at Lady Pothergill's," said Mr. Underwood.

The viscount threw himself carelessly into a chair. His hooded eyes gleamed above the smile that twisted his thin lips. "I am out of favor, my friend. Her ladyship showed her true colors this afternoon."

He spoke so bitterly that Mr. Underwood and Lord Heatherton exchanged a comprehensive glance. They thereafter applied themselves to the task of pulling Lord St. John out of his black temper and, failing that, to getting his lordship roaring drunk. In the last, they were successful, for Lord St. John was completely amenable.

At the end of the evening, Lord St. John's friends stuffed him into a cab and accompanied him home. Supporting his lordship between them, Mr. Underwood and Lord Heatherton staggered up the steps of the viscount's town house.

"We'll have to pour him into bed," grunted Mr. Underwood.

"Better that than hear that Sinjin blew a hole in some unfortunate," observed Lord Heatherton.

"Lord, don't you think I thought of that as well?" uttered Mr. Underwood scornfully, banging on the door while endeavoring to keep Lord St. John from slithering to the ground. "Though I suspect he'd much rather thrash the lady."

"You don't say. I never pegged Sinjin to be in the petticoat line," said Lord Heatherton. He blinked rather owlishly as the door opened and the viscount's butler peered out. "Craighton. Just the man we want."

The butler had taken in the situation at a glance and opened the door wide, directing the gentlemen to help his lordship upstairs. Mr. Underwood and Lord Heatherton looked dubiously at the stairs, then at each other. Lord Heatherton shrugged. "Nothing for it. What set Sinjin off?"

"Lady Pothergill's rout," supplied Mr. Underwood, panting as he navigated upward.

"Ah, that explains it. One of m'mother's cronies. Awful woman. Can't think why her ladyship is so in vogue. Never has a decent layout," said Lord Heatherton disapprovingly.

"Lady Althea likes Lady Pothergill," said Mr. Underwood.

"Ah," said Lord Heatherton, frowning heavily. Silence fell between the gentlemen until they had rounded the landing and were proceeding to the viscount's bedroom. Lord Heatherton's countenance suddenly cleared. "Ah!"

"Just so," nodded Mr. Underwood.

The butler ran ahead to alert the viscount's valet. The gentlemen tumbled Lord St. John onto his bed and Tibbs took over the task of making his lordship comfortable.

Mr. Underwood and Lord Heatherton contemplated the unconscious viscount for a moment. "Poor Sinjin. Much better to get drunk," said Lord Heatherton.

Realizing that they had given over their charge into the capable hands of the viscount's valet and butler, they withdrew from the bedroom and left the town house, weaving slightly as they made their way down the sidewalk.

Chapter 6

The terraced residences in Islington were respectable addresses, though so far removed from the haunts of the fashionable as to be almost another world. Night had fallen and at one quiet house the occupants were enjoying their after-dinner respite from the demands of the day.

In the drawing room, candles had been lit to augment the glow from the hearth fire so that there would be no need for the elderly gentleman or the young lady to strain their eyes against competing shadows.

The portly gentleman rustled the newspaper. "Here is an interesting item. The Duke of Alton has wed. The gentleman must be twenty years my senior! I wonder what his grace's heir thinks of it. Nay, I suspect I may guess. 'Tis a wonderment, don't you think, Mary?"

"Indeed it is, Papa," agreed the young lady opposite the wide-striped settee, without looking up from her embroidery. Beside her was a basket holding silks of various colors, folded work, a small scissors and assorted other supplies. She reached for the scissors and snipped a finished thread. Deftly knotting the end of the silk on her needle, she started a new bit of stitching on her hoop.

Mr. Pepperidge peered around the edge of his newspaper, his spectacles glinting in the firelight. He regarded his eldest child with strong fondness. She was a comely young woman, her brown hair smoothed into a coronet of braids, her capable fingers evenly and surely drawing the needle through the fabric on the embroidery hoop. The design she worked would be one of her own creation, he knew, for she had proven to be quite artistic with her needle. The expense that he had been put to in sending Mary to that select seminary had been a worthwhile investment, for he could not think of another young woman of their social standing who was as refined or educated as his own dear Mary.

Mr. Pepperidge lowered the newspaper to allow his appreciative gaze to go round the comfortably appointed drawing room. Mary was talented in other ways. She had a knack of making a room appear warm and welcoming, a quality much prized by an old gentleman such as himself, or for that matter, any other gentleman.

On the thought, Mr. Pepperidge sighed heavily, for it occurred to him, and not for the first time, that his daughter should have been stitching chair covers for her own house instead of for her father's.

Mary looked up upon hearing the regretful sound, a smile coming at once to the full curve of her lips. "What is it, Papa? Have you read another item that does not quite meet with your approval?"

"I have been a selfish old man, Mary. I should have seen you wed and the happy mistress of your own house years ago."

Astonished, Mary lowered her embroidery to her lap. "Papa! What an extraordinary thing to say. I am quite content as I am."

"As am I, dear child. Your being here has meant all the world to me since your sweet mother died. But you are a lovely young woman. You should have pretty dresses and choose a suitable gentleman of our acquaintance for your husband," said Mr. Pepperidge.

Mary laughed, a rich throaty peal of amusement. "What a funny you are, Papa. I do not pine after frivolity or furbelows, as you well know. And as for a husband, well, I suspect I am a little too long in the tooth to expect to receive a suitable offer. I am all of one-and-twenty since last week and had a lovely locket from you and a scarf sent by Tabitha and a beautiful nosegay from William. Now, Papa, pray do not scowl. I could scarcely wish for anything dearer than the affection of my family."

Mr. Pepperidge shook his head, sighing again. "I have kept you locked away too long with me, Mary. I see it now. I have been blinded by my own selfishness. You have spoiled me too well, Mary."

The door to the drawing room opened and the housemaid entered with the coffee tray. Mary set aside her embroidery in the basket, saying, "If I have done so it is because you are such a darling. Now, Papa, we will have no more of this nonsense if you please. I am well content to go on just as we are. Do we not have everything we could possibly wish for our comfort?" Mary quietly thanked the housemaid and dismissed the girl until she was needed again.

"Oh, aye, we do well enough," agreed Mr. Pepperidge. "Business is very good since the South American market has been tapped. However, that is not to what I am referring, as well you know, child."

Mary shook her head. "Really, Papa. I confess I do not understand this strange tack you have taken this evening." She fixed the coffee precisely as her father preferred with a generous dollop of cream and sugar. He accepted the cup and upon tasting the coffee, nodded his approval. Mary poured herself a cup and sat back comfortably against the settee. She said serenely, "How was business today, Papa?"

"You would make a delightful wife, Mary."

"Papa," she said warningly.

Mr. Pepperidge shook his heavy finger at her. "I know of what I speak, daughter. You always do my coffee just as I prefer. My favorite dishes are always at table. The rooms are clean and bright and cheerful. You always inquire after my concerns with the right mixture of interest and intelligence. These are little things that a gentleman appreciates. You are a treasure, Mary, and one that any gentleman would be honored to have to wife."

"Very well, Papa, I am a treasure. I shall not pull caps with you on that score," said Mary, her eyes twinkling. "But what gentlemen do you refer to? I have not a score of suitors waiting outside the door, as did Tabitha. Nor do I possess my sister's rare beauty. I am myself and only that."

"You underrate yourself, Mary. You have an abundance of excellent qualities. Poor Tabitha possessed little else but her beauty. She had to make the most of it," said Mr. Pepperidge with an air of regret.

Mary looked over at her father in surprise. "Papa, whatever has gotten into you this evening? I have never heard you speak so before."

"Perhaps I feel my own mortality more than is my usual wont. Certainly things appear uncommonly clear to me these days," said Mr. Pepperidge.

"I do wish you would not speak so, Papa. Why, you are a prime specimen of the stolid respectable Englishman. You shall undoubtedly enjoy many more years of my spoiling you," said Mary. "I am only glad that Tabitha and William are not here to listen to your foolishness."

Mr. Pepperidge chuckled. "Aye, Tabitha would give us floods of tears, would she not? Tabitha was always a spritely little thing, pretty as a picture, but not near as clever as you or William."

"William would undoubtedly scold you, just as I have," said Mary, smiling.

"The boy has no proper respect for his elders," Mr. Pepperidge grumbled, but it was said indulgently. He said, suddenly pensive, "I would have liked my son to follow me into trade, but I have come to recognize that it will never be. William has always been unsteady. Now he is wild for the army and I will not be able to hold him in England much longer."

"But he is only sixteen, Papa! A mere boy!" exclaimed Mary as she returned her nearly empty coffee cup to the tray.

"Aye, old enough to know his mind but not old enough to have acquired good sense," said Mr. Pepperidge. "I worry about some of those friends of his, Mary, I shan't disguise that from you."

"As do I, Papa. His last visit he spoke quite glowingly of a fellow who sounded to me to be suspiciously knowing for a schoolboy," said Mary quietly.

"It is a pity you were not born a man, Mary. You've the sensible discerning character required for business that William so deplorably lacks," said Mr. Pepperidge.

"If I had been a man you would not now be sipping coffee made perfectly to your liking," Mary said wryly. She got the rise that she had expected as Mr. Pepperidge chuckled and agreed it was so.

"Still and all, I wish more for you than keeping house for an old man. 'Tis a pity that you were never taken with any of the gentlemen who called on Tabitha."

"I think it was as much the other way around, Papa. None of the gentlemen was taken with me," said Mary matter-of-factly. In the beginning, a few of the gentlemen had been her callers; but their interest in her had never survived once they had met her sister.

"Idiots, one and all," said Mr. Pepperidge forcibly.

Mary laughed. She shook her head at him reprovingly. "Really, Papa. How can you say so when you have just expressed the wish that I had wed one of them?"

"Aye, tie me in knots with my own words. I still wish something better for you, child," said Mr. Pepperidge.

"Perhaps I shall surprise you one day. Papa," said Mary. "Now do finish your coffee so that Maud may take back the tray. It is getting very late."

Mr. Pepperidge obeyed, grumbling a little. "Aye, fuss over me and send me up to my bed. I am just an old man. What do I know, after all?"

Mary laughed again. "Dear Papa." She rose and walked over to drop an affectionate kiss on his wrinkled brow. "I shall see you in the morning, shall I?" She turned to the bell-pull and tugged it.

"Of course; of course. You recall that I shall be wanting to go to Dover on the morrow?"

"Yes, Papa. I gave the orders for the packing hours ago. We shall be able to leave at first light," said Mary.

He regarded her with his head cocked to one side. "It is to be a holiday, is it?"

"I do love the sea, and though it is not Brighton or Bath, I shall still be able to smell the salt on the air," said Mary.

The housemaid entered and Mary gestured at the tray. "Thank you, Maud. That will be all this evening."

"Yes, miss." The housemaid exited, the tray in her hands.

Mr. Pepperidge chuckled as he got up out of his chair. "You've merchants' blood running strong in your veins, my Mary. 'Tis a pity that females are not welcomed on board ships."

"I have often thought so, indeed," said Mary imperturbably. "Are you going up directly?"

"No, I think that I shall watch the fire for a few minutes," said Mr. Pepperidge.

Mary knew from her father's slightly guilty expression that he meant to light one of the abominable cigars that he had taken a liking to since receiving a box as a gift from an associate in the South American trade, but she did not tease him about it. It was a small vice and hardly one to greatly concern her. "Good night, dear Papa."

She left the drawing room and went up the narrow staircase to the upper hall. In her bedroom, she dismissed her maid once the woman had unbuttoned the innumerable tiny buttons down the back of her gown, saying that she would prepare herself for bed.

The maid left without any undue curiosity. Miss Pepperidge often preferred to do for herself.

Mary finished undressing and slipped on a nightgown. She got into bed, but she did not immediately blow out the candle. Feeling somewhat restless, she decided to read. But after a time, she found that her thoughts wandered from the printed page so often that she had no idea what she had read. Finally she set aside the book and surrendered to the direction of her overpowering reflections.

Her father's astonishing comments that evening had set up a regrettable train of thought. Mary had often wondered what her life might have been like if circumstances had been a little different. If her mother had survived the influenza, Mary would not have taken over the supervision of the house, nor have learned so much about the workings of her father's business during the time of his deepest grief.

Certainly she would have enjoyed small outings into the family's limited but respectable society more often and perhaps she would have attached a suitor or two of her own. She might even have become betrothed. It was a giddy thought, for Mary had never considered herself to be attractive in the same sense as her sister.

Tabitha had been only fifteen when she began to receive gentlemen callers. Looking back, Mary could not quite recall how it had happened that the gentlemen had discovered her sister; but discover her they had and nothing was ever the same for Tabitha.

Tabitha had never liked lessons of any sort and she had been the bane of her governess's existence. When the frustrated governess had given abrupt notice, Tabitha had refused to go to the select seminary which had so benefitted Mary. Instead Tabitha had announced her intention of entering society and finding herself a rich husband. Mary had always been puzzled by her father's acquiescence to Tabitha's declaration, but in light of his revelations that evening, she finally understood. For Tabitha, there could be no other respectable alternative but immediate marriage.

Tabitha had made her choice and entered wedded bliss.

Mary had not liked the gentleman. He had been a great deal older than her sister and was somewhat boorish in manners, which she had suspected hinted at a similar indifference of character.

When she had voiced her reservations during the courtship, Tabitha had pooh-poohed her concerns. "It is all that fancy learning you have had, Mary. It has made you too nice by half. Mr. Applegate shall suit me very well, I promise you. Why, only look at this ravishing hat that he bought me just this morning. Isn't it simply too precious for words?" She had set the bonnet on her head at a rakish angle and turned to her sister, anticipating oohs of admiration.

The hat had been a frivolous confection of lace and silk and flowers and dipping feathers, quite inappropriate and quite obviously very expensive. "Don't you think it a bit . . . fast to accept so extravagant a gift from the gentleman?" Mary had asked hesitantly. She knew that she would not have accepted such an intimate gift, nor one so outré.

"Oh, do not be such a sad stick, Mary. We are very nearly betrothed, after all. What difference now or when we have actually wed?" Tabitha had said blithely, swinging around to preen herself in front of the cheval glass.

Mary held her tongue after that, but at the wedding ceremony she had not been able to summon up the happiness that she knew that she should have felt for her sister. But three years later, they still received the rare, laboriously written letter from Tabitha expressing her continued happiness, while Mary herself remained unwed and unsought.

Mary sighed and reached over to put out the candle. A whiff of smoke teased her nostrils as she slid under the bedclothes. Mary closed her eyes against the dark of the bedroom. As she fell asleep, she had an undefined yearning that was all caught up in the unclear face of a very special gentleman.

Chapter 7

A few nights later it rained, a steady monotonous sheet of gray obscuring the streets. The wind blew in ill-tempered gusts, sending bone-settling chill nipping at the heels of anyone foolish enough to be out in it.

The bleak weather suited Lord St. John's mood perfectly. He slumped in the rattling carriage, hands thrust deep into his pockets. He had just come from a card party with friends—Miles Trilby, the Earl of Walmsley; Lord Edward Heatherton; and Mr. Carey Underwood. They were arguably the only true friends that he had left.

Lord St. John turned his face to the window. The play of lightning cast jagged shadows over his grim expression. He had won at cards that night, but it had not seemed to matter very much. He had tossed his winnings over to Lord Heatherton, preferring to have nothing than to give the monies over to Witherspoon and know that it was but a hopeless drop in the bucket compared to what he had to have.

A muscle worked in his jaw. He rolled his shoulders, attempting to release the tension of his pent-up rage. He had not been particularly good company that evening. His thoughts had ultimately proven too strong to be diverted by a card game with friends. And so he had flung down his best hand of the night, spurning his winnings, and taken abrupt leave from the Earl of Walmsley's town house.

Mr. Underwood had followed him out to the cab and insisted upon sharing it, saying that it would be impossible to find another in such weather. Lord St. John had reluctantly given way, but he had directed the driver first to Mr. Underwood's lodgings so that he could be rid of his well-intentioned friend.

"I do not want your company, Carey. I prefer to deal with my own demons in private," he had said pointedly.

Mr. Underwood had objected. "I had hoped for a drop of that excellent brandy you have laid down in your cellar." The viscount had been insulting in turning aside the suggestion and in the end Mr. Underwood had no choice but to accede to the viscount's wishes.

Before he left the carriage, however, he had said, "You will call on me, Sinjin?"

Lord St. John had grimaced and said bitingly, "You need not be so anxious, Carey. Your wager is safe enough. I am not likely to forfeit the race by putting a period to my existence."

Mr. Underwood had nodded. "I never thought that you would," he said casually, before leaping out into the driving rain and racing for the shelter of his door.

Recalling that conversation, Lord St. John gave a short bark of laughter. The last several days since his return to London had been hellish. It could hardly be wondered at if his demeanor reflected it.

His position was untenable. He had been given the cut direct by personages who had previously afforded him affable recognition. Amongst those acquaintances who shared his interests in driving and other sports, he had detected the slightest withdrawal, as though his cronies waited to see whether he was still one of them.

Matrons who had previously beamed when he had approached their daughters to stand up with them for a dance now received him with frozen smiles and quite pointed remarks designed to warn him away. Before his betrothal to

Lady Althea, he had been a favored party and it had been audibly regretted that his lordship, with his prospects of becoming a duke, had been snatched up by the Earl of Cowltern's daughter. Since it had become known that his grand prospects had gone up in proverbial smoke, and that the betrothal was no longer existent, Lord St. John was looked upon as a gazetted fortune hunter. Society's well-bred daughters must therefore be protected from his unwanted attentions.

As for many of the other ladies, their eyes had reflected an avid, even malicious, interest as they commiserated with Lord St. John on his recent misfortunes. His pride had been exacerbated almost beyond endurance by the insult and hypocrisy that was directed to his face, but it had been the certainty of ridicule directed at his back that had been the most difficult to accept.

But no, contrary to Mr. Underwood's delicately expressed concern, he would drive the race. It was one for time between London and Dover. In his present frame of mind, there was nothing that would suit him better than the wildest drive that he could manage short of killing his horses.

The cab stopped. Lord St. John got out and paid the fare. He sauntered up the steps of his town house without regard for the rain. He was soaked when he entered and his butler regarded his drenched appearance with horror.

"My lord! I shall ring up at once for Mr. Tibbs."

Lord St. John brusquely waved aside the butler's concern. "No, do not concern Tibbs just yet. I shall go up momentarily. First bring me a bottle of brandy in the sitting room."

The butler hesitated. "My lord, there is a gentleman in the sitting room who has been waiting to see you. A Captain Hargrove."

Lord St. John put up his brows. A stir of curiosity entered his indifferent eyes. "Indeed? I wonder what the good captain could possibly want of me?" Heedless of the water dripping from his garments onto the entry tiles, he strode down the hall to the sitting room and flung open the door.

Inside, the fire had burned down to red embers. On a settee a lanky gentleman was sprawled in sleep, his arms crossed over his chest, his long legs stretched before him toward the fire. A horrible strangling sound punctuated by a loud snore issued forth from his slack mouth.

Lord St. John regarded his somnolent visitor thoughtfully before turning to inquire of the butler, "Craighton?"

The butler coughed discreetly and said in a hushed voice, "Captain Hargrove was somewhat the worse for drink when he arrived, my lord. I suggested that perhaps he might wish to return at a more conventional time, but he insisted that he would wait upon your return."

"And so he has," said Lord St. John. He motioned the butler out of the room and followed, closing the door. "I am going upstairs to bed. Pray inform Captain Hargrove in the morning that I shall be glad to have him join me for breakfast."

"Very good, my lord. Shall I bring up the brandy, my lord?"

Lord St. John, already in the act of mounting the stairs, paused with his hand on the balustrade. There was a rare smile lighting his eyes. "I think not, Craighton. Captain Hargrove has effectively persuaded me that the better course is to address my pillow sober. Otherwise I might wake myself with my own hideous snoring."

The butler permitted himself a prim smile and wished the viscount good night.

Lord St. John slept soundly for the first time in several

days. When he wakened, he lay still for a moment wondering why he should feel a hint of anticipation for the day. Then he recalled his unexpected visitor and swung himself out of bed, calling for his valet, Tibbs.

A short while later Lord St. John entered the breakfast room. He saw that Captain Hargrove was already before him. The gentleman's coat was rumpled and his cravat bore the signs of having been unsuccessfully smoothed, while his hair stood up in unruly waves. The captain was morosely staring at a cup of coffee.

"Good morning, Hargrove. I trust that you slept well?" asked Lord St. John, crossing to the sideboard to make his selection.

Captain Hargrove, having glanced up quickly at the sound of his voice, grimaced. "Aye, as well as any man could stone-drunk on a sofa too short for the purpose."

Lord St. John laughed as he filled his plate. "I apologize for my remiss hospitality. Perhaps I might make up for it with a decent repast." He looked round with a hint of mockery in his eyes. "The kippers are particularly good, I think."

Captain Hargrove gave a perceptible shudder. "Thank you, but no. I could not look a kipper in the face. I shall stick with coffee."

Lord St. John took his plate to the table and seated himself. He started on his kippers with every appearance of appreciation, while Captain Hargrove, somewhat green about the mouth, watched him with revolted fascination.

At length, Lord St. John said, "I must admit to curiosity, Captain. I had not thought us such particularly good friends that you would feel able to make free with my settee."

Captain Hargrove flushed. "My apologies, my lord. I

68

had no intention of doing so. I meant only to call on you briefly. Though now that I am sober, it seems a dashed stupid thing to do at all."

Lord St. John leaned back in his chair, having finished with his breakfast. He waved aside the footman's offer of coffee. Drawling, he said, "Not at all, sir. I am quite willing for you to call on me, for I enjoyed immensely our last encounter. Are we to try pistols at twenty paces with the pips of playing cards for targets?"

Captain Hargrove laughed. "Not this morning, my lord. My head is not in it and I fear my hand would shake so that I would disgrace myself."

"A pity, for I would like nothing better than such a contest." Lord St. John regarded his guest for a moment. He dismissed the footmen and when the door had fallen shut behind their retreating backs, he then asked softly, "Why *have* you come, Captain?"

Captain Hargrove again flushed. He looked uncomfortable. "As I said before, it was a dashed stupid thing to do. I had a notion, you see, that—well, it is neither here nor there now. Pray disregard the intrusion, my lord. I should get back to my quarters before my batman decides I have been abducted."

Lord St. John played with his knife. He looked up as the captain rose from the table. "But I fear that I cannot disregard it, Captain Hargrove. We are scarcely acquainted; yet you felt so strongly about this notion of yours last night that you insisted upon waiting for me to return. I really cannot let you go without understanding something of what was in your thoughts."

Captain Hargrove appeared acutely uncomfortable. "My lord, I would rather not say."

Lord St. John smiled thinly. The bare warmth in his eyes

had disappeared. His voice turned cold. "Indulge me, Captain.

For a moment the gentlemen measured each other.

Captain Hargrove smiled then, and shrugged. "You will likely plant me a facer for it, but I suppose that even with this head I shall survive. The plain fact of it is, my lord, I come to offer you whatever might be in my power to give. I-I have heard of your reverses and having taken a liking for you, I determined that I, at least, would not turn my back." There was resolution, as well as an underlying echo of anger, in his voice.

Lord St. John heard it and understood. He felt a surge of fury at the hypocrisy of society. He drew in a breath to steady himself. "My name makes the rounds, is that it, Captain?"

Captain Hargrove balled his fingers on the table. "However reluctant I am to say it, yes, my lord."

"It is not unexpected."

Lord St. John rose abruptly, flinging his napkin to the table. He saw the gentleman opposite squaring his shoulders as though preparing to receive a blow. "No, I have no intention of brawling with you, Captain. I am not an ancient Greek to punish the bearer of unpleasant tidings. Instead, I accept the gesture that you have made on my behalf. It is a rare thing to find friendship in my present position."

Lord St. John's lips twisted, then eased into a genuine smile, faint though it was. "Are you up to seconding a race, Captain?"

"A race, my lord?" Captain Hargrove's eyes reflected startlement, then the instant of his understanding. "I should like nothing better. When do you leave?"

Lord St. John's glance raked the captain's figure, still attired in evening clothes. "I shall take you up at your lodgings in a half hour. That should be time enough to effect a change."

"More than ample, my lord! I shall be awaiting your arrival," said Captain Hargrove with the flash of a grin. He gave the viscount his address at an hotel that catered to military gentlemen when they were on leave from the Peninsula.

Lord St. John went around the table and clapped the gentleman's broad shoulder. "Good. I shall alert a few of my acquaintances to the start of the race and then be with you." He showed his twisted smile. "Though I am somewhat out of favor in certain quarters, I can yet command attention over a sporting wager."

Captain Hargrove shook his head. After shooting a keen glance at the viscount's flinty expression, he wisely did not attempt to express his sympathy. Instead, he said, "I trust that the book is not yet closed, for I should like to place a small wager of my own. I have a shrewd notion that one could pocket a tidy sum from backing you, my lord."

Lord St. John glanced at his companion as he reached for and opened the breakfast room door. He felt a vague disappointment. He had not thought the gentleman to be a toadeater. As he crossed the threshold into the entry hall, Captain Hargrove matching his steps, he said with cynicism, "Surely that is a far-reaching assumption, sir. You have never seen me drive."

"But I have seen your team, on the occasion of our duel. I've never laid eyes on a finer set of cattle. As for your driving skill"—Captain Hargrove smiled faintly as he met the viscount's cold eyes.—"I am a fair dab at judging my man, and in addition I have had the rare privilege of measuring a length of steel against you. Aye, I think it safe enough to risk my blunt on you, my lord."

Lord St. John cracked a laugh as he accompanied Captain Hargrove to the front door. He saw the gentleman out, much to the astonishment of his wooden-faced porter. "I am humbled, indeed. Captain, I look forward to furthering our acquaintance."

"As shall I, my lord," said Captain Hargrove, flashing his dazzling grin once more. He ran lightly down the steps to the curb and hailed a hackney.

Lord St. John turned back into the town house, a rare smile easing the severity that had lately come to deepen his characteristically cynical expression.

Chapter 8

Lord St. John took up Captain Hargrove at the curb in front of that gentleman's lodgings. Several fashionable acquaintances, some of whom had given the viscount a scarce nod of recognition in the days just past, and many unknowns had gathered on the walk in front of the hotel to witness the beginning of the race. A brisk business was done in the placing of last-minute wagers.

Captain Hargrove placed his own wager, remarking that there was nothing he liked better than a contest whose outcome could not be in doubt. His cheerful declaration aroused a fury of competition in the breasts of some of those who heard him and they loudly proclaimed that the viscount could not possibly shave off the necessary minutes. The odds increased sharply.

Lord St. John listened with a sardonic expression in his eyes.

The gentlemen who had taken it upon themselves to record the wagers agreed that Captain Hargrove, despite his partisan remark, had already established a reputation for fair dealing and, in addition, was just in from the Peninsula and so had no loyalties, so that he could be depended upon to give impartial witness to the finish.

Pocket watches were consulted in order to mark and record the starting time. Captain Hargrove put the yard of tin to his lips and gave a flourishing blast. Lord St. John flicked his whip and guided his team away from the curb. A few interested parties had come to the beginning of the race in their own carriages or on horseback and they accompanied the viscount's vehicle through the street, shouting cheerful witticisms back and forth among their company.

Lord St. John paid little heed to the tomfoolery. He tooled the curricle through the tangle of carriages and wagons, horsemen and pedestrians with consummate skill, coolly negotiating even the most impossibly narrow gaps without mishap.

Quickly enough the other drivers fell behind and gave way. One or two of those in hacks remained in sight of the viscount's curricle almost to the outer reaches of the congested London byways, but then they, too, turned back.

Captain Hargrove watched the viscount work, giving a soundless whistle at a particularly harrowing squeeze between two draft wagons. "You are quite good at this," he said.

He was startled when Lord St. John flashed a completely open grin. In his short acquaintance with the viscount, Captain Hargrove had taken for granted that his lordship's faintly mocking air was habitual. He recalled only one other time that he had seen such naturalness in the man and that had been on the occasion of their duel. It was an interesting insight into the viscount's character, he reflected thoughtfully.

London was eventually left behind and Lord St. John let his horses go. The countryside swept by in a blur of high green hedges and glimpses of fine estates and cottage roofs.

Lord St. John drove his horses hard but not beyond what he judged to be their limits of endurance. Barring unforeseen accidents or barriers in the road, he was completely confident of making Dover well under the designated time.

And so it proved. Upon entering the outskirts of Dover, Captain Hargrove pulled out his pocket watch. "Oh, well done!" he exclaimed, faithfully marking the hour in a small notebook he had carried for the purpose.

Lord St. John said nothing, but the unusual ease of his expression was enough to show his companion that he was also pleased.

"I think a celebration is in order, my lord," said Captain Hargrove, putting away the notebook.

"Do you indeed, Hargrove?" asked Lord St. John with the glimmer of a smile. "What manner of celebration had you in mind?"

"A pint of ale and a hand of beef are called for after such dusty work," said Captain Hargrove firmly. "There is an inn that gained my favor when last I embarked for the Peninsula. It is not the stop of the fashionable, of course, but instead lays out a man's trenchers." There was an underlying contempt in his words for the haunts of the fashionable that made St. John laugh.

"You intrigue me, sir. Direct me to it, I pray," said Lord St. John.

Captain Hargrove did so and within a few short minutes the gentleman's carriage turned into a lively inn yard. After Lord St. John had given instructions for the care of his team, he and Captain Hargrove entered into the crowded taproom.

While Captain Hargrove made known to a waiter what was wanted, Lord St. John stripped off his driving gloves and looked about him with interest.

It was as Captain Hargrove had said. The taproom clientele was of a commoner sort than he was used to mingling with, the majority being respectable tradespeople or of the same military stamp as Captain Hargrove. He was the only gentleman in the room, his identity marked by his fine apparel, and he had already garnered a few flickering glances of curiosity.

But instead of being made uncomfortable because he was so obviously out of place, Lord St. John felt a liberating sense of anonymity. None here would know or care about his financial difficulties. There would be no supercilious smiles or barbed greetings to meet and deflect.

Captain Hargrove returned to the viscount, rubbing his hands together. "We shall shortly be taken care of, my lord. Have you a preference of one table over another?"

He suddenly appeared a shade uncertain, as if struck for the first time by the incongruity of his lordship's appearance in that setting. "That is, if you do not mind remaining here belowstairs rather than taking a private parlor."

Lord St. John smiled at his companion. There was a gleam of unusual satisfaction in his gray eyes. "None whatsoever, Hargrove. As for bespeaking a private parlor, I cannot imagine anything more boring. I infinitely prefer the taproom."

Captain Hargrove flashed a grin. "Very well, then. Let us lay claim to a table at once, my lord. My dry throat is begging to be slaked."

Lord St. John and Captain Hargrove were soon toasting the successful completion of the race with good ale and a late luncheon. An hour later, replete and good-humored, the gentlemen rose and made their way out of the taproom to pay their bill. Captain Hargrove insisted that the honor was to be his and as the viscount's expression frosted, he leveled a look on him. "My lord, I would not insult you. I have made a fair profit by wagering on your chances in the race. Would you deny me the pleasure of properly showing my appreciation of the sport you have shown me?"

A faint smile curled Lord St. John's lips. "Forgive me, Hargrove. My pride is perhaps overly sensitive these days."

Captain Hargrove nodded acceptance of the viscount's

apology and turned to the innkeeper.

Lord St. John had scarcely finished pulling on his driving gloves when he was suddenly knocked off-balance by a flying figure. Instinctively his hands steadied the woman as she rebounded from her collision with him.

The edge of the bonnet lifted as a startled feminine face was raised to his own. The lady's dark eyes were wide with an incongruous distress that he realized had nothing to do with embarrassment at running into him.

"My pardon—!" she gasped. She looked beyond him toward the innkeeper, scarcely appearing aware that his hands were still on her shoulders or that she was clinging to one of his arms. "My father—I must have help!"

In that fleeting instant, Lord St. John recognized the depth of her alarm, and responded. Much later he would wonder why he did so, but the question never entered his mind at the time. He tightened his fingers, thus drawing her attention. His eyes met and held hers commandingly. "Your father, I believe you said. Perhaps I can be of service."

She did not question his authority, but relief flashed in her eyes. "Yes, yes! He has fallen and I cannot rouse him." Her hands went to cover her lips as she tried to stifle a sob.

Lord St. John released her. "Show me."

The young woman turned and hurried toward the stairs and he followed. At Captain Hargrove's startled question, he threw over his shoulder a terse explanation even as he continued to mount the stairs. Behind him, he heard the swift trod betokening that Captain Hargrove was following.

On the narrow landing, the young woman stopped and knelt. A portly gentleman sprawled over the steps, his head lower than his feet. His hat had tumbled from his head, leaving its white fringe and bald pate peculiarly vulnerable.

A bleeding cut marred the gentleman's brow and his eyes were closed.

Lord St. John dropped down on one knee to rest his hand on the unconscious man's chest. He frowned at the shallowness and irregularity of the man's breathing.

Captain Hargrove joined the viscount at his shoulder. "How is he?"

"In shock, I suspect. We must get him onto a bed," said Lord St. John, preparing to lift the man's shoulders.

Captain Hargrove caught his arm. "Hold up, my lord. Let me feel for breaks in his neck. A fellow I know of was moved too quickly after taking a tumble from his horse. His head lolled at an awful angle and he was dead in an instant." At the young woman's horrified gasp, he said, with a fleeting upward glance, "Begging your pardon, ma'am."

The innkeeper had arrived in time to hear this grim pronouncement. "There now, Miss Pepperidge," he said, patting the young woman on the arm. "I've sent a boy for the sawbones, quick-like. We'll soon see Mr. Pepperidge his own self again."

Captain Hargrove gently probed the area and pronounced himself almost positive that there had not been a break. He said coolly, "One can't be certain, of course. But I think the odds are better than even."

"Then we shall chance it," said Lord St. John.

Together he and Captain Hargrove carefully lifted the old gentleman's dead weight. At the innkeeper's instructions, they carried the man back up the stairs and through a private parlor. "Ye'll find the back bedroom straight across," called the innkeeper, coming close behind them.

At entrance of the party, a stout lady's maid came out of an opposite bedroom and exclaimed in horror at the sight that greeted her eyes. Miss Pepperidge made haste to give a disjointed reassurance, adding, "My father has suffered an accident, Smith. Pray see whether you can find a hartshorn."

"At once, miss!" The maid disappeared.

In the bedroom, Miss Pepperidge hastily pulled back the bedclothes and Lord St. John and Captain Hargrove slid the old gentleman onto the bed. They made the man as comfortable as they knew how by loosening his neckcloth and removing his coat and boots. Then Lord St. John and Captain Hargrove withdrew to the private parlor. The innkeeper left, saying that he would go see what was keeping the sawbones.

The maid had returned a few minutes before, hartshorn in hand. With a sharp glance at her mistress's white face, she said, "I shall sit with the old gentleman, miss. You go out into the parlor."

Mary left her father in the maid's capable hands with a sense of relief. She closed the door softly before turning into the parlor. She summoned up a wan but grateful smile for the gentlemen. She advanced toward them, holding out her hand. "I cannot properly express my gratitude, dear sirs. I-I do not know what I would have done without your ready and able assistance."

Captain Hargrove shook her hand. "It was our pleasure, ma'am."

In his turn, Lord St. John took her small hand briefly in his own. "I am only glad that we were available to assist you. You must tell me if there is anything more that we can do."

Mary shook her head. "Thank you, but no. Once the physician has seen my father, I shall rest easier, of course."

Captain Hargrove nodded. "Your father—Mr. Pepperidge, was it?—did not appear to have broken any bones. I daresay the old gentleman will prove to have been merely rattled by the fall."

"Oh, I do hope you are proven correct, sir," Mary said, the shadow of anxiety still in her eyes. Her face suddenly colored in a becoming way as she recalled her manners. "I do apologize. I have not even asked your names, nor told you mine. I am Miss Mary Pepperidge."

"Captain Michael Hargrove, at your service."

Lord St. John made the slightest of bows. "Lord St. John. The oversight is as much ours, Miss Pepperidge." He glanced at his companion. "Hargrove, we have more than likely outstayed our welcome. Miss Pepperidge is doubtless even now wishing us to the devil so that she may return to her father's bedside."

"Oh no; not at all!"

Mary flushed under his lordship's raised brows and the cold surprise in his eyes. She gestured slightly. "Forgive my seeming forwardness, my lord. It is only that—I have no one to stay with me, you see. I have a stupid fear of sickrooms and Smith will not allow me to stay with my father, and quite rightly. She knows my rampant imagination too well. And I-I did not think to ask the innkeeper to send up one of his maids to sit with me until the physician arrives. I-I would take it as a kindness if you could serve for a little while to divert my thoughts."

"An oversight, indeed. Hargrove, we cannot abandon the lady in her distress," said Lord St. John with the faintest of smiles. The expression in his eyes did not quite match the seeming affability of his words.

"Of course not," said Captain Hargrove, throwing a quizzical glance at the viscount's face. "Miss Pepperidge, you should sit down. You have sustained quite a shock. I see a decanter on the sideboard. May I fetch you a small glass of wine?"

She shook her head, sinking down into a wingback chair. "No, I could not drink it. But do pour some for yourself and his lordship."

Lord St. John accepted the glass that Captain Hargrove offered to him. He did not sit down, but instead stood at the mantel. Swirling the wine in its glass, he listened idly to the polite conversation that Miss Pepperidge and Captain Hargrove indulged in. He sent an occasional glance in the lady's direction, his hooded eyes enigmatic.

He judged from Miss Pepperidge's abstracted returns that her mind was not completely absorbed with Captain Hargrove's amusing anecdotes. She had not misled them, then, in claiming that her imagination was particularly engaged in times of stress. Still, she managed to convey enough interest that proved her experienced in officiating as hostess.

Lord St. John studied the lady. She was of a sort who had not before come in his way. Miss Pepperidge's manner and her tone of conversation were nothing out of the ordinary, evidencing a proper social instruction. However, her dress was decorous in cut and fabric compared to the attire worn by the fashionable ladies of his acquaintance. Even if he had not met her in a hostel that catered to those of a different social distinction than his own, it did not take great powers of deduction to recognize that she was a genteel, well-educated lady from a prosperous trades family.

By birth and by upbringing, Lord St. John had no reason to doubt the superior qualities of the ladies of his own class over those of the females from the trades. However, Miss Pepperidge was proving to be pleasant company even though it was patently obvious that her concern for her father overrode everything else. In any event, she had remained unaffected when she had learned that he was a nobleman. When he had made it plain that he had no desire to indulge in conversation she had not pressed the issue, nor pushed herself upon him in that annoying way that many members of the lower classes thought to be ingratiating.

It was borne in upon the viscount quite swiftly that though Miss Pepperidge had acknowledged his greater social position, she had not toadied to it. Her undemanding company proved soothing to his over-taxed pride and he appreciated the unusual respite.

The parlor door opened and Miss Pepperidge broke off in mid-sentence, springing to her feet. All semblance of the proper hostess was flown as she greeted the sight of the innkeeper, accompanied by a gentleman carrying a black bag. "Oh, thank goodness!" she exclaimed.

"I have instructed one of my girls to come up and attend to any needs of your own, Miss Pepperidge. I should have thought of it before, but with my own worry over Mr. Pepperidge—" The innkeeper shook his head over his laxness.

Lord St. John perceived that the time had finally come for himself and Captain Hargrove to part ways with Miss Pepperidge. He set the wineglass down on the mantel and turned to Miss Pepperidge. He saw that Captain Hargrove had already risen and was making his good-byes. When Miss Pepperidge turned to him, he took her hand in a light clasp. "You will be well taken care of now, Miss Pepperidge."

"Oh, yes. Thank you, my lord," she said, a smile warming her eyes.

He felt a momentary regret. Strangely enough, he would have liked to have prolonged the restful period that he had experienced in this lady's company. Again he realized that his feelings must have had a great deal to do with the anonymity that he had enjoyed. Miss Pepperidge had known nothing about him and therefore there had not been any undue curiosity in her eyes or her manners.

Lord St. John and Captain Hargrove emerged from the inn and climbed up into the curricle that had been brought around to the door for them. Once up behind his beloved horses again, Lord St. John did not long dwell on Miss Pepperidge. In fact, he forgot the lady almost as soon as he had driven out of the inn yard.

The return of Lord St. John and Captain Hargrove to London was one of triumph. They went at once to the club, where it had been agreed that all those interested in the outcome would meet. There it was made known that the viscount had beaten the requisite time by a quarter hour. Those who had heavily favored Lord St. John's chances raked in substantial sums and congratulated him most heartily. For a brief time, it seemed that Viscount Weemswood had back his old standing. But Lord St. John had grown too cynical to believe that it was but a momentary flash of acceptance that would cool as quickly as the memory of the day's victory.

Lord St. John himself took home a small fortune, having been completely confident in his own chances. He gave over the funds to Mr. Witherspoon, who was quite happy to see the monies. However, Mr. Witherspoon was wise enough to know that the viscount would not want to be told the particulars of how it was to be spent. It sufficed for his lordship to be assured only that the monies would go to good account.

Chapter 9

A week later the Earl of Cowltern chanced to meet Lord St. John as the viscount was leaving the club. The older gentleman hailed the viscount in a friendly fashion. "I am happy to have met you, Lord St. John. Pray join me for a bit of brandy."

"I beg that you hold me excused, my lord. I have a previous engagement," said Lord St. John.

He had no desire whatsoever of enduring amiable conversation with Lady Althea's father. His pride had been flayed by the ruthless treatment he had received from that quarter. The day following his interview with Lady Althea, a brief announcement had appeared in the *Gazette* retracting the betrothal. Its timing left him in little doubt that the announcement had been sent round to the printer before he had been given his marching papers by Lady Althea. If he had returned to town one day later, the first hint he would have had of his broken engagement would have been through the newspaper or from the lips of acquaintances. The singular lack of courtesy afforded him by Lady Althea and her family was not to be easily forgiven or overlooked. Even now the smoulderings of anger stirred in his breast and it was difficult to accord the Earl of Cowltern the polite bow required of him.

"Indulge me, Weemswood." There had come a frosty look into the earl's eyes and his mouth had lost its curve, tightening to a thin despotic line. "I have a spot of business exercising my thoughts that I wish to discuss with you."

Lord St. John saw that he had no choice but to acquiesce, short of thoroughly offending the gentleman, and he could ill-afford to make an enemy of the earl at that point. His reputation was extremely shaky as it was and it would be humiliating to find himself blackballed from his own club through the earl's greater influence. He was grimly attempting to retain as much respect as was left to him in society and to lose in even this, because of the earl's pique, was a wasteful gamble.

"Of course, my lord. I am at your disposal," he said with a negligent shrug, deliberately feigning for any sharp-eared parties the impression that it was a matter of free will that he should indulge the Earl of Cowltern in a few moments' conversation.

Lord St. John wondered briefly what possible business the earl could have with him. Their men of business were at that moment jointly negotiating the termination of the bridal agreement and undoubtedly Lady Althea's dowry settlement would be returned to her father within the week. Whatever else the earl had to say to him on the matter would be superfluous.

The earl nodded as though there had never been any doubt of the outcome of their short contest of wills. "Pray join me across the room where we may be assured of convivial quiet," he said.

Lord St. John silently followed the earl's lead, threading his way through the sparsely occupied chairs and tables. He was aware that the company he was in was engendering some speculative glances and he kept his expression carefully neutral.

The gentlemen seated themselves at a small card table against the wall. The earl signalled a waiter and requested the brandy. While waiting to be served, his lordship maintained a flow of pleasantries to which Lord St. John responded with cynical civility.

The waiter returned and served to each gentleman a measure of the club's excellent brandy. The earl and Lord St. John had both tasted the wine and the Earl of Cowltern had commented favorably on it before he finally broached the topic uppermost on each of their minds.

"I regret the necessity of that interview with my daughter earlier this week, Weemswood. Of course, you understood."

"But naturally, my lord. The matter was made abundantly clear," said Lord St. John, somewhat bitingly. It still smarted his pride that he had been deemed of such insignificance by the lady whom he had thought to honor with his name. However much he blamed the lady, though, he knew that Lady Althea's overweening sense of self-importance had been fostered and encouraged by the gentleman who sat opposite him. Lord St. John could therefore scarcely look upon his companion with any sort of friendliness.

The earl nodded, quite insensitive to the harsh undercurrents in the viscount's drawling voice. He sighed heavily, swirling the brandy in his glass. "I knew your father. Excellent man. You remind me much of him, St. John. I was quite pleased when Althea's choice fell on you."

Lord St. John smiled, but his eyes did not reflect anything close to amusement. His voice came very soft, very ironic. "Indeed, my lord? That is a high compliment. It is a pity that circumstances became such as to alter your good opinion."

The Earl of Cowltern nodded in ponderous regret. His own consequence was such that the viscount's sarcasm passed quite over his head. "Who could have foretold such misfortune? However, that is not what I desired to discuss with you, St. John. It is this business of the betrothal that perturbs me. My daughter's reputation has inexplicably suffered since it became known that the agreement between you has been dissolved."

"Indeed? How unfortunate," said Lord St. John politely. Lady Althea's woes were of supreme indifference to him. It crossed his mind that a small modicum of poetic justice had been served. He swirled the brandy in his glass before tossing it off, mentally toasting the whim of fate that had discomfited Lady Althea.

"Weemswood, I should like you to put it about that the betrothal was ended at your instigation," said the earl.

Lord St. John straightened suddenly in his chair. With a snap of his wrist he set down the empty wineglass. A touch of temper ignited in his eyes. "What possible reason should I have for doing that, my lord? I was perfectly willing to fulfill my obligation toward Lady Althea, if you will recall."

The earl nodded, waving aside the viscount's reminder with condescension. "I am aware of all that transpired, Weemswood. My daughter told me the whole. She was made quite upset by the necessity of releasing you from the betrothal."

Lord St. John recalled the thorough kiss that he had pressed so ruthlessly on the lady. He doubted very much that Lady Althea had discussed everything with her pompous parent. He grinned faintly, a mocking light in his eyes. "I can well understand the lady's sensitivity over the matter. It is a credit to you, sir, that Lady Althea feels comfortable enough to confide . . . all to you."

The Earl of Cowltern pursed his mouth. He stared at the viscount with the dim suspicion that gentleman was somehow making game of him, but as instantly he dismissed such an absurd thought. "Yes, well, that is precisely the point. My little Althea has always had the most delicate of sensibilities. These last few days have proven most trying to her nerves. The vulgar will talk, you know."

"As I know all too well," agreed Lord St. John with bitterness.

Since losing his privileged position as heir presumptive to a rich dukedom, the unpleasant reality that gossip could go far in breaking a man had been forcibly borne in upon him. With the loss of his expectations had gone his credit, his betrothed, several of his acquaintances, his pleasures and comforts—in short, everything that he had taken for granted that were his to enjoy and that he had expected to continue to enjoy during his lifetime. His life had literally been turned upside down by the freak pregnancy of the duke's mistress.

Brooding, Lord St. John abruptly realized that the Earl of Cowltern had begun speaking again and when he comprehended what the gentleman was saying, his temper flared brighter. It was insulting that the earl would assume that he would meekly acquiesce to publicly shouldering the responsibility of breaking off the betrothal between himself and Lady Althea.

He had had humiliation enough. Let Lady Althea retain her newly won title of heartless jilt.

Interrupting the earl, he said, "You are in error in your assumption, sir. I have no wish to be known as a bounder. Quite frankly, my lord, I do not care to further blacken my character when I already have so many legitimate black marks against me now."

The Earl of Cowltern's lips thinned. His voice turned frigid. "I do not appeal solely to your sense of chivalry in this matter, Weemswood. Though I would have thought that alone would have decided you to do the proper thing."

"You were mistaken, my lord," said Lord St. John, equally cold.

The earl raised his brows and looked down his long nose. His eyes were extremely hard. "You forget yourself, Weemswood."

Lord St. John smiled, a peculiarly unnerving expression in his own eyes. The black temper sat full upon him now. He no longer cared that the earl could very possibly add to his humiliation by having him blackballed from the exclusive men's club. He threw out a challenge in the very teeth of superior force. "Do your damnedest, my lord."

Staring into Viscount Weemswood's utterly cold eyes, the earl abruptly comprehended that a change of tactic was expedient. He thought, with a great deal of annoyance, that he could appreciate and understood the viscount's pride. Certainly he would have felt contempt if the viscount had shown anything less worthy of his personal honor. Nevertheless, it was an irritating impediment to his own present determination to protect his daughter. If it were not for that overriding desire, he would wash his hands of the overly arrogant young lord.

The Earl of Cowltern reeled in his own towering displeasure and altered his tone to one of reluctant conciliation. "I assure you, Weemswood, that I am quite sincere. Out of my genuine liking for you, and in fond memory of your father, I am prepared to release to your sole discretion the previously agreed-upon bridal settlement."

Lord St. John stared at the earl for a bare second. Then he rose to his feet. His lips twisted in contempt as he regarded the older man. "You insult me indeed, my lord. I am not a lackey that you may direct through your purse. If I agreed to your proposal at all it would be for honor, not for penurious considerations!"

The Earl of Cowltern allowed a small smile to cross his lips. He had never been in any real doubt of the outcome of this meeting. The viscount had made his protestations as his honor demanded, perhaps more stridently than expected, but in the end he would bend to a greater will. "I would be more than satisfied to accept your word of honor, my lord. However, as a favor and out of the esteem in which I continue to hold you, I shall send round my man of business to yours with the papers concerning this other. A mere formality, you understand."

"I have not agreed to this thing, my lord," said Lord St. John, his eyes blazing.

The earl rose in his turn, as much because he misliked the younger gentleman to tower over him as to signal an end to the discussion. He smiled condescendingly at the viscount and at last the full coldness of his considerable personality entered his expression.

"You are at *point non plus,* Weemswood. Already the word whispered about town is that you shall shortly find yourself in debtor's prison unless you come about and quickly. For this small favor on my daughter's behalf, I offer the means to stave off such an ignoble fate for the son of my former noble acquaintance. Your pride does you credit, Weemsworth, but it is misplaced in this instance. I do not think your excellent father would have countenanced such false pride in his only son, my lord. Nor will I."

The threat was implicit in the earl's eyes. Then he smiled in a genial fashion. "Good day, my lord."

Lord St. John stood with his fists clenched at his sides. He desired nothing more in life than to wipe the expression of pompous satisfaction from the Earl of Cowltern's face. But breeding and protocol would not allow him to do so. He could only stand by while the earl sauntered away. Marginally, through his rage, he was aware of whispers and a soft laugh from others in the room.

"There you are, Sinjin."

A hand clasped his forearm and when he attempted to shrug it off, it tightened. Lord St. John looked around, a ready curse on his tongue, to meet the cool gray gaze of Lord Miles Trilby, Earl of Walmsley.

"I had hoped to find you here this morning. Come; I would have your advice on a new hunter I am thinking of acquiring," said Lord Trilby. He smiled lazily, but there was an underlying intentness in his eyes. Lowering his voice, he said, "The avid eyes of vultures surround us, my friend. If you value your reputation, behave as a gentleman."

"What the devil do you care, Miles?" Lord St. John demanded. His eyes still blazed in a countenance that was whitened by tightly reined rage.

Most who had the ill-fortune to come face-to-face with the viscount while he was in such a state took care to sidestep him, not wishing to attract that awful tempest onto themselves. However, Lord Trilby was made of sterner stuff. His acquaintance with the viscount was of long duration and had survived turbulent times. More than anyone else, he was familiar with the roiling depths that drove Lord St. John, Viscount Weemswood.

"Absolve me, Sinjin. It is not I who cares, but you," said Lord Trilby gently.

Lord St. John stared at his lordship, then gave a short harsh laugh. The taut look about his mouth eased to a degree. "You persuade me, Miles. I will be glad to give you the benefit of my opinion."

"Excellent. I had hoped you would be so kind," said Lord Trilby. Resting his hand on the viscount's shoulder, he sauntered toward the club's entrance, keeping up a relaxed discourse until together they emerged onto the street.

Lord St. John's burning outrage was such that he could scarcely give the semblance of interest and he did not make an effort to enter the conversation, but he did give a nod as it seemed appropriate. Even through his temper he recognized and appreciated the effort that Lord Trilby was making upon his behalf.

The gentlemen continued down the crowded walk, to all appearances deep in friendly conversation, and altogether proving a disappointment to those who had lingered at the entrance of the club to watch them or to those acquaintances that they chanced to pass.

At the corner, Lord St. John immediately shook off the earl's hand. He ground out, "Was it truly necessary to bear-lead me, Miles?"

The Earl of Walmsley smiled faintly. "I feared that you would think twice about it and bolt back in after that pompous pouter pigeon."

Lord St. John's eyes glittered. "I should like to have him in my sights at twenty-five paces."

"Your good sense is beginning to assert itself. When I first laid eyes on you, I could have sworn that you were on the point of pounding him with your fists," said Lord Trilby.

Lord St. John's expression did not lighten, but became grimmer. He said softly, "You know my freakish temper, Miles."

The Earl of Walmsley sighed. "I shan't attempt to keep you, Sinjin. Get on with the exorcism."

Lord St. John sketched a mocking salute. He left Lord Trilby and directed his steps straight to his town house. The extreme control he had exercised while in the Earl of Walmsley's company was completely worn away by the time he reached his address and had run up the steps to his front door.

When he thrust open the door, he fairly knocked the porter aside. He did not pause in his swift progress down the entry hall toward the stairs. "Send round for my phaeton," he barked, not breaking stride as he took the stairs three at a time.

"Aye, my lord!"

The porter left his post at a run to carry the message. After the fleeting look he had had of his lordship's thunderous expression he had no wish to be caught loitering about the business.

In ten minutes Lord St. John had changed from morning coat and pantaloons to driving coat and breeches. He swept out the town house, down the steps to the curb, and sprang up into the waiting carriage. His groom stood at the horses' heads and as the viscount shook out the reins, he let go the leads and came round to climb up to his place.

"I shan't need you," said Lord St. John shortly.

Without a backward glance he swung the team into the flow of traffic. The groom stood on the curb, watching until the phaeton disappeared from sight, and shook his head.

Chapter 10

Lord St. John put his team through the midday traffic with ruthless precision. Once he had won free of the London congestion, he sprang his horses. The wind and thunder of hooves was accompaniment to the wild rage that consumed him.

It gave him savage pleasure to give the rushing go-by to the more sedate carriages and wagons that were on the road, sometimes by only inches. Often his passage left behind startled, frightened countenances staring after the dust that boiled up from the wheels of his phaeton.

At a narrow turn in the hedgerowed road, Lord St. John came from behind and drew level with a wagon. On the curve an oncoming private coach appeared directly before him. The coach was moving at too great a speed to be able to avoid the imminent collision, though the distant coachman could be seen desperately hauling on his reins.

Lord St. John's eyes gleamed. His mouth curved in a reckless grin. The devil was on him. He whipped his leaders to top speed, sweeping past the wagon.

The viscount's phaeton whipped out of the path of the approaching coach with but inches to spare between their respective wheels. The coach's occupants had the most fleeting glimpse of a wild-faced gentleman before the image was gone in a whirl of dust and wind.

Mr. Pepperidge thrust himself to the window. Shaking his cane, he shouted after the swiftly disappearing carriage, "Jackanapes! You should be whipped from your own carriage axle, sirrah!"

"Papa, pray calm yourself. See, he is already gone. He cannot possibly hear you," said Mary soothingly. "And besides, you shall have Smith thinking that you will do yourself harm, making it necessary to bring out the hartshorn."

The maid seated primly on the opposite seat nodded her grim agreement.

"I am quite well, thank you! There will be no cause for waving that nasty smelling bottle under my nose." Mr. Pepperidge subsided back onto the seat, but he was still red faced with anger. "The gall of some of these so-called gentlemen is incomprehensible—making a mockery and a danger of the King's roads!"

"Yes, Papa. It is very bad, indeed. But there is not the least thing that you can do about it, after all," said Mary.

"Is there not? Someone must report this outrageous distress visited upon peaceable travelers, Mary."

"Then do as you will when we have reached London, Papa. Now come, you must compose your thoughts or I promise you that I shall trounce you finely in this last contest," she said coaxingly.

Mr. Pepperidge's high color was already fading as he bent his attention again to the cribbage board. "Aye, you've proven yourself a worthy opponent this day. I must be upon my mettle if I am to redeem myself." He sighed even as he moved his peg, his thoughts obviously still reluctant to let go of the outrage he felt. "To have the name of that scoundrel would please me."

Mary said nothing. In the split second as the passing gentleman had been framed in their coach window, she had recognized him.

Lord St. John, Viscount Weemswood. There could be no two gentlemen with the same harsh profile, nor the same aura of leashed power.

She had been unable to forget the brief time that she had spent in Lord St. John's company, though they had exchanged scarcely three sentences. She had cause to be grateful for his lordship's swift comprehension and quick action, of course. But it had been his bored eyes and cold features that had disturbingly haunted her dreams. Once her father had been made comfortable, Lord St. John had retreated so thoroughly behind that arrogant mask that she had been momentarily taken aback. It had seemed impossible that the fathomless depths of his eyes had ever held a spark of compassion.

She had told her father very little about that chance meeting, other than the names of the gentlemen who had come to her aid. Captain Hargrove she could have spoken about with ease. He had been all amiability and had exerted himself to divert her thoughts, for which she had been very grateful.

There was no reason not to have conveyed to her father every word of that odd interlude, but she had not done so because it had included Lord St. John's presence. His lordship had not attempted to engage her in conversation; on the contrary, he had made it plain without giving true offense that he was uninterested in casual interchange. It would not have been wonderful if she had altogether forgotten that he was in the room, but such had not been the case. She had been acutely aware of his tall, still figure leaning against the mantel. She had known when his considering gaze had rested upon her: she had been sorry to say good-bye to him.

At the time that her father had inquired about the gentlemen who had shown such true Christian mercy, she had been strangely reluctant to confide what was only intuition, however strongly it had stirred in her.

Before the mask had slipped into place, she thought she had glimpsed the viscount's soul. He was a man tortured and vulnerable. She could not begin to comprehend what had reduced such a man to that depth of pain.

She wondered at herself. She was a strange daughter indeed not to confide the whole right then to her father. She did not think that her silence was due to a desire to protect Lord St. John from her father's complaint, for Mr. Pepperidge would more than likely never actually lodge it. In any event, a noble gentleman such as Lord St. John was not one to be worried overmuch by the bad opinion of a merchant.

Mary knew herself too well to be deceived by anything that her mind might fabricate. She reflected upon the matter, paying only superficial attention to the cribbage board. She began to frown, not liking what she found to be lying lodged in her heart.

It seemed that Lord St. John had made a quite lasting and deep impression upon her.

"The round goes to me, my dear. Those last few moves lacked your usual precise logic."

Mary looked over at her father. She felt an unusual sense of forlornness that had nothing whatsoever to do with losing the match of cribbage. "Am I such a logical creature, Papa?"

Mr. Pepperidge chuckled as he put away the cribbage board. "I dare say there is not another female with so few fanciful flights as yourself, Mary. Aye, you've got your head firmly attached to your shoulders and better than several young men of my acquaintance, too. I need never be anxious that you shall have call to do anything in the least foolish."

Mary smiled faintly at her father. She understood now

why she had remained silent about Lord St. John and her speculation concerning him, for to have confided in her father would have completely deflated his good opinion of her.

She had quite foolishly tumbled head over heels in love with a gentlemen completely beyond her reach.

It was a flight of fancy of positively epic proportions.

Caught up in the struggle with his own private demons, Lord St. John did not realize where he was headed until he had actually turned in at the gate to his family seat. It seemed somehow symbolic that he should flee to the place where he had been given birth and had learned his earliest lessons in disillusionment.

He was not amused by the workings of his unconscious mind.

However, since he was already in sight of the front door, he thought he might as well put his unplanned visit to good use. He stopped his team at the steps and snubbed the reins. Before he had leapt down to the graveled drive, the front door opened.

One of his retainers came hurrying down the steps. "My lord! This is an unexpected pleasure, indeed."

"Is it? You astonish me, Jessup," Lord St. John said, pulling off his driving gloves as he went up the steps and strode inside, his man hurrying behind him. "Have my horses attended to. I shan't be here above an hour or two, so tell the boy not to founder them."

"Of course, my lord." The manservant nodded to an underling to carry the message to the stables, then turned back to the viscount in time to receive his lordship's whip and gloves and curly brimmed beaver. "Will you be wanting a glass of brandy, my lord? Accompanied by a small collation, perhaps? Mrs. Jessup would be pleased to see to it."

Lord St. John paused to actually read the man's expression. He was startled by the real desire to please that was in his retainer's eyes. He said slowly, "My compliments to Mrs. Jessup and a cold collation would be welcome. I shall be in my study. Pray send Mr. Todd to me straightaway."

"Aye, my lord." The retainer hurried off, bearing the viscount's belongings.

Lord St. John shook off the unaccountable balm that the man's greeting had proven to his spirits and stepped into his study. He sat down behind the massive desk and opened a large drawer where the estate accounting records were kept. He took out the unwieldy books and proceeded to study the entries. He was soon absorbed in the task.

Several minutes later a knock sounded on the door. At his word to enter, Jessup ushered in a short plump woman who was carrying a tray. Mrs. Jessup bustled over to the occasional table, saying, "Now then, my lord, it isn't what you're used to, I know. But I fancy my meat pies and the apple tart will be pleasing enough. Jessup, you'll be getting his lordship his brandy now." As she spoke, she had swiftly laid out the contents of the tray and serving utensils. She dropped a curtsey, her round face beaming, and left the room. Jessup had obediently performed his duty as well and, assured that his lordship wished for nothing else, he also exited.

Lord St. John frowned at the closed door. He did not have long to reflect on the unexpected warmth of this homecoming, however, before the door opened once more and the burly figure of his bailiff entered.

"M'lord, ye wished to speak wi' me?"

Lord St. John waved the man to the chair beside the desk. "I have been going over the records, Mr. Todd. I would like your report as well."

Mr. Todd settled into the chair and placed his cap on his knee. "Right glad I am to give it, m'lord. Ye'll no doubt be pleased." He launched into a thorough and succinct description of all the estate business, including the status of the tenants and the rents. He ended by giving it as his opinion that his lordship's policy of putting monies back into the estate was at last beginning to win against the sad air of disrepair that had hung over the estate for too many years.

Mr. Todd held up a thick cautioning finger. "Now make no mistake, m'lord. There's still work to be done; but wi' a bit more effort this place will do ye proud."

Lord St. John thanked and dismissed the bailiff. Mr. Todd nodded and made known where he might be found if his lordship wished to speak to him again before his lordship's departure. Lord St. John thought over all that he had heard while he did justice to the meat pies and apple tart. When he had had his fill, he crossed the study, opened the door, and called for his retainer.

Jessup appeared so quickly that Lord St. John realized the man had been hovering nearby for just such a summons. With the hint of a smile at his lips, Lord St. John said, "My compliments to Mrs. Jessup for a satisfying meal. I shall not be leaving as quickly as I anticipated, Jessup. I have decided that I wish to ride about the grounds with Mr. Todd, so that I will in all probability be staying for dinner. Please inform Mrs. Jessup of my change in plans."

"Aye, my lord." Jessup fairly beamed approval.

Lord St. John went down to the stables. As he walked past empty stall after empty stall he recalled that as a boy the stables had always been a scene of activity. Even in his father's direst days there had been hunters and jumpers and hacks and brood mares. Now the once-scrubbed stone walls had an air of desolation and the roof sagged in places.

An unexpected melancholy tugged at him. He had spent the brightest moments of his lonely, unhappy childhood in the stables. He thrust away the unbidden memories.

As expected, he found his own horses at the end. The boy whose responsibility it was to care for the few animals left in the stables was tongue-tied at the unexpected appearance of the master, but at the sharp admonition given him by the elderly stable groom, he saddled up a rawboned hack that had seen better years.

Mounting the gelding, Lord St. John set off over the estate. He found Mr. Todd at the far end of a fine meadow, directing the final stages in the repair of a stone wall.

The bailiff appeared somewhat surprised at the viscount's appearance but he agreed readily enough to join his employer in a closer look at the management of the estate. Leaving his crew with precise directions, he clumsily mounted his own horse and offered to act as his lordship's guide. "Not that ye need one, my lord, but it was my thought that ye might like details pointed out, so to speak," he said. The viscount agreed to it, relieving the bailiff of having given possible offense.

Lord St. John spent the afternoon meeting his tenants, putting questions and listening to explanations. When the shadows had lengthened to dusk, he took final leave of Mr. Todd and returned to the manor. He was pleasantly tired and hungry and it came as a welcome surprise to find that Mrs. Jessup had laid a fine table for him. It occurred to him that he had not found such a welcome for many, many years.

Upon Jessup's inquiry whether he wished a bedroom prepared for his use, Lord St. John required only a brief reflection. He had been sitting in the drawing room with his after-dinner wine, staring at the flames on the grate, his thoughts engaged by very little of consequence. He looked consideringly at Jessup. There was nothing for him in London that night and he discovered that he was reluctant to part from the unexpected respite of peace that he had found that day at Rosethorn.

"How are you at valeting, Jessup?"

At once the man beamed. "I can do as well as any, I suppose, my lord."

Lord St. John laughed, his somber face lightening to a surprising degree. "My man, Tibbs, would undoubtedly take quick insult at that assertion, Jessup. Have the bed prepared, then. You can help me out of this coat."

"Aye, my lord." Jessup went away to spread the glad word that the master would be remaining the night even though his lordship had come away from London without a change of clothes. "I am to valet his lordship."

"Well, do your best for him, Mr. Jessup. His lordship is proving himself a better master than his father before him," said Mrs. Jessup.

If there were unhappy ghosts haunting the halls of Rosethorn, none entered the chamber occupied that night by the viscount. Lord St. John slept well and deeply, the rest of the truly exhausted.

When he arose the next morning, he managed the inadequate toilette that was necessitated when there was no clean shirt to put on or freshly ironed cravat. He found that Jessup had brushed off his coat and breeches and cleaned his boots, however, so he was fairly presentable when he went down to breakfast. The table spread for his edification made his brows rise in pleased surprise. Mrs. Jessup had outdone herself in the kitchen. He set to with a good appetite.

Afterwards, replete and somewhat more at peace than when he had come down, he took leave of his retainers and drove back to London.

Chapter 11

Upon reaching his town house, Lord St. John's improved frame of mind was instantly banished by the intelligence that a small package had been delivered from the Earl of Cowltern.

"Put it in my study," he said shortly, before going upstairs to change into fresh clothes. A scarce half hour later he returned downstairs, his hair still damp from the bath but otherwise a sartorial picture of the gentlemen of fashion. Lord St. John closed the door to his study and walked over to his desk. He took up the package, weighing it for a second in his hand.

Lord St. John, his face carved in forbidding planes, opened the small package. He was unsurprised to find a bank draft written for a familiar and substantial amount along with several large pound notes. The earl had fulfilled the terms of the bargain he had proposed in the confident expectation that it would buy Viscount Weemswood's cooperation.

"Rot his arrogance," said Lord St. John with controlled fury.

He was consigning the entire contents of the package to the flames when Mr. Underwood and Lord Heatherton were shown in.

"Ah, Carey, Nana! Pray join me. I am burning my bridges behind me," he said sardonically. He gestured at the swiftly charring mess. "My once-prospective father-in-law holds the mistaken opinion that he may buy my honor. I intend to return the ashes of his largesse to him, and be damned to the consequences."

"Your honor? I thought all was at an end between you and Lady Althea," said Mr. Underwood, going to the occasional table and helping himself from a decanter of wine.

Lord St. John gave a hoot of unamused laughter. "Not quite, according to his lordship. He wishes me to declare that it was at my behest that the engagement was severed. In short, I am to preserve Lady Althea's precious brow from the crown of jilt."

Mr. Underwood shook his head. "I am not altogether surprised. Pride is the earl's watchword. His lordship is a shark and his wife a cold fish, while his beauteous daughter—"

He grimaced and raised his glass. "Here's to a fortunate escape, Sinjin."

Lord St. John dropped carelessly into a chair. His rakish smile was grim. "That is an utterly laughable sentiment, Carey."

Mr. Underwood stood quite still, uncomfortably staring into his wineglass. He abruptly set the wine aside with a sudden show of repulsion. "It was a tasteless bit of nonsense."

"Pray do not castigate yourself, Carey. The entire business is tasteless and I am sick to death of it," said Lord St. John with suppressed violence.

Lord Edward Heatherton, hitherto silent, cleared his throat. "One doesn't like to tell one's friends their business, of course."

"Pray feel free to unburden yourself, Nana," said Lord St. John, turning a glittering gaze on his lordship. "I assure you that I shan't take undue affront."

Mr. Underwood glanced sharply at the viscount. He did not like the way that Lord St. John lazed in the chair, yet still managed to convey the impression of a tightly coiled spring.

"A delicate matter and all that," said Lord Heatherton anxiously.

"For God's sake, Nana!" exclaimed Lord St. John impatiently.

Lord Heatherton fingered his fob. "What I mean to say is, wedlock is not so bad a notion. A wealthy wife, the problem is solved."

Taken by surprise, Lord St. John forced a laugh. "That's rich, by God!"

Lord Heatherton looked at once relieved and bewildered by the viscount's reaction. His soulful brown eyes turned from the viscount to Mr. Underwood and back again. "I do not understand."

Lord St. John merely put his head back against the chair squabs and closed his eyes in a weary fashion.

It was left to Mr. Underwood to point out the obvious objection. "There isn't an heiress in society who does not know how things stand with Sinjin. He's not likely to be accepted as a serious suitor, Nana."

Realizing that his suggestion had not been completely understood, Lord Heatherton coughed again. "Not society. The trades."

At Lord Heatherton's elaboration, Lord St. John opened his eyes and lifted his head to stare at him, while Mr. Underwood's expression could only have been described as openmouthed.

Lord Heatherton's countenance fell. "I see that the notion doesn't strike your fancy. Well, we must think of something else, then."

"A bride from the trades," Mr. Underwood repeated slowly. His eyes met Lord St. John's. The viscount gestured abruptly, negatively, and Mr. Underwood leaned forward. "No, but consider, Sinjin. You were fixed to be leg-shackled in any event. You were not enamored of Lady Althea. It was purely duty in expectation of the title that made you offer for her. You told me so at the time. What matter now another woman, as long as she is rich as Croesus?"

"Aye, we mustn't forget that," said Lord Heatherton, gratified that his idea had actually become worthy of discussion. "No point in it unless the lady is rich."

Lord St. John suddenly erupted from the chair to his feet. He strode to the mantel to stare fixedly down into the fire. With tight control, he said, "I dislike this discussion intensely."

There was a moment of silence, before Mr. Underwood drummed up the courage to fly in the face of all civility. He said quietly, "Sinjin, it is a sound solution. The alternatives are not pleasant."

Lord St. John looked round. His mouth was twisted in self-derision. "No, the alternatives are not pleasant. If I remain in England, I can go to the sharks or let myself be carted away to prison."

Lord Heatherton frowned heavily. "It is my opinion that you shouldn't choose either of those, Sinjin. You'd not like prison. Murderers and cutpurses and lice. A distressing experience altogether. And as for dealing with the sharks, I daresay you would kill the first bloodsucker that demanded payment on his loan. That would be a hanging offense, even though I've never heard that anyone cares for those fellows in the least. Quite the contrary, in fact. You would not care for the scandal, of course."

"No, I prefer not to have my neck stretched on the gallows," said Lord St. John, his expression lightening at the trace of black humor.

"There you are, then," said Lord Heatherton.

"There is one other alternative. You could accept a loan from your friends," said Mr. Underwood quietly, his glance intent on the viscount's face.

Lord St. John threw up his head as though struck. Revulsion prominent in his eyes, he said with loathing, "I thank you, but no. I am not a leech."

Lord Heatherton looked astonished. "No such thing. Carey has made a very proper suggestion. It would be an agreement between gentlemen—a debt of honor." He gave a discreet cough. "Be happy to oblige you in any way, Sinjin."

"As would I or would Miles, I am certain," said Mr. Underwood. "We are your friends, Sinjin. There is nothing more to he said than that."

Lord St. John hit the hard mantel with his fist. There was a moment of tense silence during which he made a visible effort to control himself. Then with a hard-won crooked smile, he said, "The offers are appreciated. I shall not . . . easily forget them."

Mr. Underwood chuckled sympathetically. He understood perfectly the viscount's aversion, as it would be much the same feeling he would himself have had if their positions had been reversed. While it was acceptable to accept funds from one's peers for betting purposes, one did not ask loans of one's friends for such things as the expense of maintaining one's town house. "Oh, very well, Sinjin. We shall not press you further on that head. It was ill-considered, but I promise you not ill-meant."

Lord St. John allowed his smile to ease. "My damnable pride, Carey."

Mr. Underwood nodded, accepting the oblique apology.

"Aye. I am fortunate that you have not called me out for such temerity."

The expression in Lord St. John's eyes hardened briefly. "That is not so farfetched, Carey."

Mr. Underwood smiled faintly. "I know it. But I gambled that you have so few true friends at this hour that I stood a fair chance of escaping that particular terror."

"Damn your eyes, Carey," said Lord St. John, quite mildly.

Mr. Underwood laughed.

Lord Heatherton had not paid attention to the conversation, having been caught up in his own deep reflections, but now he abruptly rejoined it. "It will have to be a bride from the trades. But the lady must be genteel and thus worthy of Sinjin's consequence. He won't stand for a vulgar woman."

"Spare me altogether," said Lord St. John.

"Nor a squint-eyed, harelipped harpy with thick ankles," quipped Mr. Underwood, grinning at the viscount.

Lord St. John grimaced.

Even as Mr. Underwood acknowledged Lord St. John's dislike of the topic, however, his connoisseur instincts rose with the exercise. He dropped into a chair and crossed his ankles. "The lady must be passable, at the very least, so as not to give the man a fright. One does not like to face an ugly woman across the breakfast table."

Lord Heatherton considered the point and nodded gravely. "She must be pretty. Sinjin ain't the skirtchaser you are, of course, Carey, but one's wife should be pleasant to look at, and to listen to, as well."

"Too right. Nothing is more disillusioning than when a lovely ladybird opens her mouth and shrill twitters issue forth," agreed Mr. Underwood feelingly.

"You have between you described an ideal lady of

breeding, distinction, and beauty. Now all that must be done is to discover this paragon of the trades," said Lord St. John sardonically. He had turned his back to the mantel and stood leaning against it with his arms crossed over his broad chest so that he could better regard his friends, a mocking smile touching his lips.

Mr. Underwood appeared to be somewhat abashed at the viscount's observation, but Lord Heatherton merely gave a somber nod. "I shall ask my mother," he said.

"Your mother!" exclaimed Mr. Underwood, starting upright in his seat. "Good God! What madness has snagged your brain?"

"My mother is very respectable," Lord Heatherton pointed out.

Lord St. John laughed. "None more so, Nana."

Lord Heatherton bowed solemnly at the compliment.

Mr. Underwood put his head in his hands. "Nana, Lady Heatherton is arguably one of the starchiest ladies of my acquaintance." Dropping his hands, he raised his head. "Pray explain what possible use she could be to Sinjin?"

"M'mother's respectable. She knows any number of respectable people. Stands to reason she'd know respectable tradespeople, too," said Lord Heatherton patiently. "In fact, m'mother refuses to have dealings with anyone who isn't respectable."

"Quite true, Carey. You and I have been barred from her house these two seasons, past," said Lord St. John with the glint of a mocking smile.

Mr. Underwood was unheeding of the viscount's irreverent contribution. Instead, he regarded Lord Heatherton with the expression of one who has seen a revelation. "Very true, Nana. I had not thought it completely out, but of course you are right. Quite, quite, right."

"Carey, this ludicrousness has gone on long enough," said Lord St. John sharply. He had straightened abruptly. "It does not amuse me to think of my affairs displayed to Lady Heatherton's disapproving gaze."

"She doesn't like Sinjin above half," agreed Lord Heatherton. He sighed with regret. "It's a rare pity, but m'mother doesn't like you much either, Carey. She says that you are both bad influences upon my character."

Mr. Underwood dismissed this dismal observation with the indifference it deserved and continued with the point of the matter. He turned to the viscount. "We shan't tell Lady Heatherton what we are about, of course. Nana shall tell her simply that someone he knows is looking for a solid investment in trade. Yes, that is it. The acquaintance in question will deal only with a respectable, wealthy family man, as those qualities signify sound judgment and proper moral values."

Lord St. John glanced toward Lord Heatherton and observed the effects of Mr. Underwood's discourse on him. What he gathered from Lord Heatherton's expression greatly amused him.

"I congratulate you upon your fertile imagination, Carey. It is an excellent ploy. Lady Heatherton will undoubtedly be hooked like a large trout by such a challenge," he drawled. "I am not so certain that the hook can be set, however."

"What do you mean? Why, it is very nearly foolproof," said Mr. Underwood indignantly. "All Nana has to do—"

"That is precisely the point," said Lord St. John softly as he gestured toward their companion.

As Lord Heatherton had listened to the unfolding of Mr. Underwood's plan his eyes had begun to bulge. Now he

111

pulled out a handkerchief and mopped his sweating brow. "I can't lie to m'mother, Carey," he said apologetically. "She always knows somehow. She'll pull out of me just what I don't want to tell her. Always does, I don't know how."

Mr. Underwood's jaw hardened and his brown eyes glinted with determination. "Well, she shan't get anything out of me. *I* shall lie to her, Nana."

"Oh, will you indeed? I would be more grateful than I can say, Carey," said Lord Heatherton, a huge relief in his face.

"Is Lady Heatherton in town, Nana?" asked Lord St. John idly.

There was a short silence as it was realized that Lady Heatherton was not then enjoying one of her rare sojourns in the city.

"Curse you, Sinjin. You are determined to play devil's advocate," said Mr. Underwood, understandably put out.

"I am so very good at it, you see," said Lord St. John in mock apology.

"I shall write m'mother. I shall tell her that Carey has introduced me to an actress," said Lord Heatherton as though setting himself to face a hideous ordeal.

Lord Heatherton's brave announcement did not go unappreciated. Mr. Underwood looked at him in surprise and approval. "Oh, well done, Nana! That will bring her ladyship to town like a shot."

"Aye," agreed Lord Heatherton, very gloomy. "And then I shall have to make up some farradiddle about this actress that I don't know and don't want to know and before I know it I shall truly be in the basket."

Surprising himself, Lord St. John said, "You will not have to go to such strenuous lengths on my account, Nana.

Instead write to Lady Heatherton that I have taken you to a gaming hell. It will have one and the same effect on her ladyship; but at least you shall derive some pleasure from it as well for I mean to introduce you to a certain establishment that will curl your conservative locks."

"That is damned decent of you, Sinjin," said Lord Heatherton gratefully, much cheered at the faintly alarming prospect of stepping foot into a notorious hell.

"I take it that you are willing to tread this road, Sinjin?" asked Mr. Underwood.

Lord St. John shrugged irritably. He had not realized that he was actually giving the ridiculous notion real consideration until he had made his offer to Lord Heatherton, but now that he had done so, he might as well play out the hand. He was a drowning man in any event. "This road or another—what matter?"

"Then it is settled. We shall find Sinjin a worthy—but more importantly—a wealthy bride," said Mr. Underwood.

He looked thoughtfully across at the viscount's deep-carven face. Lord St. John had turned again to contemplate the flames. The fire's flickering light caught the bleakness in his lordship's eyes. Hesitantly, Mr. Underwood asked, "Unless you dislike the notion, Sinjin?"

Lord St. John made a weary gesture.

For a moment he toyed with the notion of actually taking sail the very next evening for parts unknown. Then, unbidden, he recalled the honest countenances of his retainers, Jessup and Mrs. Jessup; the calm determination of Mr. Todd and the favorable report he had had from the man; and the visible signs of improvement in his tenants' lots. If he left England behind, it would be a betrayal of all that he had tried to accomplish and of the unexpected trust of those who depended upon him for their living.

His expression altered and became so hard that it was unreadable. "What true choice have I, if I am to remain in England? I am not precisely enamored of the notion of exile. The other alternatives open to me are bleaker still."

"I am sorry," said Mr. Underwood quietly.

"Your pity be damned. Find the lady whose sorry fate it is to be shackled to me," Lord St. John said harshly.

Chapter 12

As Lord St. John had anticipated, the Earl of Cowltern did not appreciate the return of the bridal settlement and the monies as a box of ashes. Some weeks later, at a ball, when he chanced to come face-to-face with the earl, that gentleman deliberately turned his back upon him, causing a sudden frozen silence and then a flurry of forced conversation.

Lord St. John shrugged, his lips prominently twisted in his most sardonic smile, and sauntered on to the refreshment table. He did not address anyone on his way, merely acknowledging a few acquaintances with a slight nod, some of whom subsequently appeared slightly embarrassed to be even so mildly singled out by a gentleman just given the cut direct by the powerful Earl of Cowltern.

While standing at the refreshment table, Lord St. John was surprised when Lord Heatherton led up to him a grande dame of stern visage. "Sinjin, m'mother desired to speak with you," said Lord Heatherton in a worried tone.

Lord St. John bowed to the lady. With an ironic smile, he said, "Lady Heatherton. It is a pleasant evening, is it not?"

Lady Heatherton snorted. She regarded the viscount with a frosty gaze. "You are in a strange humor, my lord. However, I suppose it is to be expected of one of your stamp. You do not seem the worse for wear for the earl's slight." She unfurled her fan with a snap as she directed a cutting glance in the Earl of Cowltern's direction. "A more pompous man I have never seen."

115

"Forgive me, ma'am, but I am amazed that you speak in my defense," said Lord St. John.

"Hardly that, Lord St. John," retorted Lady Heatherton. "I have no misguided sympathy for your plight. Your hell is of your own devising. However, I take exception to the earl's assumption that you should bear up his daughter's reputation at the sacrifice of your own. One's reputation is to be prized, and what little of yours remains to you should be safeguarded."

Lord St. John looked thoughtfully at Lord Heatherton. He wondered just how much his friend had revealed to Lady Heatherton. "You have heard more about my business than you should have, my lady."

Lord Heatherton had the grace to flush. He sent a pleading glance in the viscount's direction. "No help for it, Sinjin. You know how it is."

Lady Heatherton did not bother to even glance at her son. "You must not blame Edward, Lord St. John. He is not capable of standing up to me and never will be, as you are well aware. In any event, it is for the best, for I intend to stand firm for you to the extent that my conscience allows. I shall see that the earl's machinations are seen in the proper light. In return, I wish to extract your word of honor that you will not escort Edward to any other gaming hells."

Lord St. John laughed. He regarded Lady Heatherton with more friendliness than he had ever shown that redoubtable lady. "I understand perfectly, ma'am. You have my word on it, but not so much to gain what you offer but because Nana proved himself a dead bore in that company."

Lord Heatherton cleared his throat in a distressed fashion, but Lady Heatherton's expression actually eased into the faintest of smiles. "You greatly relieve my mind, my lord." She snapped shut her fan and held out her gloved hand.

Lord St. John bowed over her ladyship's fingers.

Lady Heatherton looked at her son. "I know that you will wish to talk privately with Lord St. John, so I shall leave you with him. But do not linger overlong, Edward, for I wish you to escort me into dinner."

Lord Heatherton agreed and Lady Heatherton moved off. When Lord Heatherton was assured that his mother was out of earshot, he turned at once to the viscount. "Sinjin, I know what you are wondering. I swear to you that I did not betray your confidence in regards to that certain matter that Carey and I discussed with you. It was a close-run thing, I don't mind telling you, but once I had m'mother onto the gaming hell I was safe enough."

Lord St. John shrugged. His cold eyes roamed the ballroom. "At this juncture I am not so certain that it would be a bad thing, Nana. Perhaps if it was known that I was hanging out for a wealthy bride my reception would not be so damnable."

Lord Heatherton's heavy brows lowered. "You do not mean that, Sinjin. Your pride is such that you could not bear the added talk that must arise over such an *on dit*."

Lord St. John gave a short, harsh laugh. "Ah, Nana. How easily you thrust to the truth. No, it would not gratify me to hear speculation concerning my chances of taking the sort of bride I require."

"I have made inquiry of m'mother, you know, just as we decided I would do. She was very well pleased to hear that Carey was giving such sober thought to the future." A rare smile lit Lord Heatherton's face at the recollection of actually hoodwinking his uncannily sharp mother in so small a way. He cast a glance at the viscount's shuttered expression and said in a hopeful fashion, "I have taken the liberty of composing something of a list."

Lord St. John looked at his companion. The thought of a list of candidates revolted him. It was on the point of his tongue to brusquely dismiss Lord Heatherton's announcement, but he thought better of it. He sighed. "Very well, Nana. Bring your list to my town house on the morrow. You may as well stay to supper and afterwards I shall hear you out."

Lord Heatherton brightened. "Very good, then. I shall do just that, and I'll bring Carey along as well. He is a discerning man when it comes to the ladies and he might be of some use to you in making your decision."

Dinner was announced and Lord Heatherton, seeing that his mother was summoning him with her fan, made a hasty apology and hurried to lend his escort. Lord St. John was devoid of appetite and had no desire to remain longer in that company.

He quit the ball and went to a gaming hell, where he remained until the small hours of the morning. Rising from the table the loser, he made his way home and tumbled into bed, greatly the worse for quantities of bad brandy, bad company and high self-disgust.

The following evening his table was enlivened with the company of his friends, but it was not until the gentlemen had retired to the parlor where they could be assured of privacy from the servants' ears that the subject uppermost in each of their minds was broached.

Mr. Underwood and Lord Heatherton discussed animatedly for several minutes the various qualities recommending each of the ladies on Lord Heatherton's carefully composed list. Lord St. John listened, but indifferently. It mattered little to him what lady his friends would finally agree upon as the best possible candidate for his bride.

At last, after numerous applications for an expression of his preferences had been met with a shrug or a monosyllabic reply, Mr. Underwood exclaimed, "Dash it, Sinjin! It is your future we are deciding here. Do you not have anything to say to the point?"

Lord St. John's mouth twisted in a bitter smile. "But you see, Carey, it is of infinite indifference to me. I care so little. One shopkeeper's daughter is the same as any other."

His lordship's pronouncement was met by strained silence. Mr. Underwood and Lord Heatherton stared uncertainly at the viscount.

At last Lord Heatherton ventured a mild reproof. "But you must take an interest, Sinjin. It is your future lady, after all."

Lord St. John, on the point of a savage retort, met Lord Heatherton's worried gaze. In the face of such patent, honest concern he could not bring himself to say what had sprung to his lips. It would have wounded Lord Heatherton's uncomplicated nature too deeply. His voice harsh, he said, "Very well, Nana. You have outlined the ladies' antecedents and probable worth. There does not seem to be much to choose out from among them in that way. Read me their names; perhaps I shall be struck by inspiration."

"There are only five candidates," said Lord Heatherton, anxious to lessen the viscount's black scowl.

"God help me," murmured Lord St. John.

Thus encouraged, Lord Heatherton plunged into the list of the ladies deemed most suitable to be elevated to the station of viscountess. He was but halfway through when the viscount threw up his hand.

Lord Heatherton faltered to a stop, looking over questioningly. "What is it, Sinjin?"

Lord St. John was frowning. There had been something familiar about that third name. It teased at his memory, until abruptly he recalled the lady's wide, dark eyes and the circumstances of their meeting. In an instant he made his decision. "That is the one: Mary Pepperidge. I'll have my man begin the negotiations at once," he said shortly.

Mr. Underwood was moved to sharp protest. "No, really, Sinjin! This is too much. For the last hour you have not paid the least heed to anything that Nana and I have said. Now of a sudden you have made up your mind."

"I do not understand your objection, Carey," said Lord St. John. "You have been urging me to choose one of the fair ladies and I have done so."

"You've not given fair hearing to the lot. You know that you haven't. Besides, you are never going to offer for a woman whom you have yet to set eyes on!"

Lord St. John smiled, but his cold eyes were not warmed by the expression. Coolly, he said, "But I have seen this particular lady, Carey. I have even spent several minutes in her company. That is enough upon which to base an informed decision, is it not?"

"No, it is not!" exclaimed Mr. Underwood.

Lord St. John's countenance became even more sardonic. "I am but following your own example, Carey. One glimpse of a beautiful face and you counted yourself well lost."

Mr. Underwood stared at the viscount, a flicker of pain crossing his expression. "That is quite beside the point. You cannot persuade me that you have tumbled head over heels for this young woman."

"No, I leave such follies to you," retorted Lord St. John.

"Damn you, Sinjin," said Mr. Underwood tightly, somewhat white about the mouth.

Lord Heatherton consulted his list with a thoughtful pursing of lips, unwilling to enter into the unpleasant scene.

Lord St. John yanked the bellpull. A footman entered at the summons and was given a curt message to convey to his lordship's secretary.

The footman withdrew. Mr. Underwood, having mastered his emotions, tried once again. "You are surely not earnest, Sinjin."

"I was never more sober of purpose in my life." Lord St. John turned to the decanters of wine on the occasional table. He poured himself a measure of brandy and tossed it back with a careless flick of the wrist.

"But this-this—" Mr. Underwood turned in appeal to Lord Heatherton, "What the devil was the woman's name, Nana?"

"Miss Mary Pepperidge," said Lord Heatherton. He had taken a pencil out of his pocket and was engaged in carefully underlining the name. He looked up, adding helpfully, "Her father is in the mercantile business."

"Aye, that's the one. Sinjin, you know nothing about this Miss Pepperidge except the meager bits that Nana has gathered. By your own admission you have scarcely exchanged three words with the lady, and how you came to manage even that I cannot begin to fathom. You cannot in all seriousness enter into marriage settlements armed only with that!" said Mr. Underwood.

Lord St. John's tone was biting. "Was that not the whole object of this amusing exercise, Carey? Was I not to make my choice of wife from that pitiful list in Nana's hand?"

Mr. Underwood avoided the viscount's hard stare. "I did not expect you to do so without reflection, nor without making an effort to satisfy yourself to their suitability."

Lord St. John gave a short, harsh laugh. "Come, my friend, be honest. It was never anything but an agreeable exercise to you. It was not your neck in the noose, after all. You could afford to derive amusement at my expense."

"That is not true, Sinjin. It does not amuse me to see you reduced to such shifts," said Mr. Underwood quietly.

Lord St. John smiled again, this time mockingly. "Though you urged me to the course, it appears that you never truly expected that I would stay it to the finish. But I must, Carey, if I am to survive. That is the devil of it. I have had to accept that grim reality. But it is otherwise for you. After all is done and said, you will return to your lodgings secure in your own easy existence. What will you tell our mutual acquaintances, Carey? Shall you shake your head and offer an amusing witticism at the conclusion of another passing diversion? Be damned to you, Carey!"

Mr. Underwood had withstood the viscount's tirade without comment, but now he rose from his place. There was a certain bleakness in his brown eyes. "Perhaps everything you say is true. Perhaps I have treated the circumstances with greater levity than was called for. Nevertheless, I have stood your friend, my lord. That did not, nor shall not, change." He bowed and turned on his heel.

As Mr. Underwood turned to the door, it opened and Mr. Witherspoon entered. The secretary offered a greeting to Mr. Underwood, but that gentlemen did not acknowledge it as he exited. Mr. Witherspoon looked round questioningly at his employer.

Lord St. John stood at the mantel, impassive and appearing unmoved by Mr. Underwood's abrupt leavetaking. He did not appear to notice the awkward strain that was in the room.

Lord Heatherton went over to carefully set the list down on the mantel near the viscount's hand. "You'll want privacy, I expect," he said, almost apologetically. He took punctilious leave of Mr. Witherspoon and glanced once more at the impassive viscount before he, also, left.

The secretary stood uncertainly a moment. "My lord? I was told that you had need of me."

There was a long moment while Mr. Witherspoon thought Lord St. John had not heard him. Just as he was about to bring himself again to the viscount's attention, his employer made a startling announcement.

"I am to be married, Witherspoon," said Lord St. John neutrally. "You will find the lady's name and direction on this paper. It is the third on the list. Pray see to the business of making known my interest to the lady's parent."

Mr. Witherspoon numbly took the sheet of paper, his eyes drawn as to a magnet to what was written on it. He found an underlined name. "Miss Mary Pepperidge, my lord? I-I do not believe I am familiar—"

"She is a merchant's daughter," said Lord St. John harshly. "I have it on good authority that it is a wealthy family. You will find out more about that, I trust. Pray keep me informed as to the progress of the negotiations."

The enormity of what he was hearing, and the significance of the other unknown names on the list, hit Mr. Witherspoon so strongly that he was startled into indiscretion. "My lord! Surely you cannot actually contemplate—"

"I can. And I will." Lord St. John's voice was steely, its very harshness not brooking question. He turned his head to stare at the secretary. "That will be all, Witherspoon."

It was dismissal, utter and final. Mr. Witherspoon knew the futility of addressing the viscount when his lordship wore that particular implacability upon his face. Without

123

further words, the secretary bowed and left the room, his bearing stiff with shock. Softly he closed the door behind him.

Lord St. John returned to the occasional table, where he poured himself an ample glass of wine. He lifted it, but instead of setting it to his lips, he stared down into the depths of the fine burgundy for several seconds.

With a violent gesture, he threw the wineglass against the wainscotted wall. The glass shattered, showering wine and sharp shards of crystal.

He felt the sting of tiny cuts in his face and on his hands, but he merely leaned over the occasional table, his head bent, his weight borne by his rigid arms and hands.

The door flew open and a footman rushed in, alarm on his countenance. "My lord! Is there aught amiss?"

Lord St. John turned his head. His eyes were murderously cold. Low and savage, he said, "Get out."

Visibly recoiling, the footman instantly obeyed.

Chapter 13

Mr. Pepperidge came home early from the City, an unusual occurrence in itself. His mind was obviously exercised by something of grave import. His forehead was deeply creased and there was an expression of fierce inner concentration in his eyes, so that his response to his daughter's surprised greeting was somewhat vague.

Mary recognized that her father was faced with a puzzle of great proportion. She did not inquire into her father's abstraction, being familiar enough with his habits to know that eventually he would unburden himself to her once he was in a fair way to making a decision.

After dinner, when they had retired to the drawing room as was their comfortable custom and the coffee had been served, Mr. Pepperidge finally came out of his preoccupation. "Mary, I have had an extraordinary communication today."

"Indeed, Papa? Has it to do with the South American trade?" Mary asked, calmly embroidering.

"Nothing so mundane as that, my dear," said Mr. Pepperidge, a troubled note in his voice.

Mary looked up, surprised. That her father would term his greatest mercantile venture as mundane portended something in truth quite extraordinary. "Then whatever can it be?"

Mr. Pepperidge seemed strangely hesitant to launch into an explanation. He uncharacteristically fidgeted in his chair and Mary felt the first stirrings of alarm. Her fingers stilled. "Papa, it is not Tabitha? You have not had ill news, surely. Or William?"

"No, no, nothing of that sort," Mr. Pepperidge said, making haste to reassure her. He waved his wide hand dismissively. "If it were that simple I should have no difficulty in deciding what would be for the best."

Mary let her embroidery hoop drop to her lap as she regarded her father with liveliest concern. "Papa, you have succeeded in riveting my attention to an uncommon degree. I do hope that you mean to spare me unnecessary suspense."

Mr. Pepperidge grunted. He put his hand inside his coat and withdrew a neatly folded parchment. "This is what has exercised my mind so powerfully. It is truly an extraordinary communication. You cannot imagine my astonishment, nor my feelings of mixed dismay and hope, upon reading its content. I am unable to form a proper reply to its author until I have discussed its content with you, for, in short, it has to do with you."

"I? What could anyone possibly write you about me?" asked Mary, bewildered and astounded.

"Mary, I have received an offer for your hand in marriage," said Mr. Pepperidge, quite baldly.

Mary received the news in stunned silence, her lips parting. She stared at the parchment in her father's hand for a long moment. Then her eyes lifted to his somber face and she gave a breathless, disbelieving chuckle. "You must be jesting, Papa."

"I have never been more sober in my life. I could have been knocked over with a feather when I first read it. Indeed, I am just now coming to accepting its content," said Mr. Pepperidge.

He leaned over to hand the parchment to his daughter. She accepted it hesitantly, bending her head as she began to unfold the pages. He settled a keen gaze on her. "You should know that this offer has been proffered by Lord St. John, Viscount Weemswood."

Mr. Pepperidge, watching his daughter, was not disappointed by the impact of his revelation. She looked up quickly, shock showing plainly in her face.

"Lord St. John?" Mary shook her head, seeking to clear the strange suspended feeling that threatened to overtake her. It was impossible, of course. One's close-held fantasies did not become suddenly cloaked in reality. Her hands trembled, making the parchment rustle. She shook her head again. "Quite, quite impossible."

Mr. Pepperidge misinterpreted her reaction. "Now, Mary, before you reject the matter out of hand, let me give to you my considered opinion. I have reflected on little else since this communication arrived this afternoon. It has not been so long ago, in this very room, that I revealed to you my misgivings that you had no family or establishment to call your own."

Mary could scarcely command her voice, but she forced it out. "Papa—"

Mr. Pepperidge threw up one hand. "Pray let me finish, Mary. You have had suitors; never as many as Tabitha, I grant you. But I suspect that one or two, given proper encouragement, might have come up to scratch. However, I was not entirely disappointed that you did not entertain the notion of offering such encouragement to them, for the simple reason that none of these gentlemen ever seemed completely worthy of you."

Mary smiled at her father, rather mistily. "You are biased on my behalf, sir."

"Of course I am. I would be an unnatural parent if I was not," said Mr. Pepperidge stoutly. He leaned forward with earnestness written large on his countenance. He tapped the parchment with a finger. "Read it, Mary."

As she obediently turned her eyes to the careful copper-plate on the parchment pages, he continued, "The point of it all, Mary, is very simple. I never aspired to such heights as this for you; but now that this offer has come, I ask that you give it the gravest consideration. I will not condemn you if you decide that you cannot accept this suit from Viscount Weemswood. Your happiness means more to me than seeing you elevated to such an exalted position. However, I shall not conceal from you that the thought of my daughter taking her place in circles far above my own touch warms my heart, as well as justifying my pride and faith in those ladylike accomplishments that I have particularly encouraged in you."

Mary scarcely registered the import of her father's words through the haze of thickening disbelief that enveloped her as she read the document. It was an extraordinary thing. She glanced again and again at various statements in the formal paragraphs.

Her heart rose as she began to believe what she was reading. The impossible had truly happened. She had received an offer of marriage from Lord St. John, Viscount Weemswood. Her idiotic fantasy was on the way to being realized.

The signature at the bottom of the document was one unknown to her. There was nothing to disappoint her in that. The proposal had obviously been drafted at the viscount's direction. She was her father's daughter; she understood how business was conducted. A marriage contract was no less a matter of business than any other contract and it would naturally be approached in the same manner. It was enough to know that the proposal would never have been made except through the viscount's express instructions.

The prospect represented by the proposal both dazzled and terrified her. She looked up to find her father's gaze intent upon her face. "But why, Papa? Why should Lord St. John offer for me?"

"I suppose his lordship was impressed enough by you in that unexpected encounter in Dover that he recalled you to mind." Mr. Pepperidge's gaze sharpened. "I trust that the viscount made an equally agreeable impression upon you, Mary?"

"Yes, of course. How could it be otherwise? His lordship was so quick to recognize my distress and he came at once to assist me after you had fallen on the stairs. I have never forgotten his compassion," stammered Mary. She did not voice but kept to herself the knowledge that she would never have forgotten the viscount for quite another reason than gratitude. In truth, she did not think that she could have uttered more, for her heart was behaving in such an erratic way that she felt thoroughly discomposed.

Mr. Pepperidge was satisfied, and even pleased. He settled deeper into his chair. "I am glad of it. I trust your instincts, child. You've a level head, as I have often said. I must rely upon your good sense in this matter. It is for you to best judge the possibility of happiness that you might find in such a marriage as this."

Mary could not shake aside the doubt that suddenly formed in her mind. Surely she had not made such a striking impression upon the viscount that he had felt the same blinding flash of love that she herself had experienced. Surely it was not possible, and yet his lordship had sent a formal proposal of marriage.

She could not still that lamentable practical portion of her brain and she said, with a small frown, "Papa, I still do not understand. Surely Lord St. John could have his pick of ladies from his own class. Why should he offer for me?"

"It is just like you to put your finger on the crux of the matter," said Mr. Pepperidge approvingly. "You do not know, then. The viscount was the heir presumptive to the old Duke of Alton. Do you not recall my mentioning that his grace was wedded? The talk is that the new duchess will present a babe to his grace. Without ducal expectations, and with his own inheritance mortgaged to the hilt, Lord St. John must naturally marry for substance."

"Of course. How stupid of me not to have realized," said Mary, as she felt something plummet leadenly to her toes. There was a curiously hollow feeling where her heart had been. She very meticulously refolded the document to its original creases.

"It is disgraceful how the nobility squanders their substance. I shall never understand it," said Mr. Pepperidge. He shook his head in utter bewilderment.

"Do you advise me to marry a profligate then, Papa?" she asked dully, her interest not actually engaged by the question. There were such swirling emotions inside her that she did not know what to think, let alone what to say. But one must say something.

Mr. Pepperidge frowned thoughtfully, completely unaware of his daughter's state of mind. "I do not recall ever hearing that Lord St. John is himself a reckless steward. I believe that his lordship stepped into an inheritance already devastated by his father. But do not be anxious, child. I shall make it my business to discover the truth. Once more you have touched upon a point of importance." He sighed. "It is a pity that you were not born to business, Mary."

Mary made a credible effort to smile. If the warmth of her expression did not quite reach her eyes it was because the pain of disillusionment was so strong. She shook her head, admonishing herself that she should not mourn the loss of something she had never actually possessed. She took a deep breath to steady herself. "It is to be a marriage of convenience, then. My inheritance, conveyed by my person, is to be exchanged for a title."

Mr. Pepperidge frowned deeply, misliking the manner in which she had reduced it. "You make it sound as though I have put you on the block, Mary."

Mary did smile then. "No such thing, Papa. I do know how truly you value me. This is but a simple business arrangement. You have the commodity which Viscount Weemswood deems essential to the survival of his world, whilst I stand to gain a title and every advantage imaginable for myself and my descendants." The calm timbre of her voice did not reflect her inner turmoil. "I hope that you do not allow his lordship to skin you, Papa."

Mr. Pepperidge's face reflected his pleased amazement. "Mary! Does this mean that you are willing to accept his lordship's offer?"

"Yes—no! I do not know." Mary pressed her hands to her temples for an instant. When she raised wide confused eyes to her father, all appearance of tranquility had vanished. She whispered, "Papa, I never wished to sell myself."

"My dear Mary!" Mr. Pepperidge was deeply shocked.

Mary dropped her hands to her lap. "Oh, I do not mean that precisely. But I-I had always hoped to find that same affection that was always to be witnessed between you and my mother."

"Aye, so I would have wanted for you, Mary." Mr. Pepperidge rose and came over to place his heavy hand gently on her shoulder. "It is not a romantic beginning, child. But marriages of convenience have been known to deepen into love. You must be guided by your own heart. You have already made plain that you have found something worthy of respect in the viscount. That is not a bad start, Mary. Many begin with much less."

She did not reply, nor did she raise her bowed head.

Mr. Pepperidge sighed and awkwardly patted her shoulder, "I will not press you. Reflect on it before you give me your answer. Now go to bed, child. You must be wearied indeed by the shock I have given you this evening."

Mary obeyed, not because she was in truth tired but because she craved solitude in order to think everything through. She let her tiring-woman make her ready for bed, submitting to the brushing out of her hair before the maid departed. Mary unfolded the pages that had brought her, all in the space of a few minutes, unutterable happiness and despair. For a very long time, she pored over and over the marriage proposal. She had it practically memorized word for word when at last she folded the parchment and laid it aside on her bedstand. She cupped the candle flame and blew it out, then settled beneath the bedclothes.

Once she had composed herself for sleep, she discovered that sleep was eluding her as determinedly as peace.

She rose, shivering in the cool night air, and slipped on a robe over her gown. She crossed the darkened bedroom to her window and parted the muslin curtains. Laying her forehead against the cool glass, she murmured, "Dear Lord, whatever am I to do?"

"La, Mary! There's practical and then there's pound foolish."

Mary glanced about her sharply, even though she knew that the amused voice sounded only in her imagination. "Oh, do be quiet, Tabitha," she told the mind's-eye image of her sister. "What know you of it, after all?"

In her imagination, her sister tossed her head, and a familiar gleam lit Tabitha's eyes. "I married the man I wanted. Why shouldn't you?"

Mary stared out of the dark window, the question echoing in her mind.

Chapter 14

After a week of vacillating, of weighing the positive aspects against the worst factors, of being borne up by high-winging happiness, then plunged into the chasms of fear and uncertainty, Mary finally decided, somewhat timorously, to accept the viscount's proposal. She would be staking her future on a rare risk that, as her father's daughter, she was aware was foolhardy.

Yet she knew in her heart that she would never love another. Her sometimes regrettable levelheadedness assured her of that certainty. Perhaps, given the chance, she could cause the viscount to come to love her as well. As her father had said, many marriages began with less and she at least had the advantage of knowing her own heart.

Mr. Pepperidge was delighted by her decision, and added, "I am confident that you shall have no reason to ever regret it, my dear. I have done as we discussed and looked into his lordship's private affairs. He is indeed in desperate straits and it will cost me a pretty penny to bring him about, I make no doubt. However, I was encouraged to learn that Lord St. John is apparently not the profligate his parent was before him, having it on excellent authority that he has been making a push to save his birthright, Rosethorn Hall. I gather it is a snug property, greatly neglected in past years and hopelessly mortgaged, of course, but held by his lordship in such esteem that the restricted rents he derives are put straight back into the land. I therefore consider it to be a moderately safe investment on my part to bring his lordship to safe port."

Mary laughed, shaking her head at her father's manner of expression. "I know you to be too shrewd to put your money into a foolhardy venture, so I am reassured indeed. Lord St. John will undoubtedly prove to be an excellent husband for me."

"I hope that he may be that indeed, Mary, for you know that my fondest wish is for your happiness," said Mr. Pepperidge.

She stood on tiptoe to kiss his cheek. "Indeed, and I do know it. I promise you, Papa, I shall be as happy as I can contrive."

"Good girl," he approved. He rubbed his hands together as his thoughts turned to the details that needed to be addressed. "I shall send round to Lord St. John's man of business—this Mr. Witherspoon—and get down to brass tacks. We shall see what sort of negotiator is this fine gentleman."

Mary knew that her father was already anticipating the part of business that he most enjoyed. "I shall leave it all to you, Papa. Only do, pray, keep in mind that I wish a few weeks at least to have my bridal clothes done up."

Mr. Pepperidge nodded as though surprised. "But of course, my dear. I know well what is due you. In fact, I wish you to go down to the warehouse and choose whatever pretty fabrics and laces you desire. Do not think to spare the expense, for I am of a mind to send you off in grand style. This shall be no scrambling affair, you may depend upon that."

So Mary turned her attention to patterns and fabrics, engaged a fashionable modiste and a team of seamstresses, and set out on a shopping spree that quite eclipsed any that she had ever engaged upon. Bonnets, gloves, reticules, boots, and slippers; corsets, camisoles, and slips; gowns of sheerest lawn; several pairs of silk stockings, and a number of other feminine fripperies, constituted the bulk of her purchases. There were innumerable fittings to be endured, and letters to write to her married sister and her brother and a very few others that she felt able to take into her confidence.

In truth, she was glad to have something to occupy her mind and her hours. She was afraid that if she let herself reflect on the step that she was taking, her courage might fail her. Scarcely a half hour after she told her father that she would wed the viscount, then all of her worst apprehensions assailed her. Hers was an unenviable position, no matter how the connection would be perceived by others.

She was a tradesman's daughter.

Mary was all too cognizant that she was "marrying up," as the expression went. While it was true that her education had been of the best, including as it had those accomplishments thought to be the earmarks of a lady, she knew that the bar presented by her undistinguished lineage was one that she could never hope to overcome. On the surface, polite society might accept her because of the title that she would bear, but she doubted that any blueblood would actually offer friendship.

As for her intended husband, she already knew that Lord St. John was a proud man. She had seen it for herself in that one brief meeting, when he had withdrawn behind that cold polite mask. It would undoubtedly rub his lordship's pride raw to own, even to himself, that his renewed affluence was owed to her. Her only hope of ever attaining the happiness that she desired more than anything in her life was to somehow convince the viscount that she had married him for himself, not for the station in life that he could give to her. Otherwise hers would be a very lonely, friendless existence.

She was so shaken by her realizations that she actually started downstairs to her father's study to tell him that she had changed her mind. She could not possibly enter into such a cold-blooded contract. She leaned against the balustrade, closing her eyes. Behind her lids she could see that flash of compassion, and something else, in Lord St. John's expression, before his face had become shuttered. Surely, surely, she had not been mistaken.

"Miss Mary, is there anything that you need?"

Mary opened her eyes and straightened, turning her head to the maid who had addressed her. There was a shade of worry in the woman's expression. Mary forced herself to smile as naturally as possible. "No, I thank you. I was but woolgathering for a moment. Have you seen the laces that I brought home with me yesterday? I seem to have misplaced them." With that, she diverted the maid's attention, and abandoned the impulse born out of fear that had almost led her to cry off from the betrothal.

Mary was aware when the necessary negotiations had been entered into, but she asked no question of her father. She was positive that it would not have added to her tenuous peace to know in exact terms how dearly she would go to the altar. So she buried herself in preparations and tried not to dwell on her apprehensions.

Mr. Pepperidge was soon deep into the convolutions and was immensely enjoying the contest, finding the viscount's man of business a worthy opponent. Eventually the time came when the settlements were hammered out to the satisfaction of both parties, Mr. Witherspoon apparently enjoyed the full confidence of his employer, for, as he once informed Mr. Pepperidge in an aside, Lord St. John had gone into the country with friends and it was unknown when his lordship would return.

"Very cool, that," said Mr. Pepperidge as he related events to his daughter. "I will go so far as to say it was a master stroke on Mr. Witherspoon's part. We were in the midst of discussing a very fine point, and I was momentarily put off my stride by his observation, so he carried the matter. But I soon came about, being made much more alert by such crafty tactics, and not an inch more did I give him. So the thing has been done. It requires only his lordship's signature of agreement to see you inside the chapel on the date we decided upon."

Mary did not betray the disappointment she felt upon hearing that the viscount had cared so little about the outcome of the settlements that he had journeyed off with friends. Nor was the calm of her expression marred by the vague trepidation that shivered through her to learn that her future was settled past recall.

"Thank you, Papa. I know that you have done your best for me," she said quietly, setting another careful stitch in her embroidery. "Have you seen the post today? William writes that he means to come down to 'see me riveted,' as he puts it."

"William may be a sad scamp, but he is a fond brother. I shall be happy to see him," said Mr. Pepperidge. He shot a keen glance at his daughter. "I know that you wrote the tidings to Tabitha, as well. Have you heard aught from her?"

At Mary's shake of the head and tiny frown, he said dryly, "I am not surprised. You have quite put her nose out of joint by landing a nobleman, my dear."

"I do fear it, indeed," said Mary, her exasperation overridden by a faint smile of amusement.

"Ah well. Tabitha was never able to hold two thoughts together for long. She will come about," said Mr. Pepperidge comfortably.

"Oh, of course she shall. I only hope that it is before the wedding, for I should like all my family with me," said Mary.

As it chanced, however, her sister and her brother-in-law were not present at the wedding. The ceremony took place at ten o'clock on a gray Wednesday morning. There was scarcely a handful in attendance to witness the event, numbering Mr. Pepperidge, two school friends of Mary's, who had accepted the honor of being her bridesmaids, and her brother, William.

The company included as well the viscount's friends, Lord Heatherton and Mr. Carey Underwood, who would stand with him, and Captain Hargrove. Lord St. John had given a twisted smile when he had sent off an invitation to Captain Hargrove, who was, after all, the veriest acquaintance; but it afforded him amusement to have present the gentleman in whose company he had first met his future bride.

The wedding took place quietly by license in a small chapel in Islington. The viscount had been indifferent to the location of the ceremony. Since he did not attend any church, he had acquiesced without objection when the site was specifically requested by his betrothed.

Mary had wished to take her vows in familiar surroundings. She had been christened in the chapel and some of her earliest memories were of services in the soft candlelit interior. The memorial service for her mother had been said there, and there, also, Tabitha had been wed. It seemed appropriate that she should embark on her new life accompanied by the comforting reminders of times past.

As Mr. Pepperidge escorted his daughter to the altar, those gathered to witness the exchange of vows turned to watch their progress. Lord St. John, Viscount Weemswood, awaited his bride with an unfathomable expression in his cool gray eyes. His was a commanding presence, set off by an impeccably cut dark blue dress coat with gilt buttons. An intricately tied cravat fastened with a jewelled pin above a white velvet waistcoat, topped the quilted undercoat and frilled shirt. And buff-colored breeches and silk stockings with pumps completed his toilette.

One glance at the viscount's finery and his remote expression was enough to set Mary's equilibrium wavering. She knew that she had never appeared to better advantage in the long-sleeved gown of lace over white satin, but it was one thing to judge oneself in a mirror and quite another to brave the unreadable gaze of one's betrothed. She was very glad of her cottage bonnet with its lace veil, concealing her face from too-penetrating scrutiny. Her courage sank lower at the bridesmen's expressions; it was as though the gentlemen disapproved of, but yet were resigned to the proceedings. Her trembling spirits were somewhat heartened when Captain Hargrove at least offered a kind smile as she passed him.

It was a brief ceremony. The minister did not give a sermon, instead simply setting forth the duties of husband and wife. The viscount made his vows in a strong, decided tone; Mary repeated the vows in a clear, unwavering voice. Those observing the couple had no inkling of the inner emotions and thoughts that swirled through their beings.

With the exchange of rings and the lifting of the bride's veil for a chaste kiss, the ceremony was speedily concluded. Entry was made into the register immediately following the service and was duly signed by the minister, the newly wedded couple, and their witnesses. There was not to be a reception—to Mr. Pepperidge's disappointment, neither the viscount nor Mary having wished for one. There were quiet well-wishes all round as the few in attendance began to take their leave.

Mary was saying good-bye to her old school friends, who were properly impressed and genuinely happy for her that she had done so well for herself. They regarded with sentimental awe the viscount's splendid figure. "His lordship looks just like a prince," one commented.

If Lord St. John had been privileged to overhear the extravagant observation, he would have laughed it to contempt. The morning had been a singularly wearing one. It had clouded some hours before dawn and begun to rain on the way to the chapel, an ill omen if one was to believe in such. The wedding ceremony had seemed little but a mockery to him. He had set out to find a means to restore his fortunes and he had succeeded; but in the process he had sold his freedom, signified by the heavy gold band that now encircled his finger. The lady whom he had made his wife also stood in some way as his gaoler. It was not a thought that set well on one of his temperament.

Lord St. John's lack of equanimity was not improved when his new brother-in-law, young William Pepperidge, seized the opportunity to assure him that he would personally knock his lordship's teeth down his well-bred throat if he, William, ever got wind that Mary was being made unhappy.

Lord St. John tightened the leash on his ragged temper, biting back the hasty retort that sprang to his lips. Instead, he said coldly, "Rest assured, Mr. Pepperidge. Your sister has nothing to fear from my hands."

"See that she doesn't. Good day to you, my lord," said William Pepperidge. He made an awkward bow and moved off to make himself known to Captain Hargrove, who had attended the wedding in his regimentals.

Mr. Underwood had come up in time to catch the youth's last utterance and he glanced curiously after the young gentlemen. "Whatever was that about, Sinjin?"

"A piece of infernal impertinence," said Lord St. John, dismissing it impatiently. "I suppose that you and Nana are doing the pretty and making your excuses?"

"We've done our duty, old boy, and have seen you through to the end," said Mr. Underwood with a shrug and a laugh. He held out his hand and, suddenly somber, said, "Good luck to you, Sinjin."

Lord St. John took his friend's fingers in a hard grasp. "Be damned to you, Carey. You know that I've the devil's own luck. I always come about."

"So it would seem," said Mr. Underwood, glancing in the new viscountess's direction. "I see that Nana is mightily taken by her. That is positively the most elegant leg I have ever seen him make." As Lord Heatherton took leave of the bride, Mr. Underwood hailed him. When his lordship came up, he said, "I have been telling Sinjin that you've taken a liking to his bride."

"Of course I like Lady St. John. Why shouldn't I?" said Lord Heatherton, surprised. He frowned at Mr. Underwood. "Don't you, Carey?"

"A home question for you, my friend," murmured Lord St. John sardonically.

"And a most improper one, which I am honor bound to ignore," said Mr. Underwood. "Come, Nana, let us be off. Sinjin and Lady St. John must naturally be anxious to return to London."

"We will he gone from London for an indefinite time," said Lord St. John shortly. "Witherspoon will handle any inquiries that are made in connection to the announcement that has been inserted in the *Gazette*."

Mr. Underwood's brows rose. The inquisitiveness of the ton would naturally be fanned to white heat by the announcement of Lord St. John's marriage, but with the passing of a few weeks something new would be going the rounds of the gossip mill and the advent of Lord and Lady St. John on the social scene would then occasion only mild curiosity. All in all, he thought, his lordship was behaving most wisely. It crossed his mind to wonder what Lord St. John meant to do with his bride once his lordship had established her in the town house.

His understanding of the viscount was such that he did not tax Lord St. John to reveal his plans, however, but instead he adjured Lord Heatherton again to finish taking leave of those of the wedding party who still lingered.

Mr. Pepperidge had reluctantly let his daughter be led off by her maid so that she could change into traveling clothes. His gaze clung for a sentimental moment on her graceful figure, then he harrumphed and turned about to stump up to his son-in-law. "Lord St. John."

Lord St. John, where he was standing inside the open door giving onto the chapel porch, had been contemplating the dreary weather outside. His expression was still frowning when he turned his eyes to Mr. Pepperidge, but he met the gentlemen's hand readily enough. "Mr. Pepperidge."

"I shall not beat about the bush with you, my lord. I know well that this is not the connection that you had wanted for yourself. But I wish you to know that my daughter is as true a lady as if she had been born to it, which you shall learn soon enough," said Mr. Pepperidge.

"I am certain that I shall," said Lord St. John.

Mr. Pepperidge looked sharply into the viscount's eyes, but the cool gray depths gave nothing away. "I wish every happiness for her, my lord."

"I am pledged to provide all within my power," said Lord St. John. He wondered if he was to sustain a threat of bodily harm from another of his wife's relations and the thought caused a thin smile to rise to his lips. His expression was wiped clean by his father-in-law's next words.

"You need not be anxious that I shall embarrass you, my lord, by forever taking my ease in your parlor. Well I know that you are above my company. I shall be happy only to be allowed to visit with my daughter on the rare occasion, if you will consent to her coming to my home."

Though his countenance revealed nothing of his thoughts, Lord St. John was uncharacteristically startled. He could discern in his father-in-law's stiff posture the effort it had taken to ask for such a concession and he felt a reluctant admiration for the gentleman's strength. Quietly, he said, "Thank you, Mr. Pepperidge. I assure you, however, that I am not as high in the instep as you think me. I shall not forbid my wife from associating with her family."

Mr. Pepperidge smiled, a somewhat shrewd look coming into his eyes. "You've pride enough, my lord. I know that, even though you are polite to a point. Never fear; I know the bounds and shall keep to them. I'll not keep you longer, my lord." He bowed and moved away to meet his daughter, who had changed into a smart traveling pelisse and was coming toward the door of the chapel with her maid in tow.

Mr. Pepperidge's place was taken by Captain Hargrove. He grasped the viscount's hand. "I wish you well, my lord. You've embarked on a campaign that I, for one, would not have the courage to contemplate," he said.

Lord St. John stiffened slightly. There came a cold

glitter into his eyes. "What precisely do you mean, Hargrove?"

Captain Hargrove grinned, quite understanding the viscount's suddenly softened, deadly voice. "I mean nothing but that the notion of wedded bliss makes my blood run cold." He paused momentarily, then said, "My lord, ours is too short an acquaintance to allow for liberties, but nevertheless I offer this observation. You cannot call out every man who appears to slight your bride."

Lord St. John locked gazes with the captain for a long moment. Then his expression eased into one of those quick, natural grins that came so rarely to him. "I shall remember that, Hargrove." He held out his hand again. Captain Hargrove grasped it a short moment, turned to bid goodbye to the new viscountess and her parent, and swiftly left.

Mr. Pepperidge saw that the viscount's carriage was waiting at the curb. He, also, made his good-byes, tears standing in his eyes as he kissed his daughter. She clung to him, her own eyes awash. "There now, dear Mary. You are to be happy." She nodded, smiling tremulously, and turned away to find her husband awaiting her.

The viscount handed her up into the carriage before entering it himself. Then the carriage swept them away.

Chapter 15

For their honeymoon, Viscount Weemswood took his bride to Rosethorn Hall. Mary saw the manor from the window of the carriage, very late in the afternoon. The sun was slanting off the mellow stone and glinted in the leaded-glass windows of the Tudor manor. She fell in love at once with the house set in the rough grounds. "It is a beautiful place," she exclaimed.

Lord St. John glanced over at his bride, feeling surprised pleasure that she should like her first sight of Rosethorn Hall. "Do you think so?"

"Oh, yes. How very happy you must have been here as a child," said Mary.

At once the faint smile in his eyes vanished. "I believe we are expected," he said coolly.

Mary did not reply, having realized instantly that she had inadvertently said the wrong thing. The viscount had briefly told her where they were going and had mentioned that Rosethorn had been his birthplace and childhood home. She had erroneously assumed that Rosethorn must hold pleasant memories for him, but obviously that was hardly the case. She wondered why, then, he had chosen to bring her here rather than take her to his London town house.

When the marriage settlements had been signed, the viscount had authorized his secretary to inform the staff at Rosethorn of his wishes. Mr. Witherspoon's communication, coupled as it was with instructions to increase the household staff and make ready for the newly wed couple, had thrown the viscount's retainers into a flurry of activity.

Under-footmen, upper-housemaids, and a scullery maid had been hired. The question of whether a cook was necessary had been settled and a worthy woman had been engaged for the post. "For it's of no use to think that his lordship will be satisfied with my cooking when his lady wife will need me as housekeeper," said Mrs. Jessup comfortably.

The manor house had been turned inside out in a mammoth cleaning. Holland covers had been whisked away; furniture burnished free of dust and cobwebs; floors and woodwork polished; windows washed; and carpets beaten. The larders had been filled. For those items easily perishable, standing orders had been left in the village. Mr. Jessup descended to the cellar to take inventory of the wine stock and was pleasantly surprised to discover a few treasures. As he told Mrs. Jessup, "You could have knocked me over with a feather, for I had thought the Frenchy brandy had all been tossed down the late lord's throat long years past. But there it is and very pleased I am to have it."

When the carriage swept up to the front steps, all was in readiness. The staff was hastily assembled in the front hall to greet the viscount and his lady. Mr. Jessup swept the stiff company with a stern eye, then nodded for one of the footmen to open the door. He himself went forward to be the first to bow the newlyweds into the house.

Lord St. John was surprised by the reception awaiting himself and his bride, but he instantly saw his secretary's hand in it. Witherspoon, estimable and foresighted man that he was, had taken it upon himself to provide for their real comfort. With a smile, then, Lord St. John said, "Jessup, I am happy to see you. Let me make known to you Lady St. John."

"It is an honor, my lady," said Jessup with grave dignity.

Mary inclined her head with a smile. She felt a flutter of trepidation at the sight of the formal ranking of the servants but she steeled herself. She was no longer mistress of her father's house with its staff of three servants and she must become accustomed to her new rank. "Thank you, Jessup."

Lord St. John had given his beaver and gloves to a footman. He shot a swift glance about the gleaming entry hall. "I cannot recall when I have seen the place appear to better advantage."

"Thank you, my lord." Jessup bowed his appreciation. "Allow me to make known the staff to you, my lord, my lady."

The reviewing of the staff took several minutes as each was introduced and made his or her obeisance to the master and mistress. In the middle of it all, the second carriage carrying Lord St. John's valet and her ladyship's maid arrived, requiring that the baggage be carried inside and upstairs. The resultant lengthening of the review caused a frown to deepen on Lord St. John's face. Mary, acutely aware of her husband's impatience, drew a thankful breath when it was at last done.

"You will undoubtedly want to refresh yourself and rest before dinner. Mrs. Jessup will show you up to your rooms. I have some estate matters to attend to this afternoon, but I will see you again at dinner," said Lord St. John.

Mary smiled and nodded as she turned toward the housekeeper, who awaited her. She felt she had been quite effectively dismissed. She was not surprised and even felt a little relieved. The viscount had been unfailingly polite toward her during the drive to Rosethorn, but it had not taken any degree of intelligence to realize that he had no real desire for her company.

Mary was shown into her bedroom by the housekeeper. Mrs. Jessup explained that beyond the bedroom was her ladyship's private sitting room and the dressing room for her ladyship's dresser. Mary glanced about as she stepped inside. The bedroom was nicely appointed in the style of a past era, though the draperies were faded and the carpet was somewhat worn. Nevertheless it was a welcoming apartment with fresh-cut flowers on the side table and a cheerful fire in the grate.

"If you need anything at all, my lady, there is the pull beside the bed," said Mrs. Jessup, anxious that her new mistress be satisfied.

Mary drew off her gloves, saying, "It is all quite nice, Mrs. Jessup. I see that Smith has the unpacking of my trunks well in hand, so I think that will be sufficient for now."

The housekeeper curtsied. "You'll likely want to rest an hour before changing for dinner, so I will leave you."

The day had been an exhausting one and the hour was far advanced by the time they had reached Rosethorn Hall, so Mary received the suggestion that she rest with relief. She allowed her maid to remove her pelisse and lay down on the bed. She was asleep almost the instant her head had touched the pillow.

An hour later, she was awakened and her maid helped her to change for dinner. When she was ready, she found a footman waiting outside her door to guide her downstairs to the dining room.

Lord St. John was already seated but he rose at her entrance and came round the table to take her hand. "My lady. I am honored that you have joined me."

"I see that I am tardy. Pray forgive me for making you

wait," said Mary diffidently, glancing up at him as he seated her.

Lord St. John took the chair opposite. "It was of little consequence. I am not one to demand rabid punctilio from my friends, nor shall I do so with my wife."

Mary did not know how to respond. The indifference in his expression and his voice precluded anything she might say. She was saved from embarrassment when the butler began to direct the serving of the first course.

The first dinner at Rosethorn was one that Mary would always recall as uncomfortable and unbearably polite. Lord St. John scarcely addressed her, except with a courteous inquiry into her likes and dislikes as each course was presented. When the interminable repast ended with an offering of creams and tarts, which she refused, Mary was not reluctant to accede to custom and retire to the drawing room, leaving his lordship to enjoy his wine in private.

She found her embroidery basket thoughtfully placed beside a wing chair close to the fire and with relief entered upon the familiar and restful task. An hour later the butler entered to inquire whether she wished to be served coffee, but she declined it. Sometime later, when she glanced up at the clock on the mantle, she discovered that it was after ten o'clock. Certain, then, that the viscount did not intend to join her in the drawing room, Mary calmly put away her handiwork and went upstairs.

When Mary entered her room, she found that her maid had already laid out a nightgown on the wide four-postered bed and had put a screen around the steaming brass tub that was set before the fire. "How inviting this looks," Mary said.

The maid began to help her to undress. "Aye, it has been an exciting day. I'll warrant you are tired, my lady."

Mary shook her head, the faintest of smiles on her lips. She stepped into the warm bath. "How odd it sounds to hear myself addressed in such a fashion."

The maid grunted an assent as she gathered up the discarded clothing. She bustled about, tidying up for a few more minutes before she was needed to throw the nightgown over her mistress's head.

Mary went over to sit in a chair before the fire to dry her hair. Behind her, the maid turned down the bedclothes and ran a bedwarmer between the sheets.

"I shall be in my room if you need anything more, my lady."

"No, nothing. I shall go directly to bed," said Mary, smiling. The maid wished her a quiet good night and left the bedroom through a door that obviously led to the dressing room. Mary turned back to contemplate the flames, her fingers combing slowly over and over through her damp hair.

Several minutes later, when the fire had begun to burn down and the warmth generated by her bath was fading, Mary thought it was time to seek her bed. Just as she rose from the chair, a door set into the paneling beside the fireplace opened and a masculine figure entered. She took an inadvertent step backward, a startled gasp escaping her.

It was Lord St. John, attired in a silk dressing gown, his hair glistening with drops of water. Mary felt her heart thudding. She had not expected anything like this. "My-my lord!"

He regarded her with an ironic lift of his brows, a mocking glint in his eyes. "I am sorry if you assumed that ours was to be a strict *marriage de convenance*."

Mary's throat was dry. It was exactly what she had thought, and she realized the depth of her naïveté. "No, my lord. It-it is just that you surprised me a little."

"Did I? But you will know better in future," he said.

His hand reached out to caress her cheek. She caught his fingers with her own, stilling them. The eyes that she lifted to him were very wide and very dark. "I am frightened, my lord," she whispered.

There was a flash of something strange in his eyes, then their expression became inscrutable. "You have no need to be, not here, not with me." Then he swept her up, lifting her high, and carried her to the bed.

The succeeding days, and nights, at Rosethorn settled into a pattern. Mary was shown over the manor house by Mrs. Jessup and she discussed with that happy lady various improvements and changes that were designed to increase the comforts to be found at Rosethorn. It occurred to Mary almost at once that she no longer had unquestioned command over the household monies; that prerogative belonged to her husband. Mary subsequently inquired of the viscount what latitude she was to be granted in finances.

Lord St. John regarded her from where he sat behind his desk. His gray eyes were exceedingly cool. "My dear lady, you have complete carte blanche. You may do whatever you wish. The settlements were more than generous."

Mary felt the color rise in her face. "That was not my question, my lord."

"My apologies. I thought perhaps that it was," he said. "Nevertheless, it is as I said. You may do whatever you wish. I attach no sentimental value to the furnishings in this house. You may gut it with my goodwill."

Mary thanked him quietly and retreated from the study, more shaken than she cared to admit by his lordship's attitude. It was just as she had feared. The viscount resented that it was her father's money that had saved him. Beyond even that, she found his supreme indifference to what should be done inside Rosethorn shocking. Surely he had some feeling for the things that had been familiar to him from childhood.

She paused just outside the door of the study, her brows knit. Perhaps, just perhaps, the viscount had expressed the essence of his wishes in those hard, dismissive words. The more Mary thought about it, the more certain she became that it was indeed so. She went away to the library to write a letter to her father, requesting that fabric samples for draperies, curtains, and upholsteries be sent to her. She would take her husband at his word and begin to rid Rosethorn Hall of all that was worn and out-of-date.

Thus Mary's days became full of plans and inventories and consultations with an enthusiastic Mrs. Jessup, who could be relied upon to know which tradespeople and crafters in the village would do the best work. Her dealings with her husband retained the polite, reserved tone that had been established from the first. Lord St. John's time seemed to be quite taken up with the company of his bailiff, Mr. Todd, and he spent very little of any given day indoors.

The newly wedded couple met only occasionally during the daylight hours, but every evening, over the dinner table, they spoke stiltedly about what had taken place during their time apart. Lord St. John began to join his wife in the drawing room for coffee. There was little conversation. She was content with her embroidery and he with reading.

Once, he surprised her by asking whether she was a card-player. "Why, only a very little," confessed Mary. "I fear you would find my skill sadly lacking as an opponent, my lord."

"Never mind; I shall teach you," he replied with the glint

of a smile. She acquiesced, nothing loath when his eyes contained that unusual warmth. She proved an apt pupil and it was not long before it became an established thing that they indulge in a game or two of piquet during the evening.

Little by little, Mary began to piece together something of her husband's preferences. She knew what dishes and wines he enjoyed, which of her toilettes he liked and those he didn't, what he preferred to converse about—in short, she took note of everything about him and tried to make of herself and of Rosethorn all that was most appealing to him. She was rewarded in small things, such as the occasional glance that had the power to bring warmth to her face, the rare invitation to join him in going about the estate, and the offhand comments approving the menus or the new draperies that hung in each room.

As for the nights, the connecting door between her bedroom and the viscount's was never locked.

Chapter 16

Several weeks later, Lord St. John sat at breakfast with his wife. He regarded his lady with a lazy half-smile, his memory dwelling on the hour before dawn, before he had left her bed. She looked remarkably composed and very fine in a pale yellow morning dress.

Mary glanced up, meeting his gaze, and color stole into her face. She smiled and asked, "Would you like more coffee, my lord?"

Lord St. John's rare smile lighted his face. "Thank you, my lady. I would, indeed." He watched her graceful movements as she poured, idly reflecting upon the woman he had wed. His wife had a pleasant voice. She was easy to look at over the breakfast table or, indeed, any other time. She was not vulgar or waspish or demanding of him. She had been uniformly cheerful and even tempered from the day of their marriage. In short, his bride from the trades possessed in a remarkable degree every attribute that his friends had considered necessary in his prospective viscountess.

He considered himself very fortunate. He could scarcely imagine what his life might have been like if his lady had been in any way less compatible.

He had been a damned man, with nothing to anticipate but disgrace. Soliciting the hand of a bride from the trades had been a desperate gamble and one that he had detested with all of his heart. It had left a bitter taste in his mouth to acknowledge the necessity. But he had done what his circumstances demanded of him in order to salvage his pride and his heritage.

Lord St. John had gone into the marriage with his eyes open and with the absolute certainty that he would regret having married outside his class. He had not thought to gain except in a financial sense, but it had gradually been borne in upon him that the lady who had become his wife had a special gift of bringing comfort and a sense of contentment to everything she touched.

Since he had come into his own, it had not once over the years occurred to him to change anything about Rosethorn Hall, even though every time he had entered the manor he had been reminded of unhappy times. The welcome he had that once at the Jessups' hands had surprised him and eased his exacerbated pride, but it had not dispelled the general distaste he had always felt while at Rosethorn. The furnishings, the carpets and drapes, the very arrangement of the paintings on the walls, had all remained as they had been when he had endured his miserable childhood. Whichever way he turned, the past had always haunted him.

However, in recent weeks a metamorphosis had overtaken Rosethorn. New draperies and carpets accented the rooms; the ponderous furniture of his father's day had been replaced with the elegant, neat fashion currently in vogue; faded family portraits had been exiled to the attic or circumspectly placed amidst magnificent hunting prints; and prettily embroidered pillows adorned the newly upholstered settees. The faintly dusty smell that had always hung over the house had been replaced by the scents of beeswax and lemon. The once-gloomy rooms had come alive with the light of day spilling through open draperies, and at night were bathed with soft candlelight.

The shadows of his childhood had been banished.

The transformation of Rosethorn Hall represented a fortune, but Lord St. John cared little enough for that, for he knew that he had never been more content. He could easily eschew his former life in London and remain at Rosethorn indefinitely, he thought, as long as his lady was with him.

He realized suddenly the implication behind his thoughts. He stared across the breakfast table at his wife. Somehow this woman that he had been forced by excruciating circumstances to wed had become necessary to his existence. The disturbing insight dragged a frown between his brows.

"Is there anything wrong, my lord?"

He met her questioning gaze, instantly smoothing his expression. "Nothing of moment, my lady." Finished with his coffee, he rose from the table. "I shall be closeted with Mr. Todd for a time this morning over the accounts."

Mary smiled up at him and nodded. She saw nothing unusual in his announced intention. His lordship often spent his mornings on estate business, either in his study or riding over the grounds with the ever-attentive Mr. Todd. "Very well, my lord. I know that I shall not see you again until luncheon. I mean to keep myself tolerably well-amused, however. Mrs. Jessup desires to consult with me on any number of domestic trivialities."

Lord St. John granted her the slightest of smiles. "I suspect that Mrs. Jessup looks upon you as the savior of Rosethorn."

She shook her head, laughing. "No, my lord. You are too firmly entrenched in that role ever to be displaced by me."

The quick rise of his brows indicated his startlement. "Indeed. I had no notion."

"Oh, you are a veritable saint in the Jessups' eyes and I am certain that Mr. Todd is not far behind in his own veneration," she laughingly assured him.

Lord St. John grimaced. "The mantle of sainthood does not sit well on my shoulders."

"I know you do not like to be thought above the cut, so I shall say no more. But rest assured that you are very well thought of by all your household," Mary said, holding out her hand to him.

Lord St. John took her hand in his, but held it a moment while he quizzed her. "Have I your high regard as well, ma'am?"

A faint rose tinge came into her face. "It could be no less, my lord."

Strangely discomposed by the reaction he felt at her soft words, Lord St. John raised her hand and brushed his lips over her slender fingers. It was a small gallantry that had become a pleasing habit. But this morning, coming swift on the heels of the strong impulse to snatch her into his arms, even that small act of homage was disturbing to him.

Lord St. John quickly exited the breakfast room and strode down the hall to his study.

A little more than two hours later he had finished his business with Mr. Todd. Instead of completing the entries in the ledger books on his desk, he sat back in his chair. There was a shuttered expression on his face which would have been familiar to his friends, one that warned that there was something churning just below the surface.

Lord St. John's thoughts returned to his wife. She had somehow made a place for herself in his life that he had never thought would be filled. She was a companion, a gentle force that eased his days and charmed his nights. Her character was such that—

Abruptly he comprehended that the unease he felt in

connection with her had nothing whatsoever to do with her character, but what her presence in his life meant to him.

Lord St. John, renowned for his aloof cynicism, had actually become infatuated with his own wife.

It was a totally unanticipated state of affairs and, from his point of view, totally unacceptable.

The memories, half-faded but still potent, streamed through his mind. Innumerable hurts and disappointments had been his lot since early boyhood, until he had built up such a hardened defense for sheltering his sensitivity that he no longer believed in the innate goodness of humanity. His recent experiences had done nothing to revise his bitter opinion. The insults and innuendos since he had lost all prospect of the dukedom had been difficult to bear. Most intolerable of all had been Lady Althea's negligent shrug and her hard smile when she had rejected him. The Earl of Cowltern's overbred contempt and the absolute certainty that his will reigned supreme had been but a flick of the same heavy whip.

Lord St. John left his chair and strode over to the window. Resting one forearm against the edge of the wall, he stared down at the gardens. His expression was exceedingly grim.

His life had been filled with betrayal. He had thought himself immune to its bite, but at the last he had nearly been destroyed.

Then Mary Pepperidge had fallen into his arms and, quite unknown to him, his life had taken a turning for the better. Providence had chosen to take a merciful hand in his affairs at last and breathed fresh life into his existence in the form of a woman of generosity, wit, and kindness.

A small portion of his mind observed dispassionately that in his memory the gardens had never appeared more attractive. The overgrowth had been tamed, the dead things uprooted and replaced. It was Mary's doing, of course. She had hired gardeners. She could always be relied upon to quietly bring order out of the chaos. All he need ever do was express a desire. He could place his heart in her capable, comforting hands.

"No!"

Lord St. John turned his back on the view of the gardens, his fists clenched. He could not afford to trust anyone to that extent. The very thought of it made the small hairs rise on his neck. Surely he had been burned too many times to shuffle off his hard-won cynicism. Only a handful of people had ever stood by him. None had been women.

Not that the female was any worse than the male of the species. His own father had been a bastard of the first degree. Lord St. John gave a short bark of laughter, but it was a bitter sound even to his own ears. How well he had learned the lesson that one must rely only on oneself.

His wife had found her way to his most vulnerable part. The scarring of his soul was deep, but it had responded to her generosity and her gift of creating comfort where there had been none. If he did not act before it was too late, he would be irrevocably lost. Then, when her betrayal came, it would utterly destroy him.

Lord St. John was brutally honest with himself. It actually terrified him to think that he was in the grip of an emotion so powerful that the point of his very existence revolved around a woman; a woman whose regard he had come to desire more than anything else in the world.

He had to distance himself from her in order to save himself.

Suddenly decisive, Lord St. John sat down again at the desk. He pulled a sheet of paper over to him and began penning a short communique to his secretary, Mr. Witherspoon. When he was done, he readied the letter for the post.

After he had sent a servant off with the letter, Lord St. John stared for several long moments into space. His expression was bleak. What he intended to do gave him no pleasure to contemplate. However, it was necessary for his own survival.

He would throw his bride from the trades into the whirlpool of a ravenous society. His lady would build her own life revolving around entertainments and gossip and morning calls and shopping. He would plunge back into his own activities and seek out his former acquaintances. Eventually he would come to see less of his wife than did society as a whole and he would be safe again.

He would stand alone once more, impregnable, self-sufficient.

The future stretched before him like a cold barren landscape, its keening wind sweeping through the depths of his soul.

Lord St. John announced his decision over dinner that evening. Mary lifted wide eyes to him. "London, my lord?" There was a note of mingled dismay and astonishment in her voice.

He leaned back in his chair, his eyes gleaming from beneath hooded lids. "Have you an objection to removing to town, my lady?"

"Why, no. Of course I do not. It has simply come as such a surprise that we are to go so soon," said Mary.

"I wish to be gone from Rosethorn by the end of the week. Is three days sufficient time for you to be ready, ma'am?" asked Lord St. John.

Mary nodded. She was made only too aware by his lord-ship's abrupt tone that he would have little patience for any reservations.

"Yes, that is sufficient," she said quietly, her mind already skimming those tasks necessary to organize the move. There would be packing and instructions to the Jessups, not only for the household but for the disposition of the last of the articles that she had purchased for Rosethorn Hall. There were also letters to be written, cancelling various orders she had made for the manor, and one to her father to inform him of her new direction. Her correspondence to friends could wait until she had actually settled in London.

"Then I shall leave the details in your capable hands," said Lord St. John, rising.

Mary also rose from her chair, taking her cue from him that their repast was done. "I shall leave you to your wine, my lord." She walked to the door, feeling that she had been handily dismissed.

"Do not wait coffee on me, my lady. I will not be joining you this evening as I mean to return to my ledgers later," said Lord St. John.

"Very well, my lord. I wish you good night," said Mary, hoping that he would smile at her, however slightly.

He bowed to her, his countenance reflecting only cool civility.

Mary spent a lonely hour in the drawing room with her embroidery. She frequently glanced at the clock on the mantel. It had become so pleasant to spend the evenings in Lord St. John's company that she now felt her spirits to be somewhat depressed by his defection.

It was nonsensical to feel so, she knew. His lordship simply had work that required his attention and he probably wished to have it all well in hand before the journey to

London. Naturally he would want to leave matters in such a way as to make it most easy for Mr. Todd to continue in his lordship's absence.

Mary knew that she would regret leaving Rosethorn behind. She thought that the weeks she had spent at Rosethorn would always remain fixed in her memory as a time of peculiar happiness. She had adjusted to becoming a wife and she had become comfortable with her role as mistress of the manor. The household had accepted her without apparent reservation and the house and gardens had begun to take on a well-ordered appearance that quite eclipsed the former signs of neglect.

She thought also, though she could not be certain, that her lord appreciated the quiet changes she had made. He had begun to laugh with her and more than once she had surprised an expression of contentment in his eyes as he surveyed the lands or the refurbished rooms of the manor itself.

That was what made it so difficult this evening to accept his withdrawal into his former chilly manner toward her.

She knew when Lord St. John left the dining room. His quick hard steps sounded on the marble tiles in the hall, hesitating the slightest moment outside the drawing room door, then hurried on at a swifter pace than before. Seconds later a door slammed.

Mary stared at the impassive drawing room door for a long moment. Then she composedly folded her embroidery away and left the drawing room to go upstairs to bed.

Chapter 17

Two months after his marriage, Lord St. John set out for London with his bride. He chose to ride on horseback alongside the carriage that carried his wife and her maid. Another carriage followed with the baggage and the valet, Tibbs, while his lordship's faithful groom rode on the box.

Mary had ample time for private reflection during the journey. Her maid was not loquacious by nature; in addition, after a time the swaying of the carriage made the woman begin nodding. So if Mary's glance often strayed to the window where she could see the viscount's wide shoulders, there was no one to witness it.

Lord St. John had given no explanation for his abrupt decision to remove to London other than to observe that it was time for his wife to make her entrance into society. Mary felt some apprehension at the prospect, but she accepted the viscount's wishes in this matter as she had in every other. She would contrive somehow to be a credit to him.

The familiar sights of London caused her a twinge of anxiety for the first time. She had grown up within the city's busy environs, but she had never really paid more than passing attention to the number of smart carriages or the fashionable promenaders in the park. She had rarely had occasion to pass through the venues of elegant town houses, for she had known none of the inhabitants. Her world had never overlapped into that of the *beau monde*.

The fashionable world was a world unto itself. Frivolity, gambling, scandalous intrigue, and licentiousness were its earmarks. Lord St. John had been born into that society. He was at home in it. Now it was to become her place as well.

Mary was too levelheaded to believe that it would be an easy matter to become accepted by polite society. Her birth and background had nothing of the blueblood that would automatically recommend her to the *ton*. She was simply the daughter of a wealthy merchant, who had been fortunate enough to be handed a title when a gold ring was slid onto her finger.

Her new position demanded a rarified association that, given the choice, she would have preferred to avoid. Obviously she could have nothing in common with those who had inherited their perquisites.

However, she understood how it was that Lord St. John desired her to be presented to his friends and acquaintances. It would be strange if he did not.

The slowing of the carriage warned her that their destination was in sight. The maid started awake, putting her hand up to her bonnet to straighten it. "Have we arrived, my lady?"

"I think so, Smith," Mary said. She saw the viscount ride by the window a last time. His stern profile was presented to her and she sighed, wondering at herself. It would have been a very small thing for her husband to have turned his head to smile at her as he passed; but he had not and the disappointment she felt was disproportionate.

Lord St. John had not smiled once at her since he had told her of his decision to return to London. Certainly his mouth had occasionally stretched in that horridly self-mocking way, but his eyes had remained shuttered and she could not delude herself into believing that things were well between them.

Mary would have liked to have gone on just as they had

at Rosethorn. With the exception of the last three days, she had been increasingly encouraged that her husband was beginning to look upon her with a sort of tolerant affection.

She discounted what passed between them in the privacy of the nights as a true indication of his feelings. She had gathered from past fragments let drop by the married women of her acquaintance that gentlemen could consort with women without feeling a particle of either liking or respect for them.

As for her own emotions—

Mary felt herself blush and she was glad of the chill wind that nipped up as she was descending from the chaise, it giving her an excuse for her heated face.

Lord St. John's glance was considering, but he made no comment on her heightened color. He merely offered his arm to her. Mary placed her fingers on his elbow and allowed him to escort her up the steps of an elegant town house.

The moment that she entered the town house with Lord St. John, Mary realized that the ease with which she had taken command of Rosethorn Hall was not to be granted to her by this London household. The servants had been drawn up in the hallway to greet their lord and his lady, but their combined stares were hardly encouraging to Mary. There was not a curious or eager gaze in the lot and though Mary did not detect outright insubordination at this early juncture, she wondered whether she would not be faced with that trial before many days were out.

"Craighton, this is Lady St. John. You will see to it that her ladyship is accorded every courtesy," said Lord St. John.

"Yes, my lord." The butler bowed to the new mistress of the house. His expression was wooden as he gestured forward a footman. "Edward will show your ladyship and your maid upstairs. The rooms are naturally all prepared for your arrival, my lady."

"Thank you, Craighton," said Mary quietly.

"I will meet you again at dinner, my lady," said Lord St. John, taking his wife's hand and raising it briefly to his lips.

"Very well, my lord," said Mary, inclining her head. She mustered a smile. "I shall be glad of an opportunity to put off this bonnet and rest for an hour." She turned to the footman and nodded that she was ready to follow him up the stairs. Behind her, she heard the orders issued for the baggage to be brought in.

Dinner that evening was unexceptional. Lord St. John was civil and he spoke at some length on what she could expect in the coming days. He was brutally frank at one point. "I think you will find that our marriage will be considered something of a nine-day's wonder. Every eye will be upon us for some clue as to the nature of our relationship. I hope that you will not be put out of countenance by the stares and malicious remarks."

"Now that you have given me warning, I shall be better able to carry it off, my lord," said Mary quietly.

He smiled with that twist of the lips that she had begun to detest. "Certainly I cannot ask for more."

For Mary, the evening seemed to drag on leaden minutes. Lord St. John had withdrawn behind that polite, cold mask that she had first seen come over him in Dover. It was a burden to remain unaffected in her own manner and this, combined with the long journey, had the effect of exhausting her. Thus she was not unhappy when the viscount indicated that she was free to go to her rooms, which she did. After her maid had readied her for the night she crawled straight into bed. Within moments of her head touching the pillow she was asleep.

In the next few days Mary's intuition that she faced a difficult period with the servants was correct. Several small so-called misunderstandings arose over her orders. She was undoubtedly up for judgment by the viscount's household and she had to prove herself capable of running a well-ordered establishment.

It was not a task that she was unfamiliar with since she had had the ordering of her own father's house for many years, as well as her more recent experience at Rosethorn, to fall back on; but it was a nuisance. In any event, Mary was able to meet the challenges to her authority with a confident calm that went far in scuttling the disgruntlement of some at having a tradesman's daughter set over them.

She was aided by the unexpectedly supportive attitudes of the butler, Craighton; the viscount's man, Tibbs; and the secretary, Mr. Witherspoon. These three gentlemen, swiftly recognizing the quality of their new mistress's manner if not her antecedents, quickly abandoned their reservations and made certain that their approval was well-known throughout the household. Mary was thus able to resolve any question of her authority or capabilities.

The new viscountess's position in society was a little more difficult to establish, though it did not prove to be the insurmountable task that Mary herself had assumed it would be.

Contrary to popular expectation, Lord St. John did not merely ensconce his lady at the town house and leave her to her own devices while he plunged back into his old pursuits. His pride was too strong to let him do the easy thing. Instead, with a challenge in his cold eyes, Lord St. John escorted his lady to various functions until she was reluctantly acknowledged by society at large.

To the surprise of many, Lady Heatherton took the new Lady St. John under her wing. Her ladyship was known to be a high stickler of the first order. It was something of an established joke that she had barred most of Lord Heatherton's closest cronies from her doors because she considered them to fall too short of her standards.

However, from their first meeting, Lady Heatherton and Lady St. John seemed to establish a rapport, one that bore swift and unanticipated fruit.

Lord St. John escorted his wife to an evening squeeze guaranteed to expose her to as many eyes as possible. When Mr. Underwood had volunteered to accompany them and lend his support, Lord St. John had shrugged carelessly. "My wife needs nothing but the support of my name."

"I like that, Sinjin! You were nearly an outcast scarcely three months ago," Mr. Underwood reminded him.

The viscount's smile was at once grim and amused. "Yes, it left a certain piquant taste, I admit. But I am not now, and neither is my wife, as I shall shortly prove this very evening. All of polite society will take notice of us tonight."

His purpose was attended by such success that a dame of frosty mien, after one glance, proceeded to sail up to the newlywed couple. The gentleman who trailed the lady did so with such an alarmed expression that several personages turned and were witness to the encounter.

Lady Heatherton greeted Lord St. John with a regal nod. "Lord St. John. I had heard that you were returned to London. The notice of your nuptials came as a great surprise. And this must be your recent bride, formerly Miss Mary Pepperidge, I believe?"

Lord St. John acknowledged warily that it was so.

Lady Heatherton looked consideringly at Lady St. John. Without turning her head, she addressed her son. "You have made a humbug of me, Edward."

Lord Heatherton's brown eyes bulged. "Nothing of the sort, ma'am. I assure you, furthest thing from my mind!"

Lady Heatherton pinned him with a steely glance. "Do not lie to me, Edward. You know that you cannot do it in the least credibly."

Having withered Lord Heatherton, she swung her austere eyes to Lord St. John. "This young woman will undoubtedly be the making of you, my lord. I had not credited you with such good sense. See to it that she is happy."

Lord St. John bowed, an ironic twist to his lips. "I shall endeavor to do my best."

Lady Heatherton's smile was glacial. "I doubt it. I shall have cause to speak to you again, I am certain." She turned her attention to Lady St. John, who had for several minutes been regarding her with some inner trepidation. Her ladyship's expression unbent. "I know your father, Mr. Pepperidge, by reputation. It is my understanding that he is a most worthy gentleman."

"Thank you, my lady," said Lady St. John, somewhat dazed.

"You must come to dinner Friday next. I suppose Lord St. John will wish to bring that scapegrace, Underwood, with him. I trust the gentleman will be on his best behavior whilst under my roof. I will not have the undermaids squealing."

Mr. Underwood had unsuccessfully pretended that he was invisible. At Lady Heatherton's slur on his character, however, he flushed. "My word on it, my lady. I would not dream of causing the least disturbance."

"Of course you will not, Mr. Underwood," said Lady

Heatherton with a tight smile. With that, she sailed away.

Mary laughed at the expressions of the three gentlemen about her. "So that is your esteemed mama, Lord Heatherton. She is a most formidable lady, to be sure."

"Aye," sighed Lord Heatherton. He brightened suddenly. "We scraped through that fairly well, I think."

"Nothing else could be half so difficult," agreed Mr. Underwood. He clapped his hand onto Lord Heatherton's shoulder. "Come Nana. We have survived the worst; let us celebrate! Lady St. John, do you wish any refreshment? An ice, perhaps?"

Mary was on the point of accepting Mr. Underwood's offer when Lord St. John forestalled her.

"You may act the gallant later, Carey. I intend to dance this set with my wife." Lord St. John bent a faint grin on her startled face. "You do dance, do you not, my lady?"

"Of course I do, my lord," said Mary, swiftly regaining her composure. When he led her out onto the floor, she forgot about the curious stares directed their way and gave herself up to the exquisite pleasure of being squired by her husband, Lord St. John.

The small dinner party at Lady Heatherton's proved to be an affair of upwards of fifty people. The appearance of not only Lord and Lady St. John, but also Mr. Underwood, was met with absolute amazement. It was quite clearly seen that Lady Heatherton was on the best of terms with Lady St. John, since that redoubtable lady introduced her guest round with assiduous attention and was overheard to remark besides that she was happy that Lord St. John and Mr. Underwood had been free to grace her little dinner party. The news spread like wildfire that the breach between Lady Heatherton and her son's boon companions had been healed, and it was all due to the new viscountess.

Under Lady Heatherton's unimpeachable aegis, Lady St. John's acceptance, though grudging in certain quarters, was relatively painless. Soon invitations were received at the elegant town house and the curious began to make morning calls on the viscountess. The reports brought back by those visitors were nearly all favorable. Lady St. John's dress and manners were unexceptional. She carried herself with a self-possession that was at once ladylike and without false condescension. One wondered whether the new viscountess did not possess blueblood in her family background after all. The general concensus was that Lady St. John could be safely recognized by polite society.

Still, there were those who remained too top-lofty to acknowledge a merchant's daughter, however high she had been elevated or how personable she was. Most prominent among those sticklers were the Earl of Cowltern, his wife, and their daughter, the beauteous Lady Althea. However, the Cowltern attitude proved in the end to be not so much justified as amusing to the *ton*.

Society was always ripe for the unkindest of gossip and the Earl of Cowltern and his ladies were not particularly well-liked. Their air of self-importance had often produced ill-feeling, though few would openly express such outright censure that it would cost them a cut direct from the powerful family.

Lord St. John had been brutally used by the Cowltern faction and yet he had survived. Not only that, but he had come back with a wealthy bride on his arm. It was all thought a very good joke, and went a long way toward easing Lady St. John's path.

Chapter 18

A dusty traveling carriage drew up to the curb in front of an elegant town house. The door opened and a gentleman, stooping so that his impossibly tall beaver cleared the edge of the door, descended the iron step to the walkway. He turned to extend his gloved hand to the lady who appeared behind him.

Accepting the gentleman's support, the lady stepped down to the pavement in her turn. Her eyes never left the imposing residence that stood before them.

"Well, my love, here it is," said the gentleman, turning his own gaze on the town house.

"It is a frightfully fashionable address, isn't it?" asked the lady, still eyeing the town house with a somewhat avid expression in her bright blue eyes.

"Indeed it is," assured the gentleman, his tone one of immense satisfaction.

The lady turned a dazzling smile on her escort. Arm in arm, they ascended the steps to the front door, where the gentleman set up a rattling summons on the brass knocker.

Mary sat in the drawing room quietly sorting through her embroidery silks. When the butler entered, she looked up with a smile. She was mildly surprised by the faint hint of disapproval in his wooden expression. "What is it, Craighton?"

"A Mr. and Mrs. Applegate, my lady," he said stiffly.

A diminutive lady brushed past the rigid butler, all fluttering ribbons and exclamations. "Mary! La, but it has been an age!"

"Tabitha!" Mary rose to her feet. In her sister's impetuous embrace, the basket of silks fell abandoned to the settee.

With a trilling laugh, Mrs. Applegate drew back. Her lovely blue eyes took sharp note of Mary's pale yellow morning dress trimmed with georgette ribbons. "Don't you look fine as sixpence, Mary! Doesn't she, Mr. Applegate?"

Thus applied to, the gentleman who had entered on Mrs. Applegate's heels now came forward. He wore a large grin on his florid face. "Indeed she does, my love. But then, our dear sister has always had an air about her." He caught his sister-in-law's unresisting hand and made a flourishing bow over it.

The butler interposed a question to the mistress of the house, who appeared utterly taken aback by the invasion. As well she might, he thought. "Shall I send in refreshment, my lady?"

Mary shook herself free of her stupefaction. Her hand was still imprisoned by Mr. Applegate. She firmly withdrew it from his grasp. "Yes, of course, Craighton. Tabitha, won't you sit down? Mr. Applegate, pray make yourself comfortable."

Mrs. Applegate instantly availed herself of the invitation to settle onto the settee. She tossed aside the basket of silks, saying, "Oh, was there anything more wonderful? My lady! I can scarcely credit it still. You could have knocked me over with a feather after I deciphered your letter, Mary."

"The news was astonishing. My poor love could not be brought to believe it at first," said Mr. Applegate, with a broad wink.

"Yes, I can imagine," said Mary dryly, easily discerning

that there had been quite a scene enacted. As she seated herself beside her sister, she once more invited Mr. Applegate to avail himself of a chair.

He declined with a widened smile. "I shall be glad to stretch my legs a bit and look about while you ladies enjoy a comfortable cose."

"Oh, it is so prodigiously exciting to be here with you, Mary! I saw instantly that it is a very fashionable address, which was so very encouraging," said Mrs. Applegate.

Mary threw a glance at her brother-in-law as he wandered about the drawing room. He was openly eyeing its contents with a shrewd look on his face. It was easy to see that he was calculating the worth of all he saw. Mary decided to ignore him and she deliberately focused her attention on her sister. "But how did you know where to find me, Tabitha? I quite thought you had no wish to communicate with me when I did not hear from you regarding the wedding."

If Mrs. Applegate was aware of the rebuke implied in her sister's mild tone, she did not exhibit it. She was engaged in pulling off her bright vermillion kid gloves. "Why, I called first on Papa, of course. He very obligingly gave me your direction once he understood that I was determined to visit you, no matter what he urged to the contrary. Such stuff! As though you would be grown too high to receive *me*, your only sister! It made me stare to hear it, I can tell you.

Mary was dismayed. She knew all too well both her sister's willful manner and her father's stubborn determination. There must have been a glaring falling out between these two members of her family. She had always disliked such unpleasantness and she had often played the peacemaker in the past. "How was Papa when you left him,

Tabitha? I hope you did not cut up at him, for you know how he—"

"La, Mary! You must think I haven't the sense of a goose," said Mrs. Applegate scornfully. "Papa was in fine trim, as always. Not but what he did offer me a few harsh words, but I paid not the least heed to it. Mr. Applegate warned me in advance how it would be and so I was on my very best behavior. Though Papa was reluctant to give me your direction, we parted on very pretty terms."

Mary looked over at her brother-in-law, who had left off perusing the drawing room appointments and had at last taken possession of a wingback chair opposite. She smiled her gratitude at him. "Then I must thank you, sir, for I am certain that it was all your doing that my father and Tabitha did not come to cuffs."

Mr. Applegate bowed from the confines of the chair. "Nothing to it, dear sister, once I reminded Tabby of a few pertinents."

Mary felt her smile become fixed at hearing the pet name that had been bestowed upon her sister. She reminded herself that it was not at all her business. It was her sister's place to object to being likened to a skinny, homeless cat. Surprisingly, Tabitha, who had always been very aware of her own beauty and worth, said nothing. Mary had no alternative but to ignore the despicable nickname. "Nonetheless, it was well done of you, sir."

Mr. Applegate bestowed upon his hostess his widest smile and winked.

As little as Mary cared for Mr. Applegate's christening of her sister, she disliked even more her brother-in-law's familiar manners toward herself. She had never quite liked him and the more that she saw of him the truer that became.

With determination she turned her attention to her sister's spate of inconsequential chatter, forcing herself to play the interested hostess.

The arrival of tea was a welcome diversion. Mrs. Applegate gave a little squeak of pleasure at sight of the large selection of biscuits, creams, cakes, and fruits. "Only look, Mr. Applegate! There is enough to fill one up twice over."

Mr. Applegate sat forward, rubbing together his heavy hands. "Truly a feast fit for a king, or should I say a viscount!" He laughed heartily at his own sally, his enjoyment apparently unaffected by his sister-in-law's tepid smile.

As the tea was set out on the occasional table by the butler, it crossed Mary's mind to wonder why Craighton had taken on a task that could have been designated to an underling. The butler met her glance and apparently understood the question in her eyes.

"I've set the footmen to polishing the silver and running a few errands, my lady. I hope that I have not forgotten any requirements?"

Mary had weathered in good order the Applegates' vulgarity and faintly insulting conversation without losing an iota of her composure. But the butler's obvious understanding of the difficulty of her position made her flush. Responding to the situation, Craighton had taken immediate steps to spare her the humiliation of having the servants share gossip over her callers. None of the servants, with the exception of Craighton himself, would be witness to the visit paid by the mistress's vulgar relations.

"Thank you, Craighton. That will be all," she said quietly. She was grateful for the man's loyalty, believing, however, that it was not so much directed toward her as it was to Lord St. John. However much it embarrassed her to rely upon Craighton's discretion, she was nevertheless glad that certain of her household would not be handed ammunition with which to justify any sort of insurrection. It had not been without difficulty that she had established her authority as mistress of the house.

The butler bowed and withdrew, quietly closing the door behind him.

Mr. Applegate settled against the back of his chair, cradling his cup in his large hands. He looked at his sister-in-law with his habitual broad smile. "Well now; a viscountess. You've done very well for yourself, dear sister. In truth, better than anyone could ever have hoped for. Isn't that so, my love?"

"Oh, indeed," said Mrs. Applegate, a slightly petulant frown touching her lovely face.

"I suppose the settlements were substantial. Mr. Pepperidge has too shrewd a head not to take advantage of a favorable opportunity," said Mr. Applegate, sipping his tea and casting another appreciative glance about the drawing room.

"What has brought you to London, Tabitha?" asked Mary, deliberately turning the conversation.

Her polite query brought about an odd reaction. Mr. and Mrs. Applegate exchanged a long speaking look. Mr. Applegate nodded encouragement and his spouse said brightly, "Do you like my bonnet, Mary?"

Mary was taken aback by the seemingly random question. She glanced involuntarily at the smart confection that graced her sister's head. "Why, it is vastly pretty."

Mrs. Applegate gave a crow of delight, clapping her hands, while Mr. Applegate laughed heartily.

Mary looked from one to the other, bewildered. "What have I said?"

Mr. Applegate smacked his knee. "Did I not tell you,

Tabby, my love: You've a rare talent that but wants a bit of scope."

Mary shook her head. "I don't understand. Whatever has thrown you into such alt, Tabitha?"

"It is *my* bonnet, Mary," said Mrs. Applegate proudly. She saw from her sister's unchanged expression that her declaration had not been comprehended. She sighed impatiently. "Papa always said you were the cleverest of us all, but I don't find you so in the least."

"Now, love," remonstrated Mr. Applegate. His wife turned her shoulder on him, but he only shook his head tolerantly. "What Tabby is trying to say is that the bonnet is one of her own design. And very fetching it is, too."

Mrs. Applegate dimpled up at the compliment, her good humor quite restored. She turned her profile to her companions and put up her chin to show her headgear to better advantage. "Is it not the most cunning thing imaginable, Mary?"

"It is very clever of you, certainly, and truly it is a lovely bonnet," said Mary. She hesitated, then added, "But whatever has that to do with your coming to London?"

"Oh, you *are* clever after all!" exclaimed Mrs. Applegate, quite pleased.

Mr. Applegate leaned back with an expansive air. "Tabby has a notion of setting herself up in a shop."

Mrs. Applegate frowned at her husband. "Not a shop, Mr. Applegate. It will be an establishment of mode."

In the impulsive fashion characteristic of her, Mrs. Applegate turned back to her sister. Mary wore a stunned expression and, with a brilliant smile, Mrs. Applegate said, "And you shall wear all my creations, Mary, and set up such a stir that I will be an instant success! Why, everyone will simply beg me to design their bonnets for them. But naturally I shall not accept any but the highest born ladies. It is positively fatal to dilute one's quality by quantity. Papa's talk of his dealings always bored me to tears, but I do recall that much of it, at least."

Mary had listened with parted lips, speechless with amazement. But at this, she demanded, "Have you told Papa what you have in mind?"

Mrs. Applegate shrugged in an unconcerned fashion. "Oh, no. But Mr. Applegate does not think that Papa will cut up stiff about it once you have agreed to help me. Only think how convenient, Mary! Papa will provide me with all the silks and velvets and ribbons and—oh, whatever else I have a mind to use, while you shall discover me to the ladies of the *ton*. Isn't it the most delightfully prodigious scheme? Dearest Mary, I know that you will help me!"

Mary tried, and failed, to visualize herself as a walking advertisement for her sister's pretty concoctions to polite society. However, she could very well anticipate the viscount's expression if his lordship ever got wind of the proposed scheme.

Not for nothing had Mary observed the *ton* and listened to the gossip during the past weeks. She had seen how her husband dealt with and was received by society. Surprise had been expressed in Mary's own presence that Lord St. John had gone far out of his way to squire his wife into society. His attentiveness had been put down to pride and a determination to prove himself above society's strictures. The advent of vulgar relations could scarcely recommend themselves to him, and Mary had no illusions how the Applegates would be looked upon.

"Oh, my word," murmured Mary inadequately.

"Look here, Tabby. Our dear sister is fair dazzled by the

prospect," observed Mr. Applegate as he polished off a number of biscuits.

"I knew that dear Mary could not disappoint me," said Mrs. Applegate complacently.

Mary was moved at last to protest. "I could not possibly! It is absurd—impossible!" She caught hold of herself. "I am sorry, Tabitha, but I really cannot. It is completely out of the question."

Mrs. Applegate did not appear at all offended by the hasty rejection. She simply got to her feet and began to pull on her gloves. Nodding and smiling the while, she said, "Mr. Applegate said it would take a little time for the advantages of the notion to sink in, so you just think on it for now, Mary. Mr. Applegate says that there is ample time for you to reflect, for we have yet to find the best location for the shop."

"Establishment of mode," corrected Mr. Applegate, grinning hugely.

"Yes; and once you do see how very sensible and profitable a notion it truly is, you will be all eagerness to lend me your head," said Mrs. Applegate.

"Oh no, I shan't. I mean to keep it firmly attached to my shoulders," said Mary tartly. She almost shuddered to think what Lord St. John's reaction might be to the intelligence that his wife was setting up as a hat peddler. Though she had never been the direct object of her husband's wrath, she had observed several times the signs of a volatile temper in him. Further, she had overheard enough offhand comments by those well-acquainted with him to realize that she had been fortunate in that respect.

The Applegates laughed uproariously at what they took to be her witticism. "Very humorous, dear sister," said Mr. Applegate appreciatively.

"You are in such a funning humor, Mary. I had quite

181

thought that—but never mind. I am glad now that we have sprung it on you first thing. Mr. Applegate is never wrong about these things," said Mrs. Applegate blithely. She kissed her sister and waited while her husband also took his leave.

Mr. Applegate lavishly saluted Mary's hand before offering his arm to his spouse. "We shall be in touch, dear sister," he promised jovially as he led his wife from the drawing room.

Craighton had hovered just outside the door in readiness to show Lady St. John's callers out the front door. Once the visitors had been shown off the premises, the butler returned to the drawing room to clear away the remains of the tea. "Shall you require anything else, my lady?"

Mary was sitting quietly on the settee, staring pensively into space. At the butler's query, she turned her head. "I do wish I were not quite so levelheaded, Craighton. One cannot very well fall into hysterics when one is aware of how ridiculous it makes one appear, can one?"

"Too true, my lady," said Craighton. His expression was wooden but a faintly sympathetic note laced his voice.

She sighed. "Yes."

Craighton hovered a moment longer, unwilling to leave before he had been dismissed.

Lady St. John roused herself from her thoughts to smile at her butler. "Craighton, I shall shortly have a note readied to be carried round to my father." She gathered up her neglected embroidery and started toward the door of the drawing room. She turned in the doorway. "There is no need to mention anything to his lordship about my callers this morning, Craighton."

"Very good, my lady," Craighton approved. It would indeed be best if his lordship was not brought into the matter at all.

Chapter 19

Mary received a reply from her father within the day. Mr. Pepperidge's note requested that she visit him on the following afternoon. She did so, taking a hackney rather than the crested carriage that the viscount had provided for her use since she did not wish the coachman to be able to mention her destination to the other servants and thus have it come to the viscount's ears.

It was not that she was afraid that Lord St. John would disapprove of her going to visit her father, but that she simply preferred not to be faced with questions that she could not fully answer. She would not have been able to dissemble if Lord St. John inquired what she and her father had talked about. She still hoped that the awful business concerning the Applegates should never come to his lordship's attention at all.

When Mary arrived at her father's house, Mr. Pepperidge met her in the entry hall with outstretched hands. "My dear Mary. Come in and let me look at you." He shook his head admiringly. "You look positively radiant, daughter."

"Thank you, Papa." Mary had put her hands in his and now she stretched up to place an affectionate kiss on his cheek. Drawing back, she looked searchingly at his face. "How have you been, Papa?"

"Very well, my dear. I have William staying with me at present, you know," Mr. Pepperidge said with a hovering smile.

"William! Why, I thought he had returned to school," said Mary, surprised.

Mr. Pepperidge laughed and shrugged. "He has begged me not to send him back, promising to apply himself to the business instead."

"But that is wonderful, Papa," exclaimed Mary, glad for both her father and her brother.

"I only hope that it works out for the best. I have reservations, Mary. I shall not conceal that from you, for you know better than anyone else how impatient the boy is. But that is not what you have come to talk to me about. Come, we shall have some tea and discuss this foolish start of Tabitha's," said Mr. Pepperidge, leading her into the parlor and closing the door.

Mary walked over to sit down on the settee. She began pulling off her gloves, remarking, "I was never more astonished, Papa. How could Tabitha believe that I could agree to such a mad scheme? My credit with the *ton* is scarcely of a nature that makes such a thing even remotely possible."

Mr. Pepperidge regarded his daughter. "As bad as that, my dear?"

Mary's eyes lifted swiftly to meet his somber and sympathetic gaze. She flushed slightly. "It cannot be wondered at, Papa. I am not their sort. I am accepted to that extent bestowed upon me by Lord St. John's name, but with a very few exceptions I do not claim friendship amongst my new acquaintances."

Mr. Pepperidge nodded. "Aye, it is to be expected. And what of Lord St. John?"

Mary tried very hard to disguise the depth of her hurt and her confusion over the viscount's changed manner toward her. "My lord has always been attentive. He has very diligently introduced me to all of his acquaintances."

"There is something you are hiding from me, Mary. Has

his lordship mistreated or neglected you?" asked Mr. Pepperidge.

Mary quickly shook her head, smoothing her gloves between her hands. "Oh no, nothing like that. It is just that. . . ."

"Come, Mary, you may tell me."

She raised her head, her eyes brilliant with unshed tears. "It was so much warmer between us at Rosethorn Hall. Now that we are in London, I see so much less of Lord St. John. He still escorts me to all sorts of entertainments, but we have lost that oddly comfortable manner between us. There are so many obligations now that we seem never to have a quiet moment in which to simply talk." She could not bring herself to mention that her husband had rarely visited her bedroom since their remove to London.

Mr. Pepperidge frowned thoughtfully. "You must realize, Mary, that a gentlemen such as his lordship had well-established habits before he was wed. It is natural that Lord St. John should continue in his former ways, at least for a while."

"It is so very hard to bear at times," she confessed.

"Never fear; your own worth must eventually be seen for what it is. Mark my words, it is early days yet," said Mr. Pepperidge.

"Thank you, Papa," said Mary. She was grateful for her father's understanding and support, though she could not wholly believe in the comfort of his words. "I only wish that this thing with Tabitha had not come up just now, for I suspect that my lord will not be amused to learn that his sister-in-law means to exploit his name through me."

Mr. Pepperidge leaned back in his chair, his concerned expression deepening into a frown. "Your letter to me concerning Tabitha was disturbing, to say the least. I shall not deny that to you. Tabitha obviously has too little sense to realize the harm that she might do you with this precious scheme of hers. A fashionable milliner! It was plain when she and Applegate visited me that the pair of them had something up their sleeves, but I never dreamed that it was anything of this sort. If I had known that they meant to embroil you, I would have been more adamant concerning your privacy."

"What am I to do, Papa? Tabitha did not seem the least bit discouraged when I told her that I could not do it. Indeed, she and Mr. Applegate were quite complacent at my refusal, for they seemed to think that it was but a matter of time before I acquiesced," said Mary. "If it was only Tabitha, I would not be so perturbed. But Mr. Applegate seems to hold great sway over her and he is apparently not a gentlemen to be easily discouraged."

"Aye, that is my concern as well. Well, I shall see what I can do about the matter, Mary. Applegate has a healthy respect for my opinion which is in direct proportion to the depth of my pockets. In the meantime, stand firm against them," said Mr. Pepperidge.

"I mean to do so, Papa," said Mary, laughing a little at her father's matter-of-fact description of his son-in-law's priorities. "In any event, I'm of no mind to trust my reputation to such a heedless pair."

"Mind that you don't. Tabitha is my own daughter, but I have never let that blind me to her faults. She has always been set on having her own way. Applegate is cut from much the same cloth. Wherever there is an opportunity for a quick profit, that is where you will find the fellow. 'Tis a pity, but there it is," said Mr. Pepperidge with a shrug.

The door was flung open and a youth impetuously entered. "Papa, I—" At sight of Mary, his face lit up. "Mary! I didn't know you were here!"

Mary had risen at her brother's entrance and she held out her hands to him. "William, how glad I am to see you."

Instead of being content with a conventional greeting, he grabbed her up in a whirling bearhug. Laughing, she implored him to put her down. "I am a respectable lady, I'll have you know, William!"

He set her on her feet then. "Aye, a titled lady! I had forgotten." Instantly, he made a flourishing leg and kissed her hand. "My lady viscountess, your servant, ma'am!"

Mary snatched her hand free, again laughing. "Idiot! Papa tells me that you have given up on your schooling and have come to help him."

William grimaced, throwing an impish glance at his father. "Aye; I don't know that I shall be a *help* to him, however! Papa may wish me into the army yet."

Mr. Pepperidge rose from his chair, a tolerant expression on his face. "So that is your plan, jackanapes. I warn you, I am not easily discouraged."

"Don't I know it, sir," said William with an exaggerated sigh.

Mr. Pepperidge laughed. "I must return to the office, Mary. William, I shall leave you to enjoy this unexpected visit with your sister. But I shall expect you back at your duties within the hour."

"Aye, sir," said William. He held the door open for Mr. Pepperidge and once his parent had exited, he closed the door and turned to his sister. "Now, Mary, you must tell me how things go with you. I did not wish to speak frankly before Papa, but I wish you to know that if ever you have anything troubling you, you may rely upon me."

Mary was greatly touched by his obvious sincerity. "Thank you, William. I hope, however, that I am sensible enough not ever to require your services."

"Then you are happy?" asked William.

Mary shook her head, retaining her smile. "Silly, how could I not be? I am concerned only about Tabitha at the moment, and perhaps just a little about you. Do you really mean to apply yourself to the business?"

William grimaced. "It is dull going, Mary. I know that you cannot truly understand it, for you and Papa are cut from the same cloth. I would far rather make my fortune adventuring than doing so by counting figures. But I do not mean to complain. Papa has been very decent about my being sent down this term and—"

"Oh, William, no! You haven't been sacked, have you?" exclaimed Mary.

He had the grace to redden. "Not precisely that. Oh, it was nothing so bad, Mary. Just a lark or two with my cronies, you know."

"Yes, I know," said Mary, not a shred of confusion in her expression.

William flushed a brighter shade. "It's all very well for you, Mary! You have got what you wanted or you wouldn't have accepted this viscount's offer. Tabitha got what she wanted, though I think she could have made a better bargain than Applegate. As for Papa, I am sorry that I am a disappointment to him; but I have not the least desire to be shut into a building day after day, year after year. Papa likes it! He thinks it the most exciting thing imaginable to read those reports and deal with contracts and such. But I want something else. I want to see something of the world. I want"—He threw out his hands—"Oh, what's the point? You would never understand."

"What is your most ludicrous flight of fancy, William?" Mary asked quietly.

"Sailing the world, soldiering in foreign parts, seeing peoples strange to me," he said promptly. He stared at his sister, caught by the odd smiling expression on her face. "You felt it, too, didn't you, Mary?"

"Papa commented many times that I have a head for business and I, too, often wished that I could set sail on one of his ships. Unfortunately, I was born a female and however dear I am to Papa, it never occurred to him that I could be his successor," said Mary.

"I-I am sorry, Mary. I never knew that you felt that way," stammered William.

Mary laughed, reaching her hand to touch him lightly on the arm. "Pray do not think me to be weighed down with self-pity, William! On the contrary, as it has turned out I have attained an even more improbable wish."

"You are talking about the viscount, aren't you?" He regarded her with curiosity. "Are you really glad to have wed him, Mary?"

She was silent a moment, wondering how best to explain. "I tumbled in love with Lord St. John the first time I ever met him. I never told Papa, for it would have completely undermined his confidence in my sensible character. But imagine my feelings when I was informed by Papa that he had received an offer for my hand from his lordship. I, a mere tradesman's daughter!"

"His lordship is fortunate to have you," said William gruffly.

Mary shook her head, smiling. "I hope that he comes to believe that, William."

William's countenance darkened. "Has he offered you insult, Mary? Or hurt you? For if he has, I shall take him thoroughly to task, I promise you! And so I warned him, if he so much as laid a hand on you."

"What rot, William! Lord St. John is always a gentleman," said Mary sharply. She relented at the look on her brother's face. "I am sorry, William. But you mustn't abuse his lordship in my hearing, you see."

"Yes, I do see," he said slowly.

She could not stand his searching scrutiny any longer and she said, "William, I shall talk to Papa, if you like. Perhaps he will relent and let you go into the army."

William shook his head, a glum expression falling over his face. "You can talk all you wish, and with my good will. But Papa is adamant against it. He is afraid that I should be killed and it doesn't do a particle of good to assure him otherwise."

Mary could not stop the light laugh that escaped her. At her brother's indignant look, she apologized. Nevertheless, she said, "But, William, you cannot give him that guarantee. There is a war going on."

William snapped his fingers. "That for the war! I know that I should come out of it all right and tight, given the chance. But Papa always hedges his risks. That much I *have* learned!"

Mary laughed again, this time ruefully. "Yes, so he does. Still, I shall do my best for you. I do not wish you to fall into trouble for lack of something better to do."

"Much more of figures and reports and I am likely to go mad for some scrape or other," muttered William with a wicked grin.

"That is precisely what *I* fear," retorted Mary. She stood up and started to put on her gloves. "I must go now. I have some shopping to do before I return."

William recalled something she had mentioned. "What was it that you said earlier about being made anxious by Tabitha? Knowing our sister, she has taken some pea-brained notion into her head that will make us all uncomfortable."

Mary shook her head, unwilling to disclose the particulars to her brother. He would only set about taxing their sister the next time that he saw her and that would only serve to set up Tabitha's back. "Papa is seeing to it, so I shall not burden you."

William whistled, for he had few illusions. "That bad, is it?"

"William, promise me that you will not say anything to her. You know what Tabitha is like when she is crossed," she said.

"None better," agreed William. "You need not look so anxious, Mary. I should think I'd know better than to thrust my spoke into Papa's wheel. Whatever is the matter, I shall let him handle it without any interference from me."

Reassured, Mary took affectionate leave of her brother. She had requested that the hackney wait for her and when she emerged from her father's house, she immediately stepped up into it. Directing the driver to some fashionable shops, she settled back against the squabs.

Chapter 20

Mary made short work of making her purchases. She was on the point of reentering the hackney cab when she heard herself hailed. She glanced around and met the smiling gaze of a gentleman who appeared faintly familiar to her. "Do I know you, sir?" she asked politely.

The gentleman bowed slightly, the smile curling his mouth in a more pronounced fashion. "We met at the ridotto a fortnight ago, my lady, but obviously my name escapes you. Lady Pothergill introduced us. Sir Nigel Smythe, my lady, at your service."

He had taken possession of her gloved hand and pressed a light kiss onto its back. Mary was keenly embarrassed by her failure to recognize the gentlemen, while his overdone salute made her uncomfortable. She withdrew her hand from his grasp. "I do apologize, Sir Nigel. I am afraid that I have met so many personages of late that I do not always recall every name. Are you an acquaintance of my husband, Lord St. John?"

Sir Nigel bared his teeth in a half-smile. "Yes, indeed. The viscount and I are very well acquainted. I have found his lordship to be a most worthy opponent at the card table. Perhaps Lord St. John has made mention of me?"

Mary smiled, shaking her head. "I do not believe so or certainly I would have recognized you at once."

Sir Nigel put up his brows. The expression in his eyes was politely incredulous. "Never tell me that you pay particular attention to his lordship's circle, ma'am! It is far more the fashion to pretend complete indifference to a spouse's friends or interests."

"Then I am outside the fashion, Sir Nigel," she said, still smiling. She did not particularly care for the gentleman's mode of address, which was both familiar and faintly condescending. "I do hope that you will excuse me, sir, but I am in a rush to return home."

"Of course, my lady. What am I about to keep you standing on the pavement? I had not noticed before that you had so many packages. Let me hand you in."

Before Mary knew it, she had been handed into the carriage and settled on the seat with her packages. She was rendered speechless when Sir Nigel followed her inside and knocked on the wall to let the driver know to start. The hackney gave a lurch forward just as Mary found her voice. "Sir! I do not believe that I invited you to share my cab."

"The invitation existed only in your lovely eyes, Lady St. John, but I flatter myself that I am too seasoned not to understand it when a lady looks just so," said Sir Nigel.

"Then you flatter yourself too highly, sir, for nothing existed but what you conjured up in your own imagination," said Mary with asperity. "I will thank you to exit this carriage immediately."

Sir Nigel appeared to give her request a moment's rumination. Then he shook his head. "I cannot possibly do so, for that would leave you quite bereft of an escort. A lady does not jaunt about London in common hackneys without even a maid with her."

"I do not need your escort, sir, I assure you," said Mary quite coolly. "It is not at all the thing, as I very well know. We are but the slightest of acquaintances, after all."

"I hope to become much closer in your affections very shortly," said Sir Nigel.

The look in his eyes suddenly made a frisson of foreboding race up Mary's spine. She sat up very straight and her eyes did not waver from his smiling face. "What can you mean by that, sir?"

His glance slowly appraised her. He shrugged. "I think it need not be spelled out, my lady."

Mary threw herself toward the door, a scream tearing from her throat. Rough hands dragged her backward and threw her against the squab. Sir Nigel's weight imprisoned her. She stared up into his face, which was very close. There was a hard light in his eyes. "The driver will have heard me," she warned.

Sir Nigel laughed softly. His breath feathered her skin and she involuntarily flinched. "The driver received a small remuneration for becoming deaf for a few minutes, my dear Lady St. John."

"Why?"

"Why?" Sir Nigel eased his weight slightly as he reflected upon the question. At last he said, "Shall I say simply that I intensely dislike the viscount? His lordship once beggared my pride. I thought merely to return the favor."

"I shall not make it easy for you," she stated.

"My God, you're a cool one." Sir Nigel brought up a hand and traced the curve of her cheek. She jerked her head away from his touch, but he merely followed her movement. "Relax, dear lady. It will all be over quite, quite soon."

Mary fought, then. His first attempt to possess her mouth backfired as she jerked away, the hard rim of her bonnet cracking against his nose. He swore and caught her chin cruelly in his fingers. His mouth crushed hers, driving her lips against her teeth. She felt his hand at her throat, pulling aside the front of her pelisse. Her mouth was abruptly freed and she gave a sob of relief. Then in horror she felt his lips descend to the bare skin just above her breast. She renewed her struggle, pounding him with her fists. His heavy legs imprisoned hers, but strangely enough he did not attempt to slide her skirts up.

Mary was marginally aware when the hackney slowed. Suddenly she was freed. She scrambled upright, putting as much distance between herself and Sir Nigel as possible. That gentleman sat across from her very much at his ease, smoothing his hair. It was as though he had never forced his attentions on her; at least, until she met his malicious smile.

"As charming as you appear, dear lady, perhaps it would he best if you tidied your appearance," he said insultingly.

Mary felt heat rush into her face. With trembling fingers she swiftly did up her pelisse and smoothed her clothing. She felt battered and bruised and thoroughly frightened. "Where-where have you taken me?"

Sir Nigel laughed. It was not a pleasant sound. "Gather your packages, Lady St. John. I shouldn't think that you wish to leave them on this filthy floor."

Mary shot him a scorching glance before bending to retrieve the tied packages.

The hackney stopped and Sir Nigel opened the door. He jumped down and then turned to offer his hand to her.

Mary ignored his hand, preferring to descend under her own power even though one arm was full of her purchases. When she was safely on the pavement, she glanced around for familiar markers. Then she stood rooted to the spot.

She was standing outside her own town house.

The door had opened and Mr. Underwood emerged onto the top step. He gave a visible start upon seeing Lady St. John standing so cosily with a gentlemen known to him to hold the viscount in intense dislike. In that unguarded moment his expression was very plainly read and Mary knew that what had happened in the hackney would not end there on the sidewalk.

She turned a stricken gaze onto Sir Nigel. "What have you done?" she whispered.

He smiled down at her. "Why, I have but escorted you home, Lady St. John."

For the first time in her life, uncontrollable fury coursed through Mary. She drew back her hand and slapped Sir Nigel full across the face. Then without a second glance she trod up the steps and swept past the stupefied Mr. Underwood.

She had given her packages to a footman and was removing her bonnet when Mr. Underwood appeared beside her. He took her elbow and waved away the footman. "My lady, I'd be grateful for a word with you," he said, leading her into the drawing room.

Mr. Underwood closed the door, then turned to regard the viscountess. There was a grim look in his eyes. "What happened with Sir Nigel, my lady?"

Mary bit her lip. Her face was burning with embarrassment. She knew from Mr. Underwood's slightly accusing tone that she could not sidestep the question, as much as she would like to do so. She sank down on the settee dejectedly. "I had gone to visit my father. When I left there, I went to the shops. Sir Nigel accosted me and insisted upon sharing my cab. He-he made unwelcome advances." Unwillingly recalling those turbulent minutes, she covered her face with her hands, shuddering violently.

Her wrists were caught in iron grips and her hands were dragged down. Mr. Underwood's furious brown eyes stared down into hers. "Lady St. John. You must tell me at once. Did you take hurt from Sir Nigel?"

She stared up at him, uncomprehending for a split second. Then the mists in her mind cleared and she under-

The Desperate Viscount

stood. She went paperwhite. "No! I thought at first that he meant—But he let me go when the hackney stopped."

Mr. Underwood released her and slowly straightened. His expression was very tight. "Sinjin will have to be told."

Mary flew up, catching at his arm with both hands. She felt sick panic. "Carey, no! He must not know. Pray do not tell him! He would be so very angry."

Mr. Underwood gave a short, sharp laugh. "That is a mild understatement, my lady. You have not yet seen Sinjin in a wild black temper, have you? Believe me, you do not wish to."

"Then you must not say anything! Promise me that you will not," said Mary urgently. "Oh, you must see! I-I could not bear it if he were to turn on me like that."

Mr. Underwood covered her hands with his own and squeezed her fingers. There was a pitying expression in his eyes. "My dear lady, I have no choice. Which do you think will do the most harm—hearing the tale from me or from some tattle on the town?"

If possible, Mary turned whiter. She whispered, "Surely Sir Nigel would not—"

Mr. Underwood smiled grimly. "Who might have seen Sir Nigel get into your hackney?"

Mary shook her head. "I don't know. I didn't notice." She pressed her hands against her cheeks. "You are saying that anyone could have done so. Anyone could carry the tale to my lord at any time."

"Sir Nigel meant to ruin you in Sinjin's eyes, at least, if not in the eyes of society," said Mr. Underwood brutally.

"What am I to do?" she whispered, her face stark in its despair.

"You will do nothing. You will go about your business as though nothing at all has happened. I have heard that Lady

Caroline Eddington is in town to shop for her trousseau. I will send at once to her and she will put about the story that you were in her company this afternoon. She'll do it, never fear, for she's a lady who stands staunch beside her friends," said Mr. Underwood, striding over to the desk standing in the corner even as he spoke. He pulled a sheet of paper toward him and scrawled a short note; then sanded and folded it. He yanked the bell rope and waited impatiently for a servant.

"But I have never met her ladyship. I am not an intimate of hers," said Mary, feeling dazed. The dizzying speed with which he was ordering her life left her feeling stupid.

"I am, however. You will need to meet Lady Caroline as quickly as possible so that neither of you will give the game away by not recognizing one another if you should encounter her in public."

The door opened and a footman entered. Mr. Underwood entrusted the folded note to the man with terse instructions for its delivery. As the door closed, he turned once again to his companion. "Now, as for the rest, you must trust me. I will wait here until Sinjin comes in so that I can break the tidings to him."

"I cannot face him," said Mary faintly. She actually felt unwell at the thought.

Mr. Underwood's expression gentled. "You will not need to do so just at first. By the time that you do talk to Sinjin, the worst of his temper will have cooled. I give you my word on it."

"Thank you, Carey. You are a good friend to him," said Mary. Her smile wavered. "I hope that you will excuse me now. I must change before going out this evening." She gave her hand to him, very briefly, before leaving the drawing room. Her carriage was graceful and proud.

The gentleman who watched her exit the room could not but admire her courage. He only hoped that it would be enough.

Lady St. John had already gone out, making up one of Lady Heatherton's party, when Lord St. John returned to the town house. He was informed by Craighton that Mr. Underwood had been waiting for him in the drawing room since earlier that day. Lord St. John's brows drew together in a frown. "Has he, indeed?"

He stepped across the hall and thrust open the door to the drawing room. As he entered, he said, "Carey, what is this? I had no notion that you pined so for my company. I swear that I am flattered."

Mr. Underwood rose from the wingback chair in which he had made himself comfortable. "So you should be," he retorted, grasping the viscount's hand.

Lord St. John narrowed his gaze. "So what is the story, Carey?"

Mr. Underwood winced. "I wish you had not phrased it in quite that fashion, Sinjin. But since you have asked, perhaps you should close the door."

Lord St. John glanced sharply at him, then snapped shut the door. "Well, Carey?"

During the next several minutes, Mr. Underwood proceeded to unfold the particulars of Lady St. John's harrowing adventure. Halfway into the tale, Lord St. John turned away from Mr. Underwood to pour himself a glass of brandy. He lifted the glass from the occasional table, but he did not drink. He appeared oblivious to all but the rich color of the fine wine.

When Mr. Underwood at last fell silent, Lord St. John asked, "Did you believe her, Carey?"

Mr. Underwood reacted as though he had suffered a blow. "Of course I did! She was obviously in great distress. Believe me, Sinjin, I am too experienced with the intricacies of the female mind to misjudge such a thing. Your lady was the object of foul attentions."

The stem of the wineglass snapped in the viscount's fingers. He stared down at the blood slowly beading on his hand. Very softly, he murmured, "I shall kill him."

"No, you won't. Challenging Sir Nigel would only confirm whatever rumors do arise. I've already explained to you what I have set in motion with Lady Caroline. That ought to suffice in protecting Lady St. John's reputation," said Mr. Underwood. His tone altered and became harsh. "As for Sir Nigel, you may safely leave him to me."

Lord St. John looked round quickly. What he read in Mr. Underwood's expression caused a twist of a smile to come to his lips. "May I, indeed?"

Mr. Underwood nodded. His eyes were rather harder than usual. "I have to come to regard Lady St. John as a friend. I intend to have justice."

"Good enough, Carey. Though it goes hard against the grain with me, Sir Nigel is yours." Lord St. John paused, then said exceedingly softly, "Break him for me, Carey."

Mary did not encounter her husband until the following morning at breakfast. As Mr. Underwood had promised, Lord St. John did not appear to be suffering from the effects of a black fury. She almost wished that he was exhibiting anger, for then it would in a strange way have made it easier for her.

She wondered what she could possibly say to exonerate herself in her lord's eyes, but the opportunity to explain herself was lost when he broached the unpleasant subject himself.

"I understand from Underwood that you underwent a rather unpleasant experience yesterday. May I suggest that in future you take your maid with you when you go driving about town."

The expression in his gray eyes was unfathomable. She could not tell what he was thinking. "I shall do so, my lord."

Lord St. John nodded curtly.

"My lord, I—"

He threw up a hand. "There is nothing more to be said on the matter. It is forgotten."

Mary was silenced. She wanted so desperately to confide her fears to him and to be reassured that he believed her. But she could not approach him in the face of the mask he had withdrawn behind.

She was startled when he spoke again, very abruptly.

"You never cared that I was titled."

"Not much," she confessed, wondering why he should ask at just that moment. She braved a small smile. "It would have been much more comfortable to have wed a plain mister."

"You did not care for my title and you were the one with a fortune to bestow. Why did you agree to become my wife, Mary?"

Mary sat very still. How very much she yearned to confide the truth to him. Her innate honesty compelled her to do so, but she was afraid to expose her vulnerability to him in such great degree. Her poise was in a fair way to deserting her. If he had reached out for her hand, or if his expression had lightened with his rare smile, she quite thought that she would have burst into tears.

The silence demanded an answer from her. With difficulty, she said, "I-I hoped to realize a dream, my lord."

Lord St. John's lips twisted. "And have you done so, my lady?"

Mary averted her face, pretending that she required a second cup of coffee. "I had thought so, at Rosethorn."

"Rosethorn." Lord St. John lifted his shoulders in self-mockery. "Shall I tell you the fevered vision of a fool? I envisioned myself returning there one day to find waiting for me in the doorway a beautiful woman holding the hand of a child."

Her eyes flew to his closed face. There was such a frowning abstraction in his eyes that she wondered whether he knew just what it was he had said. Hesitantly, she whispered, "My lord, it is not foolish to dream of a home and family."

He glanced up, his eyes meeting hers. For a long moment their gazes clung together. He deliberately looked away. "For such as I, it is an impossibility."

Mary rose from her place to go and kneel beside his chair. She laid her hand on his thigh, and felt the hard muscle contract beneath her fingers. "You are not undeserving, my lord. I believe that with all of my heart."

He stared down at the earnestness in her expression. With a sudden movement he reached down and lifted her bodily into his arms. He kissed her with a ruthless passion.

As suddenly as he had folded her against him, he released her. Standing, he set her onto her feet. His hands still caressed her arms. "I think at times that you bewitch me," he said hoarsely.

"If I do so truly, I am glad," she whispered.

Lord St. John shook his head as though to clear it. He strode quickly from the breakfast room, leaving Mary with the distinct impression that he was fleeing from her.

Chapter 21

The following morning a calling card was taken into the drawing room for Lady St. John's perusal. Mary felt her throat go dry. "Pray send in her ladyship."

Mary waited to receive her first caller of the day with a sense of trepidation. The lady who was ushered into the drawing room was obviously of the first stare. She advanced with a smile and a quizzical look in her fine eyes. "Lady St. John, I am happy to find you at home. It might have been rather awkward otherwise."

Mary responded to the lady's wry humor. She laughed, her own tension dissipating. "Thank you, Lady Caroline. You cannot imagine how grateful I am that you have agreed to Mr. Underwood's request."

Lady Caroline sat down. "Truth to tell, my curiosity was running rampant. Carey's note to me was very brief but extremely tantalizing. Perhaps you might fill in the gaps for me."

After only the slightest hesitation, Mary decided to trust Mr. Underwood's wisdom in making Lady Caroline privy to the situation and so she related all that had happened the previous afternoon. She ended by saying, "Lord St. John was very unhappy with me for my foolishness, of course. But he has not uttered a word in reproach so I suppose that I must count myself extraordinarily fortunate."

"Fortunate, indeed." There was a small frown between Lady Caroline's winged brows, but it cleared when she smiled. "And so we come to my part in all of this. I think that we shall agree that you drove about with me all afternoon, in quite another part of town. It is fortuitous that you used a hackney. Your own carriage would have been too easily placed."

Mary was still sitting with Lady Caroline when two other ladies were shown in. Lady Pothergill and her ladyship's niece, Mrs. Nessering, greeted Lady Caroline with the familiarity of long standing and congratulated her upon her betrothal to Lord Miles Trilby, the Earl of Walmsley.

"But I had no notion that you were acquainted with Lady St. John," said Lady Pothergill with an inflection of surprise.

"Lord Trilby and Lord St. John are the closest of friends," said Lady Caroline, smiling.

"Oh, so you have just now become acquainted," said Lady Pothergill.

"I count Lady St. John one of my dearest friends, actually," said Lady Caroline, shooting a glance brimful of wry amusement to the lady in question.

Mary could not help but respond to Lady Caroline's twinkling eyes. She laughed. "Yes, indeed. I feel that I have known Lady Caroline forever and an age."

"Indeed!" said Mrs. Nessering with a sharp look.

"When I came up to London to have my trousseau made up, I took instant advantage of the opportunity to call on Lady St. John. We have since spent many pleasant moments together. In fact, I do not know what I would have done without her to help me with my shopping yesterday. She discovered the most exquisite point lace. I was never more glad of it, for we had traipsed about all afternoon before we came across it," said Lady Caroline.

Lady Pothergill and Mrs. Nessering exchanged a glance.

"I had quite thought I had heard you were seen driving about in a hackney yesterday, Lady St. John," said Mrs.

Nessering, baring her teeth.

If Mrs. Nessering had hoped to put Lady St. John out of countenance, she was disappointed. The viscountess's face remained composed, though her brows rose a fraction as though in mild query.

Lady Caroline's little laugh drew the ladies' attention back. "I hope that I have a better sense of my own consequence than that, Mrs. Nessering. We were far more comfortable in my carriage than we could ever have been in a common cab. But now I am curious, Mrs. Nessering. Who was it who thought they had seen Lady St. John and myself in a hackney?"

"I do not precisely recall. Obviously they were mistaken," said Mrs. Nessering.

The conversation turned to commonplaces then and Mary had begun to relax, when Mrs. Applegate was shown into the sitting room. Mary looked up, startled and dismayed. Her imagination could not have devised a worse coincidence.

Mrs. Applegate greeted her sister effusively. "Mary! How glad I am to have found you receiving," she said with a blindingly beautiful smile. However, a slightly glittering look in her eyes somewhat belied her assumption of good humor.

Mary knew with a sinking feeling that her staff had tried to hint Mrs. Applegate away but she, being too used to having her way, had run straight through them. How unfortunate that this was the day that Craighton had requested to have free to take care of personal business, Mary thought dismally. "Tabitha, this is a surprise. I had not expected you to call on me today," she said.

Mrs. Applegate sat down, nodding to the other ladies. She never gave a thought for the astonished expressions they each wore, merely taking it as admiration for her exquisite turn-out. She began to pull off her cherry red gloves. "I simply had to come, for I have heard nothing to the purpose from you for ages."

"Surely you had my note?" asked Mary. She could not prevent herself from uttering the hasty words, much as she hesitated to bring up anything whatever to do with her sister's importunities in this company. She had thought she had made it quite clear that she would not hear any more about the part that Tabitha and Mr. Applegate had wanted her to play in their grandiose scheme.

Mrs. Applegate tossed her head and the delightful confection of feathers and flowers on her head waved beguilingly. "That!" she said scornfully. "I did not regard it in the least. I knew you could not be so mean once you had given it more reflection."

"Mary, I do hope that you will not think it bad of me, but I really should be going. I have a few other calls to make this morning. However, I hope to see you again later today," said Lady Caroline. She turned with a pleasant smile to Lady Pothergill and Mrs. Nessering. "I am going in your direction, Lady Pothergill. May I offer you a seat in my carriage?"

"That is kind of you, Lady Caroline, but I left my own landau at the curb," said Lady Pothergill.

"Oh, then I need not be anxious on your account. Mrs. Nessering, I recall that you had a way with a crystal punch. Perhaps you will give me your arm downstairs so that I may acquire that recipe from you," said Lady Caroline.

"Oh, of course." Mrs. Nessering threw a disconcerted glance at Lady Pothergill. "Naturally I would be delighted to do so."

"Perhaps we also should be going," said Lady Pothergill,

reluctantly drawing her reticule and gloves together. She was an inveterate gossip and her antennae had already sensed the vibrations of a scandal. However, it was difficult to remain when Lady Caroline was behaving so graciously and there was not encouragement from the hostess to put off her leavetaking.

Mary rose, murmuring her regrets and assent. She was grateful to Lady Caroline for taking charge so handily and defusing a potentially embarrassing situation. Lady Pothergill and her niece had already stayed the requisite half hour, after all, and she was relieved to see that Lady Caroline had influenced them to adhere to polite convention.

"Oh, do not do so on my account. I have not met any of dear Mary's friends as yet," said Mrs. Applegate, her smile dazzling.

Lady Pothergill looked a pointed question in Lady St. John's direction.

Mary had no alternative but to perform the introductions. "Lady Pothergill, Mrs. Nessering, Lady Caroline; my sister, Mrs. Applegate."

Lady Pothergill's thin sandy brows rose into her sparse hair. Her long nose fairly quivered. "Your sister, I believe you said, Lady St. John? How interesting, to be sure."

"Quite," said Mrs. Nessering on a titter.

Mrs. Applegate seemed unperturbed by the ladies' combined stares. "You are undoubtedly admiring my bonnet. It is one of my prettiest to date, as Mary will tell you. I have settled on a number of smart confections for dear Mary, but she is such an old stick that she will say that they are too extravagant for her. But it is my opinion that now she is a viscountess she should smarten up her appearance. Why, she would be a perfect dowd if it were not for that pretty shawl."

Mary felt the heat enter her face, but otherwise she managed to keep her facial expression perfectly controlled. Mrs. Applegate's toilette was an eye-catching ensemble of lavish trim and ribbons, topped by an extravagant bonnet. In contrast, her own morning gown, through its very simplicity and excellent cut, practically shouted that it came from the hands of a very expensive modiste. The Norwich shawl that she had draped over her elbows had cost dearly, as well.

She was well aware how thoroughly her sister had exposed herself through her ignorance. A lady of breeding would have instantly recognized her mode of dress as the height of fashionable understatement. "Tabitha, I am certain these ladies have not the least interest in my appearance, dowdy or otherwise."

Lady Pothergill's expression had held a stunned disbelief, but at Mary's quiet interjection, she smiled. "Not at all, Lady St. John. I have a great interest in fashion, as it happens." She returned to her former place and laid aside her reticule and gloves. "I should be glad to remain a few minutes longer to explore the topic. My own obligations are not that urgent, but pray do not let us keep *you,* Lady Caroline."

Mrs. Nessering tittered again, a faintly superior smile crossing her thin features. "Indeed. I am myself fascinated. Your own . . . toilette is quite riveting, Mrs. Applegate."

Mrs. Applegate threw a triumphant look in Mary's direction. "La, as though all we females did not wish to furbish up our appearances. Mary is a poor creature, however, so we must all make allowances for her. I do not know how the viscount ever came to take up with her, for she has never been one to set herself to look at her best. Why, can you believe it? She has thus far refused to wear even one of my dear little hats."

Mary did not believe for a moment that it was Mrs. Applegate's fashion sense that so fascinated Lady Pothergill and Mrs. Nessering; rather, it was the discovery that Lady St. John possessed a vulgar relative.

Lady Caroline drew her aside for a moment, the expression in her eyes sympathetic. She said in a lowered voice, "I wish that I could remain, but it seems I have been outmaneuvered."

"I can only thank you for what you have already done," said Mary gratefully. Lady Caroline pressed her hand and left.

Mary returned to her remaining guests. She sat by, quite powerless to stem her sister's garrulousness in the face of Lady Pothergill's leading questions. Before Lady Pothergill and Mrs. Nessering finally rose to take their leave, they had possession of every detail of Mrs. Applegate's ambitious plan to provide the high kick of fashion in headgear.

Mary was quietly humiliated, but she refused to allow her glance to fall before Lady Pothergill's superior amusement or Mrs. Nessering's contemptuous smile. The ladies assured her that they had never spent a more entertaining hour as they took their leave. The footman showed them out, closing the door.

Mary turned slowly toward her sister. Mrs. Applegate stood in front of the large gilt mirror primping the satin bow under her rounded chin. Her satisfied expression was reflected in the glass.

Mary felt a tide of fury course through her. "Tabitha, have the goodness to leave off admiring yourself!"

Mrs. Applegate jumped and turned, her large eyes rounding. "La, Mary! What a start you have given me."

"I shall give you a shaking to rattle your teeth if you do not attend to me, Tabitha! Once and for all, I shall not help

209

you become a milliner. You may try to do so, with my goodwill, but I will not be dragged into it."

"But Mr. Applegate said—"

"Bother Mr. Applegate! He is as much flash as he is foolish to put you up to such an idiotic scheme. The *ton* does not care for my opinion and you have done my credit the greatest harm imaginable in pressing Lady Pothergill and Mrs. Nessering to order from you. It will be all over town before the day is out. Everyone will be whispering about my sister, the milliner," said Mary bitterly.

She knew it would be but a matter of time before the news came to Lord St. John's ears. After the horrid occurrence with Sir Nigel, she had hoped more than ever that her sister's desire for a milliner's shop could be handled quietly. Unfortunately, whatever her father was doing in the wings had not come about quickly enough to keep her own skin out of trouble. She had very little doubt at all that she would at last fall foul of his renowned black fury.

"But that is wonderful! For a moment, I quite thought you meant that meeting those two ladies was a mistake, but I see now that it was not. Oh, Mary! I shall be famous!" exclaimed Mrs. Applegate.

Mary slapped her sister. Instantly she was sorry, not only for completely losing her temper but because Mrs. Applegate had dissolved into tears. She tried to put her arms around her sister, but Mrs. Applegate fended her away. "Tabitha, I did not mean it, truly I didn't! Oh, you *must* see how impossible it all is! Lord St. John will not stand for it!"

"What will I not stand for, my lady?"

Mary looked around, appalled. She flushed, embarrassed to be caught in such straits. "My-my sister, Mrs. Applegate, my lord. She is overwrought."

Lord St. John closed the door behind him. There was a queer smile on his face as he advanced toward the ladies.

Mrs. Applegate stopped weeping upon the viscount's entrance, instantly struck that his lordship was a virile and attractive gentleman. She brushed her fingers over her cheeks, removing the traces of her tears, and smiled waveringly at him. She was unafraid that she had swollen or reddened eyes, for she was one of the fortunate few who could cry without suffering such ignominies. She curtsied, murmuring, "My lord, it is a pleasure to meet you at last."

Lord St. John raised her hand and brushed his lips over her fingers. "Now you must tell me what has so distressed you, ma'am."

Mrs. Applegate threw a resentful glance in her sister's direction. "Mary slapped me, my lord! She is a petty, spiteful woman and has taken on such airs as makes one positively ill!"

Mary turned sharply away, unable to bear further humiliation, especially before her husband. "Pray excuse me."

"No, stay." There was command in the two words.

She turned, throwing up her head in unconscious pride. She met her husband's unfathomable eyes. "I would prefer not to do so, my lord."

"Nevertheless; it is my pleasure that you remain."

Lord St. John's gray eyes were quite cool, but there was a ruthless quality about his stern-held mouth that warned her that he would not brook argument. Mary felt that she had no choice but to obey. She sank into a wingback chair and averted her face.

Mrs. Applegate regarded the development with complacent satisfaction. Her beautiful eyes looked up into the viscount's face. "La, my lord! I had not thought that anyone could bring Mary to heel."

Lord St. John's mouth tightened slightly, whether in amusement or otherwise it could not be said. "I believe that I have the key to the disagreement between you and my wife, Mrs. Applegate. It is the matter of a milliner's shop, is it not?"

Mary turned her head sharply, a frown pulling together her brows.

"How did you know that, my lord?" asked Mrs. Applegate, disconcerted.

"My esteemed father-in-law introduced me to your husband, Mr. Applegate. Mr. Pepperidge thought it the wisest course," said Lord St. John, glancing briefly at his wife. His expression did not warm. "The upshot of it all is that you are to have your shop, Mrs. Applegate."

Mary leaped to her feet, uttering, "No!" But it was doubtful that her protest was heard over Mrs. Applegate's squeal of delight and clapping hands.

"Oh, my lord, never say so! Why, it is a fairy tale, to be sure. Mr. Applegate assured me how it would be, but I was never certain it would actually come about!" Mrs. Applegate threw herself onto the viscount's chest and expressed herself with an exuberant embrace.

Lord St. John set her firmly away from him. "I am happy that you are pleased, Mrs. Applegate. The details are already worked out, but I shall leave the explanation of them to Mr. Applegate."

Mrs. Applegate clapped a hand to her mouth. "La, Mr. Applegate! I must see him at once. I don't know whether I am on my head or my heels! Dear Mary, I must go. No, don't trouble to show me out for I quite feel myself to be at home." Gathering up her reticule and gloves, Mrs. Applegate exited, leaving the door agape.

Chapter 22

Lord St. John closed the door and turned to regard his wife. She met his cool appraisal with obviously hard-held composure, for her hands were clenched at her sides. He sauntered to the wingback opposite her and dropped into it carelessly. "You are silent, my lady. Have you nothing to say?"

"I do not wish you to set my sister up in a shop," she said tightly.

Lord St. John shrugged, an indifferent look coming over his face. "It is already done, my lady. I could not undo it even if I wished. Your father had the contracts drawn up, signed, and witnessed not an hour past."

Mary took an agitated turn about the room. "My lord, you can have no notion what you have let yourself in for! Before-before you came in, Lady Pothergill and Mrs. Nessering had the pleasure of my sister's company. You may imagine with what satisfaction they left. Indeed, they fairly itched to spread far and wide the intelligence that Lord St. John possesses the most vulgar sister-in-law imaginable!"

"I believe that my credit can withstand one such ignoble report," said Lord St. John.

Mary turned swiftly. "My lord, can you actually believe that it will end there?" She tried to laugh, but it ended on a choked sob. "Tabitha and her husband are determined to make themselves known to the *ton* and in the process they will bring ridicule to your name."

"They will have difficulty doing so in Rio de Janeiro," remarked Lord St. John.

"Rio de Janeiro?" repeated Mary, uncomprehending.

"Mr. Pepperidge most fortuitously has connections in that thriving colonial metropolis and he is even acquainted with some members of the exiled Portuguese court. Unfortunately, the Portuguese do not have access to a talented English milliner. Mr. Applegate saw at once the advantages of a fashionable establishment in such a setting," said Lord St. John.

"South America?" Mary stared at him. "The shop is going to be in South America?"

Lord St. John rose from the chair and closed the distance between himself and his wife. He possessed himself of her hands, turning them palm upward. "I seem to recall an angry imprint on Mrs. Applegate's cheek."

Mary flushed, her shame once more rising in her. "I lost my temper, I am afraid. It is not my usual style, I assure you."

"I did not think that it was," said Lord St. John. He treated her to the rare sight of his flashing grin. "You are a constant surprise to me, my lady. I discover a hidden vein of passion in you where I thought there was none."

Mary realized he had not looked at her in just that way for a very long time. The pulse beat in her throat. "Have I seemed such a poor creature to you, my lord?"

His smile faded, taking on a shade of grimness that had not been there before. He dropped her hands and stepped away. In a clipped voice, he said, "On the contrary. You are more than I ever expected." He turned away to leave her.

His hand was already on the knob when she stopped him. "My lord!"

He waited, his brows raised in inquiry. Under that steady, cool regard, she faltered. "I-I wished to express my thanks to you, my lord. I do not know what I would have done if you had not stepped in just now. My sister is temperamental in the extreme when her will is crossed. She would have left here probably to do something that would have had uncomfortable consequences for us all."

Lord St. John acknowledged her with the slightest of bows. His eyes held an ironic light. "Without your father's intervention, I would have known nothing of the matter. Isn't that what you desired, my lady?"

"I did not wish for you to be subjected to the embarrassment that my sister and her husband would have caused if they had remained in London," said Mary. She was confused by his manner. It almost seemed that he was disappointed in her, but she could not understand how that could be.

"Yet that embarrassment, as you put it, *would* have been mine if your father had not put me into the picture," said Lord St. John levelly.

Mary realized that she had insulted his pride by going to her father instead of confiding in him. This, coming on top of her misadventure the day before, had obviously served to snap his tolerance. She drew a breath, unhappily aware that she deserved his censure. She said quietly, "I am sorry, my lord. I should have sought you out regarding both this coil and Sir Nigel's behavior. I shall know better another time that I can come to you."

He gave a short, harsh laugh. "My dear, it is my devout hope that there will not be another time. Are you engaged for the theater tonight?"

The color had flooded her cheeks at his sharp reply and Mary felt ready to sink. "Yes, my lord. Lady Heatherton was kind enough to include me in her party."

"You have cause to be grateful to Lady Heatherton. It

215

seems that she has publicly expressed censure against Sir Nigel for his unsavory habit of fleecing green youths, and to such effectiveness that it is anticipated that the baron will be barred in future from polite society," said Lord St. John.

Mary slowly whitened as the significance of what he had said penetrated to her. "It is because of what happened yesterday?"

"Do you care so much what the gentlemen has reaped, ma'am?"

Mary jumped at the fury in his tone. She grasped the back of the settee. "I regret very much that I had anything at all to do with it."

Lord St. John nodded. He hesitated, as though he had in mind something more to say concerning the matter. But he did not.

Instead, he said curtly, "I will not be joining you for dinner this evening. I am engaged at my club tonight."

He turned on his heel, not daring to trust himself to keep his hands off her, and exited the drawing room.

The gaming was hot and deep that night at the club and lasted well into the early morning hours. The card rooms were thick with smoke. Vast quantities of brandy and port had been consumed and lent a flush to otherwise pale countenances. Heavy-lidded eyes glittered feverishly at each throw of the dice or turn of a card. Harsh oaths were uttered whenever the gamester's mistress, Lady Luck, hid her face.

More than one fortune had changed hands under that august roof when Lord St. John and Mr. Underwood rose from their own game and amiably parted from their cronies. They were making their leisurely way through the card rooms toward the front of the house when a disastrously clear voice cut through the acrid air and the low murmur of conversation.

"I hear that the new viscountess is good for any number of tumbles."

Lord St. John stopped short, his head turning toward the source of the subsequent laughter that met with this sally. Mr. Underwood caught his arm, expressing himself pithily and urgently but he paid no heed. Lord St. John quietly made his way toward a certain table. At his passing, gentlemen raised their heads from their cards, at once scenting something of impending interest.

" 'Tis the truth, I swear," the gentleman insisted as the amused expressions of his tablemates faded. "She's said to have invited Smythe into the hackney."

Opposite the speaker, a gentleman coughed. "Mistake, Lawton. Lady Caroline Eddington was seen with the viscountess, you know."

Lord St. John came up to the gentlemen. "You interest me profoundly—Lawton, is it not? Pray continue, sir."

The gentleman started, staring up at the viscount with something akin to horror. "My lord!"

Lord St. John smiled, ever so slightly. "Yes, it is I. But pray continue, Mr. Lawton. I am certain I shall find your further remarks most . . . enlightening."

The viscount's expression was such that those around about ceased their desultory conversation. At table after table the fashionable abandoned interest in their pursuit of fortune or folly to witness the spontaneous entertainment.

Mr. Lawton was sweating. He wondered how he had not noticed before the closeness of the air. Meeting the viscount's compelling gaze, he cursed the idle impulse that had brought him to White's and, even more, his wretched lack of timing. Of course he would never have said what he had if he had known that Lord St. John was within hearing.

However, the combined effects of self-pity and several glasses of brandy worked upon him and through his embarrassment and discomfort a spurt of tipsy anger surfaced. Aye, and what was Weemswood even doing in the club when everyone knew that the Earl of Cowltern had set about to blackball him.

The viscount had his share of temerity, but that could be overlooked compared with this other disgrace. It was beyond anything, so it was, when a gentleman had to watch his words over some trumpery merchant's daughter.

The angered thought was followed fast by a rush of blustering words. "Really, my lord, I hardly understand what this heat is all about. I have but expressed the opinion of a great many personages. The viscountess is but the product of her low breeding."

A vein throbbed in Lord St. John's forehead. He was white about the mouth, which was held in a thin, hard slash. "Have you indeed, sir?"

Mr. Lawton spread his hands in a deprecating manner.

Lord St. John's eyes were very cold as his glance swept round the expectant, hushed circle. A curious smile touched his lips, lending the wildness in his expression a diabolical cast. His voice heavy with irony, he said, "Then certainly I am indebted to you, sir, for making everything plain to me."

Mr. Underwood clamped a heavy hand on the viscount's shoulder, saying warningly, "Sinjin—"

Lord St. John bit off a savage laugh. "I am not such a fool as to kill him here, Carey!"

Mr. Lawton suddenly turned two shades paler.

Lord St. John addressed the gentleman who had so foolishly insulted his wife. "You shall be my example, sir. Send your seconds round to Underwood here. He shall act for me."

He turned on his heel, his cold glance once more sweeping about him. Those who stood in front of him parted a way like magic before him.

Through the haze of disbelief and horror that threatened to engulf him, Mr. Lawton bleated, "The choice of weapons is naturally mine, my lord!"

Lord St. John glanced back, flicking the gentleman with indifference. "Choose what you will! It will be all the same in the end."

With that devastating pronouncement, he was gone.

Mr. Underwood remained only long enough to give his card, engraved with his direction, to the benumbed Mr. Lawton before he, too, departed from the card room. With his exit, the heavy silence was broken by a hubbub of talk.

A few gentlemen commiserated with Mr. Lawton over his ill luck, but he heard them with a curiously blank look in his eyes. Others of the company were not so compassionate. They shook their heads somberly or else regarded Mr. Lawton with mingled contempt and amusement.

Opinions ran thick and fast, breaking over Mr. Lawton's head like a cold deluge.

"Too bad, Lawton. Weemswood is such a devilish good shot."

"Heard that he nearly killed the last fellow he met."

"No, no, that was the one before. This last was with that fellow, Hargrove. Pinked him, of course, as it was only for a wager."

"Aye, nothing of this sort. He's mad for it this time around."

"The man's wife, you know."

"Shan't take above a minute or two, with swords, I should think."

"Lawton'll choose pistols, I'll warrant."

"No such thing! He'd be a fool to do so! They'll cross swords."

"A monkey against it!"

"Done! Where's the book?"

Having been rendered quite sober from the appalling encounter, which had lasted but seconds, Mr. Lawton got up from his chair and carefully made his way through the company. No one stopped him with word or glance, a sort of unspoken pact in effect which allowed him to crawl away while the question of swords or pistols was still hotly debated and cries rang out for the betting book to be brought forward.

Mr. Lawton tottered from the club, in his mind a man already dead.

Chapter 23

News of the anticipated duel flashed through the *ton*. It was thought a bad business, but titillating in the extreme. What a delicious turn-up, that the care-for-nothing viscount should go to such lengths to scotch any ill-conceived words about his ill-born shopkeeper wife.

Naturally the challenge he had flung out had been quite plain to every gentleman present. Mr. Lawton was to be held up as the sacrificial lamb as a warning to any others who dared to malign his lordship's chosen lady.

The whole matter was of such interest that some gentlemen so far forgot themselves that they let drop hints of the impending scandal to their ladies. The ladies instantly embellished the story with every nonsense that occurred to their fertile imaginations. It quickly became the *on dit* of the season.

Lord St. John was so freakish of temper and quite deadly when roused, one had always heard, ever ready for any mad piece of work. His lordship's pride was a byword, too; how it must gall the viscount to be obliged to shield the honor of his name on behalf of a wife whose background was so beneath his own.

There was certainly nothing in the rumored tryst between Lady St. John and Sir Nigel Smythe, more's the pity; but Lady Caroline Eddington had obviously not known a thing about the hackney tale when she had unwittingly vouched for the viscountess.

However reluctant Lady Pothergill was to let go of a good morsel of gossip, she had had no choice in the matter and so she had hedged her disappointment with an expression of relief. "Naturally I was glad to discover there was no truth in it. One cannot be too careful in taking these little rumors at face value, for one never knows when one has been misinformed," she remarked starchily.

Lady Pothergill's impression was confirmed by Mrs. Nessering, who commented that nothing had been less guilty than Lady St. John's demeanor when confronted with the tale.

Lawton had been a fool to dredge up that dead rumor.

He had been unlucky in the extreme to have done so within Lord St. John's hearing. The viscount was not one to let such an insult slide by, of course, and none could blame him for upholding his wife's honor over it.

However, there was no denying that Lady St. John's credit had suffered something of a blow with the discovery that she possessed such a vulgar sister.

"Why, the woman was as bold as brass in asking for my patronage," said Mrs. Nessering with a titter. "Naturally I played along, just to see how far she would go. I expect a visit from her daily to demand an explanation of my defection, I assure you!"

Lady Pothergill's and Mrs. Nessering's circle laughed themselves into stitches, but others maintained that Lady St. John could not be held accountable for bad relations when they could all point to at least one personage in their own respective families that they would rather not claim. Still, the importance of bloodlines could not be denied. Even when there was a bad sheep in the family stock, blood overrode every other consideration.

All in all, however, the consensus was that the lady was well-matched in her lord. The viscount might be of good birth, but his reputation was considered to be a bit ragged ever since the Duke of Alton had made such a surprising move and disinherited him. This latest dustup revolving around Lord St. John only served to point up his lordship's extremely volatile character.

Oddly enough, some began to wonder whether the viscount did not hold his wife in more than passing affection.

This opinion was roundly rejected by most. It was not possible that his lordship could actually care for the woman to whom he had given his name. Oh, Lady St. John was not displeasing to the eye and her manners and her comportment were surprisingly good. But after all, theirs had been naught but a marriage of convenience built upon a trade of title for a fortune.

The viscount had behaved with astonishing attentiveness in view of that fact. He had escorted his wife for weeks about the social round until he had made certain that she was acknowledged with all the courtesy due to her title. No doubt it was but an expression of his lordship's freakish nature that he had demanded such a fine adherence to protocol on the viscountess's behalf.

In truth, it was just like Lord St. John to fly in the very teeth of society and thrust his shopkeeper wife forward as a lady of the realm. The Earl of Cowltern gave it as his considered opinion that the *ton* had made a grave error in allowing so much slack to one of Lord St. John's wild stamp.

"I would not have allowed the fellow to step back inside the club, let alone put foot inside my own drawing room," he pronounced. "Unfortunately, I am not the only arbitrator of membership."

Since it was well known that Lord St. John had not even attempted to darken the doors of the Cowltern house, the earl's widely circulated statement was held up to subtle mockery amongst many, even of his lordship's own set.

The Countess of Cowltern and Lady Althea also tried their fortune at striking a blow against the touch of commonness that had invaded their august society.

"I have spoken to the woman but once, and only for the simple reason that I wished to inquire whether her merchant father would give me a good price on some fabrics that I had seen. I found her to be rather an upstart in her manners," said the countess austerely.

Her friends murmured their sympathy, though a few hid inner smiles. Most had been present when the countess had deigned to speak to Lady St. John in company concerning the expense of particular fabrics. Certainly it was shocking that a mere merchant's daughter had delivered a setdown to none other than the Countess of Cowltern, but it had been done so civilly that surely one must stand in admiration of such aplomb.

On the opposite end of the ballroom, Lady Althea was holding court with her admirers. When talk of the duel sprang up, she gave a light laugh.

"Poor Sinjin is obviously quite beside himself. Imagine finding oneself burdened with a milliner for an in-law," she observed with a pretty moue. "And now this horrid duel! I pity his lordship most sincerely, I do assure you."

Captain Hargrove chanced to be one of Lady Althea's court. Amidst the ripple of amusement around him, he alone frowned. "I count his lordship and her ladyship to be my friends, Lady Althea."

"Oh, do you, Captain? Then pray do forgive my unknowing insult, sir! It had not occurred to me that anyone with whom I am acquainted could possibly claim friendship in that direction," said Lady Althea. She was still smiling, but there was a challenging look in her blue eyes.

It was clear that Lady Althea had laid before the military gentleman a choice and onlookers waited curiously for the outcome.

"I agree, ma'am." Captain Hargrove bowed and stepped back out of the favored circle. Another immediately took his place.

Lady Althea's eyes flashed, but then she turned her shoulder and promptly deemed the captain's existence of little importance. No matter how admirably the regimentals suited Captain Hargrove's trim physique, he was, after all, of no consequence on the social ladder. She had only smiled on him to begin with because he was rather more handsome than several of her other suitors and he had been a very neat dance partner.

As Captain Hargrove left the gathering, he reflected that he could sympathize with Lord St. John's difficulties. At least on the battlefield it was immediately evident which were the enemy. He decided it was time to return to his duties; he would wait only long enough to hear the outcome of the viscount's duel before leaving England.

Though it had quickly become common knowledge that there was a duel to be fought, the actual date and location was a tightly guarded secret, known only to the principals and their seconds, against the possibility of information being lodged with the law.

The law frowned heavily on such illegal activities, but polite society awaited with collective bated breath the outcome of the affair of honor. Really, the season had never been so entertaining before Lord St. John's unfortunate reversal of fortune.

Mr. Lawton's seconds did their utmost to scotch the encounter by persuading their principal that it was in his best interests to offer an abject apology to the viscount. Mr.

Lawton did so, writing out in a shaking hand the phrases that he desperately hoped would free him from the nightmares that plagued him each night.

Mr. Lawton's profusely worded apology was not accepted.

His seconds conveyed the news to an anxious Mr. Lawton with grave countenances and shaking heads. "His lordship is determined to uphold his honor in the matter, more's the pity," concluded one with a sigh.

Mr. Lawton felt the abyss that had yawned at his feet for several days come rushing up to meet him. He knew himself to be a fair shot; but Lord St. John was said never to miss. His own skill with the rapier was considerably better than many; but the viscount was rumored to be a perfect devil with steel. Whichever way he jumped, he was sure to be the loser.

"Make it pistols," said Mr. Lawton abruptly, tossing back a reckless measure of brandy.

Mr. Lawton's seconds stared at him. "No, but think, man—!"

"I am thinking, and I'd a dashed sight rather have a hole blown in me than to be carved up into little pieces!"

The duel was fought three days later.

It was a chilly dawn. The principals laid aside their greatcoats, each revealing a somber black toilette, unrelieved by either the gleam of a white cravat or the wink of a jewel.

Each made their choice of weapon and took their position. Back to back, in time with the count, the principals strode away from one another. On the mark, the gentlemen turned, raised their pistols, and fired.

Mr. Lawton stared across the mist-wreathed green at the tall dark figure opposite. Lord St. John would not fall, for

Mr. Lawton had deliberately deloped. However, a numbness was spreading through his own side. He could feel the warm stickiness of his blood seeping into his shirt. Strangely enough, there did not seem to be any pain associated with it.

"You're hit, Lawton!" exclaimed one of his seconds, who had reached him.

Mr. Lawton's head swam. He decided to sit down, and his legs rather inelegantly gave way under him. His friends lowered him safely to the ground. The physician in attendance knelt beside him and prosaically opened a black bag. Mr. Lawton closed his eyes under the physician's probing fingers, rough treatment that seemed to bring to life searing pain.

"It is a grave wound, but he will live."

"Thank God for that. You'll not have to flee the country after all, Sinjin."

"There was never any doubt." The voice was very cold. "I meant to kill the man, but unfortunately I recalled just as I fired that he holds a few of my markers. I did not want it bruited about that I had killed a man in order to escape my debts of honor."

Mr. Lawton did not open his eyes to watch the viscount leave the field in the company of his friends. Mr. Lawton was instead breathing a prayer of thanksgiving to Providence, whom he had not realized until that instant had been at work on his behalf.

Mary was told the history of the duel and its outcome by any number of well-meaning acquaintances. She felt the sharp glances and endured the scrutiny of her face and manner, but except for a certain paleness of countenance she did not betray the leap of agitation that she had felt at the news. When she was free to do so, she fled home to her sitting room to think.

She was appalled at such barbaric behavior. She could scarcely believe that modern gentlemen had indulged in such dangerous work. But more than that, the very thought that Lord St. John could have been wounded, perhaps fatally, made her physically ill.

She could not possibly bear it if she were to be faced with the same thing in future. Though Mary shrank from it, she knew that she had to say something to her husband about his part in the duel. She had to make him understand that no insult to her was worth putting his life in jeopardy.

Mary left quiet instructions that she was to be notified when the viscount came in and then endeavored to pass the afternoon in a productive manner. Despite her attempts to remain busy, she could not help speculating about what the viscount's reaction would be to what she had to say. She was anxious that he should not misunderstand; but their relationship was not as close as she so earnestly desired.

Since the morning that Lord St. John had so thoroughly kissed her, a new wall seemed to have been erected between them. She did not feel at all secure about unburdening her heart to him.

She and Lord St. John had drifted further apart as each had become involved with their separate activities. Long gone were the days when Lord St. John escorted her to every function. It was a rarity now. She hardly saw him except to exchange polite pleasantries. The instance in the breakfast room might never have happened for all the good it had accomplished.

Mary's bedroom door had never been locked, but it might as well have been. On more than one occasion, when she was unable to sleep because of the loneliness of the night, she had wanted to go to his room. But her courage had always fallen sadly short. She did not think that she could have borne the rejection if he had repudiated such a bold advance. It was surely better to endure her longing than to have it flung back into her face, as had seemed the likely outcome.

Mary had given her unhappy status much thought and she had come to a most painful conclusion. It was overwhelmingly obvious that her husband had become altogether bored with her. The risk that she had taken in entering the marriage of convenience had been a stupid one, after all. She had loved him, but he had never come to love her.

It was said that Lord St. John had fought the duel to uphold the honor of her good name, but Mary thought she knew better. Lord St. John had fought to uphold the name that he had bestowed upon her. It was an important differentiation. In actuality the viscount cared little what was said or thought of her, as long as it did not directly insult him.

Mary's hurtful reflections did nothing to shore up her confidence. She was reduced to painful suspense as she waited to speak to Lord St. John. She had hoped that he would join her for dinner, but he did not return to the town house until it was time to escort her to the ball at Lady Pothergill's. There was no time to request an interview with him before he went upstairs to change into formal attire.

When he handed her up into their carriage, his expression was so forbidding that her courage utterly failed her. She had not regained it before they had reached Lady Pothergill's. Her best chance to capture the viscount's ear was lost. She swallowed the disappointment she felt in her craven self and summoned up a calm smile as she descended from the carriage. Accepting Lord St. John's arm, Mary entered the residence and greeted their hostess.

Chapter 24

"So delightful that you could attend my little soiree," said Lady Pothergill, bestowing an arch smile on the viscount. "One was not certain that you would be in a position to do so, my lord."

Lord St. John allowed his cynicism to color his words. "My position has proven to be more than once precarious this Season, has it not?"

Since Lady Pothergill had been one of those ladies who had originally snubbed the viscount upon his disinheritance, his lordship's reply could not have been said to be auspicious. "Indeed!" said Lady Pothergill freezingly.

Mary murmured her own greeting, very certain that Lady Pothergill did not care in the least what she had said. She passed on into the ballroom with Lord St. John at her side, determined to enjoy the evening as best she could. Perhaps an hour or so of congenial company would tease her mind away from the subject that she must eventually broach to Lord St. John.

However, that was not to be. It did not take very many encounters with other guests for Mary to realize that the duel was the uppermost *on dit*. There were so many broad allusions to it that she could not set them aside.

She endured the meaningful glances and veiled comments for a little more than an hour until she could not stand to be silent any longer. In a lull of the press of personages about them, she blurted, "Is it true, what is being said? Did you shoot that man because of me?"

The viscount glanced down at her.

Mary almost felt the anger that flashed in his eyes, but she refused to let her own gaze waver. "Pray—! Do not look at me so. But only tell me the truth."

Lord St. John's lips curled. "Would it puff up your self-consequence to know that it was true? Very well, then. It is true."

"No! You mistake me. I-I was shocked to hear of it. I do not understand how you could have done it. Indeed, I thought I would faint," she stammered. "How could you have put yourself in such appalling risk on my account?"

He narrowed his gaze. "Am I to infer that you censure my conduct, my lady?"

"Not censure, no! But I cannot believe it was necessary to shoot that gentleman."

He took her elbow in an ungentle grip and steered her over to a deserted spot near the balcony. His voice very cold, he said softly, "I will not tolerate a questioning of my sense of honor, my lady. I will not tolerate any interference whatsoever. What I do is my affair. Is that quite understood?"

She averted her face, suddenly very pale. Not trusting her voice, she nodded. His steely fingers tightened momentarily above her elbow, bruising the tender flesh, then dropped away. She heard his swift step leaving her.

Blindly, she stepped through the archway onto the darkened balcony. Placing her hands on the cool stone barrier, she squeezed shut her brimming eyes. Her heart felt shredded. The coldness of his voice, the utter palpability of his animosity toward her, had wounded her to an extraordinary degree. She did not know that one could feel such pain and still breathe.

Mary's cheeks were wet with silent tears. When she heard a hesitant footstep behind her, she hastily dashed her hand across her face. She hoped that the shadows were dark enough to hide the fact of her weeping.

"Lady St. John?"

She turned her head, pinning on a smile. "Why, Nana. Have you come out for a breath of air as well?"

"I thought you were upset, thought you might wish a friend," said Lord Heatherton.

Mary felt her smile wobble. "Thank you, Nana. That was very kind of you. But, indeed, I am quite all right."

Lord Heatherton nodded. "I thought so. But still, a friend and all that." He frowned, then offered, "Sinjin don't mean the half of what he says when he's out of temper. The very devil of a fellow, Sinjin, but he's a good sort for all of that."

Mary felt her throat closing again. She said in a strangled voice, "Yes, I know. But it is so difficult at times. He-he doesn't care much for me, you see, while I—" She could not go on, neither her slipping emotions nor her pride allowing her to do so.

Lord Heatherton cleared his throat. He felt himself completely at a loss. The situation required delicacy and finesse, qualities that he did not possess in dealing with the ladies.

"Sinjin chose you above the others," he offered hesitantly, doubtful that it was more than small comfort.

Mary turned her head. Her lips parted. "You mean he could have chosen someone else?" she asked, somewhat incredulously.

Lord Heatherton nodded, glad that his poor gambit had succeeded so well. "I had gotten up a list of the most likely candidates for Sinjin's consideration. You were not my first choice for him, nor Carey's, either. But Sinjin would have none of the rest once he had heard your name. He had already met you and insisted that he knew you well enough to make an offer."

Mary stood quite still, feeling the enormity of it come upon her. Hope blazed across her wounded soul and lit her eyes. "Oh, Nana. You have no notion what that means to me."

Impulsively she reached up to kiss his cheek.

Lord Heatherton blushed. He had not the least idea what had so pleased her, but he was happy to see that the air of dejection that had clung to her had quite passed. He protested that he was glad to be of service.

His confused air was endearing and Mary started to laugh.

A cold voice undercut Lord Heatherton's tangled disclaimer. "Indeed, Nana, and what service might that be? Or might I guess from that quite affecting kiss that my wife pressed upon you?"

Mary whirled with a gasp.

But her dismay was nothing compared to the emotion that sheered up Lord Heatherton's spine. His eyes started from his head. "Sinjin! Why—why, I don't know what you mean," he stammered, thoroughly overthrown.

Lord St. John let go of the edge of the drapery that he had crushed in his fist. His voice was insidiously soft. "Do you not? Let me make it perfectly clear, my friend. You were making love to my wife."

Lord Heatherton stood quite speechless. He had never been in such a spot in his life.

Instant protest rose to his lips, but it was not uttered before his inner censor spoke sternly to his conscience. He had not meant it to happen. Of course not. But he had done something to cause Lady St. John to kiss him, so he supposed that the accusation flung at his head was entirely appropriate. He had indeed been caught making love to another man's wife.

"I hardly know what to say. Indeed, Sinjin, I meant it all for the best."

Lord St. John's face whitened beneath its tan. He had followed his wife to apologize for his hasty, cutting words, only to he met with the sight of her bestowing a kiss upon another man. His jealousy had sprung into full flower, but it was insignificant compared to the rage that coursed his veins upon Lord Heatherton's grave admission.

"You damnable cur," he breathed. His eyes glittered like cut diamonds. "I should throttle you now, but that would be too easy. I shall take pleasure in running you through."

Lord Heatherton was not a well-rounded sportsman. He was not one of the noted whips nor did he enjoy a reputation for finesse with fists or sword. The only accomplishment he could lay claim to was an absolute dead eye with any known firearm. He was therefore much sought during the hunting season and had often won tidy sums from wagers at the shooting gallery.

Neither was Lord Heatherton a physical coward. Physical discomfort meant little to him. He was indefatigable in any weather and possessed an iron constitution.

He could be wounded by slights, when he understood them, but in general his was an even, insulated personality. Perhaps the only person he actually feared was his mother.

However, as he stared, appalled, into the viscount's cold eyes, he realized that his life was shortly to be ended in a bloody violent fashion.

But he was an honorable man and he had never skirted even the most distasteful responsibility. Therefore he straightened his shoulders and said with great dignity, "I shall have my seconds call upon you, my lord."

Lord St. John's smile was thin and menacing. "See that you do so, Heatherton."

Then it was that the lady took a hand. She stepped forward and with all the strength at her command, she slapped the viscount. His head snapped back from the unexpected blow.

"I believe that is the proper treatment for one suffering from hysteria," said Mary, her voice calm but breathless. She was vaguely aware that Lord Heatherton's mouth had dropped open, but all of her attention was held by the viscount's blazing countenance.

"You are obviously in your cups, my lord, or you would never have mistaken a sisterly kiss of gratitude for wantonness. Lord Heatherton was kind enough to offer me a word of friendship when he realized that I was in distress. That is the sum upon which you base your ridiculous challenge, as you would undoubtedly recognize if you would allow yourself a coherent thought!"

Lord St. John held himself rigidly. Without taking his eyes from his wife's pale but composed face, he said in a harsh voice, "I shall speak to you tomorrow, Nana."

"I shall hold myself at your service, Sinjin."

As Lord Heatherton retreated, he threw a glance over his shoulder. The thought occurred to him that his exit had not even been noticed.

"I think that it is time that we left, my dear," said Lord St. John, his expression shuttered.

"As you wish, my lord," said Mary.

She walked past him, her head held high. There would be no one able to point and exclaim under their breath that she had a whipped-dog appearance about her, even though that description much described her inner trembling.

Her husband's fingers closed about her elbow in a ruthless grip. Mary did not acknowledge the viscount's hurtful hold by even so much as an upward glance. Instead she smiled and nodded her way through the several good-byes required of them, her mind scarcely engaged by what she heard or said.

At last they had made their way through the company and emerged onto the steps. A porter ran to call their carriage. They waited in silence for its appearance. When it came, the viscount handed Mary up into it and then climbed in himself.

Mary turned her face determinedly to the window, staring at the passing pools of lamplight. She could feel the tightly coiled presence of the man in the opposite corner and she could only be grateful that he had chosen not to clear the air while they were riding in the carriage. The space was too contained for the explosion that was so patently on a short leash.

It was the most uncomfortable ride that she had ever experienced.

Inevitably, when they reached the town house there were consequences for her actions. Mary was unsurprised when Lord St. John followed her up to her sitting room. Smith had waited up to undress her. As her husband commanded the maid to leave them, Mary felt a sickening leadedness in her middle, but she held herself proudly.

She crossed the room to the hearth and put out her hands toward the fire to warm them. She jumped a little when she heard the door thrust shut but she did not turn about. She was tense as a bowstring but she mustered as much self-control as she could not to reveal it.

Lord St. John strode forward and threw himself into a wingback chair. He stared at his wife, noting how the firelight made mysterious pools of her eyes and caressed the fine planes of her face. She was beautiful. He felt the smoldering fire ignite in his veins.

Beneath her outward manner and the composure with which she dealt with the world, he knew her to be a passionate woman. He had distanced himself from her as he intended, denying himself the pleasure to be found in her bed. The thought that she might have found solace in another man's arms threatened his sanity.

Harshly, he said, "What have you to say for yourself, madam?"

Mary lifted her head to a proud angle. In her coolest tone, she said, "I do not believe I have anything to say at all about the matter, my lord."

Lord St. John jerked upright in the chair. His hands clamped hard about the cushioned arms. "Do not pretend to misunderstand me, my lady!"

She left the fire then and advanced to stop beside the settee. She laid a hand on its back with seeming casualness, though in reality she welcomed its solid support under her trembling fingers. "I do not pretend to misunderstand you. I understand quite well. You are angered that I dared to stand up for myself. I will not apologize for that, my lord."

"So you will not apologize for that affecting scene with Nana?" he demanded.

"I have already fully explained that to you, my lord. I have nothing whatever to add," she said quietly. The strain was beginning to tell on her nerves and almost unconsciously she tightened her fingers on the settee.

"I have never had an explanation from you, however, regarding Sir Nigel Smythe. Was he also consoling your sense of ill-usage?"

Mary gasped. "How dare you! You know what happened! If you did not hear it from my own lips, it was because you refused to allow me to speak of it. I would willingly have done so, but you would not listen!"

Lord St. John ignored her rush of pained words, too caught up in the poisonous fruits of his jealousy to understand. "What of Applegate, my lady? The mushroom sang your praises most fulsomely. Am I to believe it was to no purpose?"

A bubble of hysteria rose in her throat and Mary laughed in sheer amazement. "My brother-in-law?! What *rot* you have trotted out, my lord! I never took you before for a fool!"

Her unprecedented outburst left silence in its wake.

The viscount was still for a long moment, while he regarded her in a dispassionate, considering fashion. When at last he spoke, it was with a soft inflection that spelled danger by its very silkiness. "I am not one to be easily crossed, my lady, as you will swiftly discover if you persist in your defiance. I can be the very devil. I shall give no quarter."

"You are kinder than you pretend," said Mary.

Though chilled by his words, she recalled how he had come to her father's aid and a dozen times since then that he had come to her own rescue when she had floundered in the treacherous tides of society. He was not the unfeeling monster that he painted himself, she thought.

"Am I?" Lord St. John smiled, not at all pleasantly.

He rose to his feet. "What a very odd notion you have of me, my love."

There was such a calculating light in his eyes as he advanced on her that Mary instinctively shrank from him. The feel of the back of a wingback chair against her hip brought her up. She stood her ground then. She was trembling, but she would not flee from him.

Lord St. John stopped before her. He stared down into her widened eyes. There was scarce an inch between them.

He could see the flutter of pulse in her throat and how the breath came quickly to her. Without a word, still smiling, he reached out his hands and lightly ran his fingers up her arms to her shoulders. There, his fingers tightened.

"Shall I teach you how very unpleasant I can be, dear Mary?" he whispered.

She stared up at him. The firelight reflected the trace of fear that entered her eyes. Unconsciously she put up a hand of appeal. "Sin—"

He waited no longer, but swept her into a cruel embrace. He tangled his fingers in her heavy hair and dragged back her head. His mouth took rough possession of hers, the kiss deliberately punishing. He sought to incite her to panic or anger, but the result was far else.

She did not struggle against him nor utter a sound of protest.

Lord St. John's senses were disordered. He felt anger and hard desire. He wanted to punish her. But with the feel of her in his arms a bewildering tenderness welled up in him, turning awry his purpose.

Rosethorn . . .

He had never been more content than when he was with this woman who had become his wife. Her openness, her giving nature, her dignity, had all come to rest in the space of his very soul. Of their own volition, his hands began to gentle.

Then he tasted the salt of her tears.

With an oath he thrust her from him and she stumbled. She caught herself on the settee, turning her pale face up to him. The firelight glinted on the streaks of her tears.

White-faced, his hands in fists, he stared down at her for a heartbeat, breathing quickly. From between clenched teeth, he savagely ground out, "Damn you!"

He turned on his heel. The force of the door slamming behind him resounded in the sitting room.

Mary straightened. Mechanically she smoothed her disheveled gown. Her mouth felt swollen, violated. She could taste blood where her lips had been cut by her own teeth. But she focused on none of these things.

Instead she recalled the haunted look in the viscount's blazing eyes when he had pushed her away, the hopelessness that had flitted across his face before the rage had again erased it.

Time swirled aside and she heard once more the confession of his soul. "The fevered vision of a fool . . . returning to Rosethorn to find waiting for me a beautiful woman holding the hand of a child. . . ."

Certainty flooded her being. At last she knew that she had established a place in her husband's heart. Now all that was left to her was to teach him to acknowledge it.

Mary gave a dry little laugh at the very enormity of the task.

Chapter 25

A startling rumor swept the *ton*. The Duke of Alton had taken the unprecedented step of divorcing his duchess of three months. Infidelity and false representation were cited as the justifiable causes.

Mr. Underwood was the first to carry the tale to Lord St. John. "There will be the devil of a dustup," he predicted.

"Perhaps," said Lord St. John indifferently.

Mr. Underwood said disgustedly, "Aye, pretend that you are not thrown into agitation by the news, when it could well mean that you will be reestablished as the duke's heir."

Lord St. John gave his twisted smile. His eyes gleamed. "That would be fortune's hand, indeed, Carey. I do not look for it, however. You forget the unborn child."

Mr. Underwood made a dismissing gesture. "There's something havey-cavey about that. I always thought so. You said yourself that you doubted that Alton was the sire."

Lord St. John gave a harsh laugh. "All doubts aside, Carey, the brat is still considered to be Alton's heir. I do not forget that, my friend. It would be folly to allow one's thinking to be clouded to the issue."

"I suppose you have the right of it. Damn, Sinjin! The business leaves a bad taste in my mouth," said Mr. Underwood.

"No more than it does mine," said Lord St. John, his countenance grim.

The rumored divorce was swiftly confirmed as fact. The scandal was tremendous and was exclaimed over wherever

241

the *ton* gathered, especially when it came out that the old duke had discovered his wife *en flagrante* with her lover. Numerous speculations went the rounds but no one seemed to have any other details to add to what was already known.

It was Lord Heatherton who conveyed the sober intelligence to his friends that, in the heat of the ensuing scene, the duchess had declared the babe's father to be someone other than the duke.

"An ill-advised, rash statement on her part," he said, shaking his head. "Naturally his grace had no other recourse open to him than to repudiate both her and the babe."

"Where heard you this, Nana?" asked Mr. Underwood, astonished that of all people Lord Heatherton would have access to such sordid knowledge.

Lord Heatherton lowered his heavy brows in patent disapproval. "M'mother is an old acquaintance of the duke. She posted down to lend her support to his grace in his time of trial. The house servants were still full of the terrible row and filled her maid's ears with the details."

"Backstairs gossip will always spread one's most carefully guarded secrets. One can almost feel pity for the blow to the duke's pride," said Mr. Underwood. Since he was grinning, it was obvious that he spoke with at best a spurious sympathy.

"For myself, I sympathize with Lady Heatherton," murmured Lord St. John.

Lord Heatherton threw the viscount a startled glance. With Lord St. John's apology, the breach between them had become a thing of the past. "How did you know, Sinjin? M'mother returned to town positively livid. The old gentlemen sent her off with a flea in her ear. It ain't been comfortable to be around her, I can tell you."

"I am not at all surprised, myself being all too well acquainted with his grace's character," said Lord St. John on a laugh. "Besides, I've heard a few asides of my own. The duke is said to have insulted a fair number of well-meaning friends who had journeyed to commiserate with him over his loss by cursing them all roundly."

"A rare joke, indeed," said Mr. Underwood with a hoot of laughter.

"It is all very well for you to laugh, Carey. *You* have not got to escort m'mother about," said Lord Heatherton gloomily.

Shortly thereafter, the Duke of Alton died of apoplexy. The duke's death fired speculation whether it would mean another change in Lord St. John's fortunes. The viscount had provided grist for the gossip mill for months. The *ton* had never been more entertained.

In one particular quarter, amusement was the remotest reaction imaginable. Instead, astonishment was swiftly superseded by fury and determination.

The message that her presence was urgently enjoined was relayed by one of the footmen to Mary in her private sitting room. She gazed at some length at the name embossed on the calling card before lifting her eyes to the waiting servant. "I shall go down directly," she said quietly, and rose. The footman bowed and preceded her downstairs. He opened the drawing room door for her and stepped aside.

Mary paused in the doorway, surveying her visitor.

The lady stood in front of the huge gilt mirror on the mantel, intently studying her own reflection as she smoothed the satin ribbons of her bonnet. She presented a stylish appearance in a walking dress of palest blue which accented a perfect figure.

Although no more than a word or two had ever been exchanged between them, Mary knew much of the lady by reputation. Lady Althea had been pointed out to her on a number of occasions by not-so-friendly personages as Lord St. John's former fiancée. It had been related to her more times than she cared to count that but for the viscount's reverses in fortune, his lordship would have wed the beauteous Lady Althea.

Mary had wondered what sort of woman would spurn the gentleman of her choosing upon learning that he could no longer aspire to a grand estate. She had heard that Lady Althea, and indeed all of the Cowterns, had more than their share of pride. But surely, where there was respect and affection, there must also be loyalty.

Mary advanced into the room, hardly aware when the door was closed quietly behind her. She held out her hand in a friendly fashion. "Lady Althea? How kind of you to call on me."

Lady Althea had turned around. Her eyes raked the viscountess in appraisal. Almost disdainfully she allowed her gloved fingers to touch those of her hostess. "It is a call made from necessity only, I assure you."

Mary felt the snub. However, she had learned all too well through the past few months not to allow her expression to betray her. She continued to smile and said gently, "Indeed, Lady Althea? Then I shall not keep you overlong by offering you tea. But pray do be seated." She seated herself.

Lady Althea's large blue eyes flashed at the riposte. She followed her hostess's example and sat down on the edge of the settee. "You must wonder why I have chosen to call upon you."

"I am certain that you shall divulge it all in good time," said Mary dryly.

"You are a pert, ill-bred baggage," said Lady Althea, her lips thinning.

"Your opinion is of supreme indifference to me, my lady. Is that all that you wished to convey to me? For if it is, I can only say that you have wasted your time in coming here," said Mary.

"Yes, I certainly believe that I have. However, perhaps you shall not think so when I say that I have come to warn you, madam!" said Lady Althea dramatically.

Mary raised her brows. "Really? How utterly extraordinary of you. However, I assure you that your intentions are looked upon with just the measure of gratitude which they deserve."

Flags of color flew into Lady Althea's face. She was now thoroughly in a temper. "You shall not be so superior when I tell you that I have come on Sinjin's behalf. Oh, that pricks your interest, madam? I thought perhaps it might. I felt the greatest reluctance to come to you, but I see now that it was just the thing to do, for you must be made to understand."

"And what is it that you deem of such importance, Lady Althea?" asked Mary.

For answer, Lady Althea opened her reticule and drew out a pair of man's gloves. "This, madam!" she said triumphantly.

Mary looked at the gloves. She shook her head. "I am sorry, but I fail to understand your point, my lady."

"These belong to Sinjin. He dropped them in my boudoir when last he visited me." Lady Althea paused to gauge the effect of her words. "I shall spare your blushes and mine by not revealing the circumstances." She made a show of

245

casting down her gaze in seeming modesty.

There was a moment of silence. Mary looked at the gloves, then raised her thoughtful eyes to Lady Althea's face. Lady Althea had abandoned her pose of decorum in order to watch her hostess's expression. There was an expectant glint in the lady's hard blue eyes.

Mary knew that however those gloves had come into Lady Althea's possession, the lady hoped to use them to her present advantage. Unfortunately for Lady Althea, Mary was not so easily manipulated that she would grant her the satisfaction of a scene. "Indeed, Lady Althea. You surprise me. However, I fail to see the connection between these gloves, whomever they might belong to, and your warning to me."

"You dimwitted Cit! Must I spell it out for you?" exclaimed Lady Althea, enraged. "I am saying that Sinjin dropped these gloves in a moment of passion. There! Is that not clear enough? Your husband is in love with *me,* madam!"

Lady Althea was astonished when her hostess went into a peal of laughter. Dull red entirely suffused her ladyship's face, quite transforming her beautiful features. "He is!" she declared, incensed. "And I shall have him, too, for he wants me!"

Mary shook her head, the small smile on her face somewhat pitying. "My dear Lady Althea. Even if what you say is true and my husband did indeed leave those gloves at your residence, I very much doubt that he made love to you and vowed his everlasting adoration. No, do not speak, my lady, for you but make yourself the more ridiculous. You see, I understand my husband's character very well. He may have once been affianced to you. He may even have cared for you. But he would *never* return to anyone who had spurned him as you did. His honor and his pride would not permit it."

Lady Althea's eyes glittered. "You are so certain, madam!"

Mary sighed and made a slight gesture. Gently, she said, "I am, after all, the gentleman's wife."

There was silence, fraught with tension. The animosity in Lady Althea's expression had quite destroyed any pretense of beauty that she had.

Mary rose and pulled the bellpull. "I know that you must have other calls to make, Lady Althea," she said quietly.

The door was opened by a footman. Lady Althea stood up. Without word or glance, she sailed out of the sitting room. The footman looked inquiringly in Mary's direction. She shook her head, then stayed the footman's departure with a quick gesture. "Pray deny me to any other callers, William."

"Very well, my lady." The door closed softly.

When she was alone, Mary walked slowly over to the gloves, which had spilled from Lady Althea's lap when she had taken her abrupt leave. Mary picked up the pair. She knew before she even checked the stamped monogram inside the edge of one that the gloves were indeed her husband's. For an instant she raised the smooth leather to her cheek, breathing in the rich smell.

She had told Lady Althea the truth concerning her understanding of Lord St. John's character. However, there had been a small seed of doubt planted by Lady Althea's malicious visit.

Mary sighed, for she was acutely cognizant of the fact that she had "married up." Hers had been a contracted marriage of convenience. However much of a business arrangement it had been, however, her beliefs and the love that she had for her husband would never allow her to think less of the sanctity of her marriage. The same might not be true for Lord St. John, who was, after all, born of a class that was notorious for infidelity and casual affairs. Lady Althea's claims might have been spun out of whole cloth, but the original thread could have had some truth attached to it. For several long moments Mary stood lost in reflection.

Lord St. John received the news of the loss of his relative with apparent calm. The somber solicitors waiting upon his lordship could detect nothing in his expression beyond polite attention.

One of the solicitors offered his condolences.

There came an expression into his lordship's icy gray eyes that made more than one of the gentlemen wish that the conventional words had not been uttered. "Absolve me of hypocrisy, sir. I scarcely bleed for the duke's demise; nor would he have regarded my own death with anything more than passing indifference."

A short uncomfortable silence fell, to be broken tactfully by Mr. Witherspoon. "I believe that we may move on, gentlemen." There was a murmur of agreement and the rustle of papers.

Another of the group began the proceedings ponderously, "Of course, with the repudiation by his grace of his recent marriage, you were reinstated as heir presumptive before the time of his death, my lord."

Lord St. John nodded curtly. "What of the babe?"

The solicitors nearly all allowed themselves prim smiles of satisfaction. "The late duke made it quite clear during the divorce proceedings that the unborn child was not of his issue. In addition, we have in our possession several deposi-

tions from numerous witnesses that the former duchess herself attested to that fact. There is no question of your own
legitimate claims to the dukedom, my lord."

Lord St. John's expression did not change, though his
eyes gleamed with a strange expression. "I believe that will
be all, gentlemen."

The solicitors glanced at one another. One of them ventured to question their dismissal. "My lord—your grace,
there are details that should be discussed at some length."

Lord St. John, Viscount Weemswood, now Duke of
Alton, rose to his feet. "I am certain that there are. You
may do so with my man of business, Mr. Witherspoon, in
whom I repose the fullest confidence."

Mr. Witherspoon quickly took his cue. "Gentlemen, if
you please. Allow me to show you to my office." Without a
moment's loss of time, he ushered out the solicitors and
gently closed the door.

Lord St. John stepped around his desk to the occasional
table and decanted a measure of wine into a glass. He
picked up the half-full glass and slowly swirled the brandy,
his thoughts meditative.

Odd how his destiny had come round full circle. He possessed both a wife and a dukedom, as he had taken for
granted that he would. Matters had not unfolded quite as
he had anticipated; but it had been for the better that his
road had taken its unexpected turn.

Otherwise he would not have married Mary.

Lord St. John tossed back the brandy. Setting down the
glass, he went in search of his wife. Upon inquiry, he entered the sitting room.

His wife welcomed him with a smile. "My lord, I was
just thinking of you."

"Were you, my lady?" Lord St. John shut the door and

advanced toward her. "I am informed that you had a visitor."

Mary's smile dimmed a little. "Yes, Lady Althea. I was never more surprised than to learn she had called on me. She came to return your gloves, my lord."

Lord St. John frowned as he took the gloves that she held out to him. "My gloves? I don't recall—"

His expression cleared, before his eyes narrowed on his wife's composed face. "Yes, I remember now. I dropped them on the last occasion I called on Lady Althea. It was the day that she informed me that she no longer wished to become my wife."

Mary appreciated what he was telling her without words. He had not visited Lady Althea since before their own marriage. She smiled up at him, her own eyes beginning to dance. "I think the lady was quite piqued that that was so."

Lord St. John regarded her a moment, then said softly, "You baggage. You gave her the roundation, did you?"

Mary found that, whereas the term had been insulting in the extreme when it dropped from Lady Althea's lips, she did not in the least mind that form of address from his lordship. "My lord, I was completely circumspect, I assure you."

Lord St. John flicked her nose with his finger, an arrestingly caressing gesture. "You are a wonder, my Mary."

Pale color flew into her face as her startled eyes fastened on his. As though he realized that he was indulging in lovemaking with his wife in the middle of the day, he drew back.

"I have just this moment come from consultation with a flock of solicitors, my lady. It seems that I have come into a dukedom."

Several things hit Mary all at once. She had become a duchess, a very frightening thought for she was entirely devoid of social ambition. Lord St. John had ascended to the title that he had been denied, that denial having directly led to his seeking a marriage to her. And Lady Althea had more than likely known of Lord St. John's newly exalted state through the ever-present London gossip, thus explaining her ladyship's sudden desire to wreck Mary's marriage as thoroughly as possible.

The last thought brought a flush of real anger to her face. "I suppose that Lady Althea intended that I should divorce you on the evidence of your gloves."

He went very still, though his expression registered only polite interest. "And could you have done so?"

"Of course not. I am not such a noddy to believe every tale that is brought me," said Mary with asperity. "Especially from a lady who is vain, arrogant and so spoiled that she believes that she has only to wish a thing for it to be so."

"I possess a wise duchess," said Lord St. John.

She presented a dismayed face to him. "A duchess. I do not know how I shall go on."

"You shall go on just as you have done, my dear. I could not ask for more than that," said Lord St. John. He was at once amused and obscurely grateful that she did not seem to attach a great deal of importance to her sudden ascension.

Mary looked at her husband doubtfully. "I hope that I may accept that as a compliment, your grace."

"Consider it so, my love. However, pray do not address me so formally. I prefer that we return to the easier style that we fell into at Rosethorn, do you not?"

The expression in his eyes made Mary blush again. "Yes, indeed I do." She attempted to recover her composure under the warmth of his gaze. "I-I do not think that I shall ever become used to being addressed as 'her grace.' "

"My poor Mary. Will you divorce me for forcing you into such an unpalatable position?" he asked softly, sliding his hands up her arms.

"It is a consideration, indeed. Our original agreement never touched on such an eventuality," said Mary teasingly, though acutely aware of the touch of his hands.

His eyes darkened. His fingers tightened upon her shoulders. Almost in anger, he asked, "Would you let something of that sort come between us, Mary?"

Mary raised her hand and laid it lightly against his tense jaw. "You can be such a fool, Sinjin." She said it so gently that it took him a moment to absorb her words.

Lord St. John flashed a grin. "A fool, am I? We shall see about that!" He caught her up in a fierce embrace, his lips descending upon hers for a heart-stopping kiss. When he raised his head, he said rather raggedly, "It is true. I have been a fool, Mary. I won't deny it. I feared what I felt for you and so I tried to distance myself from you. It was the bitterest moment of my life when I thought that, because of my coldness, you had turned from me to someone else."

"So you accused poor Nana," she said, curling her fingers about his lapels.

Lord St. John laughed, albeit without amusement. "Yes. I would have killed him, too, if you had not brought me to my senses."

"And Mr. Lawton? And Sir Nigel?"

"Are you going to parade all of my follies before me?" he complained.

"Well, I suppose that I must, for you have not given me reason to stop my mouth," said Mary with a sly upward glance.

"Mary," he breathed, staring down at her through narrowed lids. "Are you *flirting* with me?"

"You did wish me to become more a lady of fashion, after all," Mary reminded him.

"As long as you confine your flirtations to me, my dear, we shall get along splendidly," he said in mock anger. "I do not intend to watch the wife that holds my heart in her hands make sheep's eyes at every male who crosses her path."

Mary smiled up at him. Her eyes lit up like a thousand candles. "Do I truly, Sinjin? I shall not break it, I promise you."

She gasped at the sudden strength of his arms about her. Then his mouth captured her own and she slid her hands round his neck.